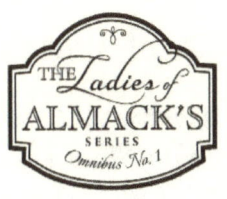

COUNTESS OF SHADOWS

Also by Marissa Doyle

The Ladies of Almack's series

The Forgery Furore
The Vanishing Volume
Lyrics and Larceny
The Cursed Canvases
Turmoil on the Thames
An Event at Epsom
The Missing Missives
Betrayal at Brighton
The Audacious Abduction

Marquis of Secrets: The Ladies of Almack's
Omnibus No.2

Skin Deep
By Jove

The Leland Sisters series

Bewitching Season
Betraying Season
Courtship and Curses
Charles Bewitched

Between Silk and Sand
Evergreen
What Lies Beneath

COUNTESS OF SHADOWS

THE LADIES OF ALMACK'S OMNIBUS NO.1

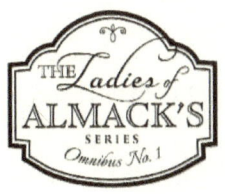

Marissa Doyle

KING STREET BOOKS

In association with
Book View Cafe

Published by Book View Café LLC
304 S. Jones Blvd., Suite #2906
Las Vegas, NV 89107

ISBN: 978-1-63632-095-3

This is a work of fiction. Names, characters, places, and
events are fictitious and/or are used fictitiously and are
solely the product of the author's imagination. Any
similarity to real persons, living or dead, places,
businesses, companies, institutions, events, or locales is
completely coincidental.

https://www.bookviewcafe.com

https://www.marissadoyle.com

For Scott,
who kept asking for what happened next

TABLE OF CONTENTS

THE FORGERY FURORE

Chapter One

Almack's Assembly Rooms
King Street, London
April 1810
A Thursday morning

The ormolu clock on the chimneypiece was striking seven as Annabel, Lady Fellbridge, slipped into her seat in the white-and-gold paneled room and glanced around the table, taking a quick count. Ah, good—she was not the last to arrive. Even after more than a year, being the newest member of the Lady Patronesses of Almack's still made her feel like a young girl allowed to dine with the adults for the first time: she'd thought about sneaking in under a concealing shadow in case she was late, but fortunately that had not been necessary.

"Good morning, Emily," she murmured, untying her hat. Seven o'clock! A bracing cup of coffee would be very welcome just now, even though she'd retired early last night.

Next to her, Lady Emily Cowper brightened. "Oh, coffee is an excellent idea, Annabel. Might we order some, Sally?"

"Hmm?" Lady Jersey looked up from the paper she'd been studying. Her forehead was uncharacteristically creased with worry lines. "Coffee? Goodness, yes. Indeed, I should have thought of it." She rang the bell on the table in front of her.

Annabel gave her friend a small smile. Emily was usually very good about staying out of her friends' minds, but it *was* seven in the morning, after all.

"I know," Emily whispered. "I do beg your pardon. I had just been hoping that someone would suggest coffee and forgot myself."

The door banged open, and Countess Dorothea Lieven stalked into the room. "At seven o'clock of a morning I am usually still asleep," she announced, glaring around the table—besides Annabel and Emily and Sally, there was Lady Sefton, Lady Frances Dalrymple, Mrs. Drummond-Burrell (who looked exhausted, Annabel thought), and grim-faced Lady Bathurst. "I trust that there is a good reason for me to be so rudely drawn from my bed at this barbaric hour."

"I enjoy getting up early." Maria Sefton smiled her sweet but rather silly smile. "The birds are more willing to talk to me then. Very useful source of news, the birds."

Dorothea snorted and sat down. Despite her complaints about the hour, she was as elegantly turned out as always in a corded muslin walking dress and Pomona green spencer. Her black curls bristled around her face like Medusa's snakes. One of them stirred and hissed, and she flicked it with a finger. "Hush. You could still be asleep, unlike me."

The curl subsided.

"I think you'll find that there's an excellent reason for our meeting so early, and not on a Monday." Unlike Dorothea, Sally looked tired and rumpled. "Ah," she said, as a footman scratched at the door. "Come in. Coffee for eight, if you will. And bring an extra cup."

Emily raised an eyebrow. When the footman had left, she asked, "Are we expecting a guest?"

"Not quite." Sally glanced at the watch pinned to her gown. "Mr. Almack will be joining us this morning."

Annabel sat up a little straighter, as did the other ladies around the table. Mr. Almack was retired from the management of the assembly rooms which bore his name and where they sat today—in fact, he'd died nearly thirty years before. But he still kept a firm (if spectral) hand on the other, more covert side of his business. Even so, he did not attend every meeting. If he were coming today, whatever was going on must be serious.

"*Can* Mr. Almack drink coffee?" Frances Dalrymple, on Annabel's other side, whispered to her. Her blue eyes were even wider than usual. "I don't see how a ghost—"

"I expect he enjoys the scent," Annabel murmured back.

"Once he arrives, we can proceed." Sally sighed and tapped her pencil on the table.

Clementina Drummond-Burrell cocked her head. "He's already here."

"William?" Sally frowned.

A deep chuckle came from the seemingly empty chair next to Maria, who jumped. "My apologies. I didna mean to startle you, Lady Sefton."

Georgiana Bathurst frowned. "Hmmph."

The coffee arrived. After Sally had poured for everyone, an expectant silence fell. She cleared her throat. "Thank you all for coming on such short notice. You will, I think, forgive me for using the new warning messenger when you hear why we have gathered."

"Doubtful," Dorothea muttered.

Annabel couldn't help agreeing with her a little. Having a ghostly footman appear in one's bedroom to urgently request her attendance at a special meeting at Almack's was a bit of a shock, though it was marginally better than the talking pigeons that had done the job last year, when Annabel first joined. They had frequently been incomprehensible and almost always left messes on the windowsills—

"Annabel?"

She started. "I'm sorry, Sally. Waiting for the coffee to take effect."

Mr. Almack chuckled again. Annabel wondered if he'd been so jolly whilst in corporeal form. "So am I, Lady Fellbridge, though I expect my wait will be a wee bit longer than yours. Pray begin again, Lady Jersey."

Sally sighed. "Very well. You weren't at last night's ball, Annabel—we understand, of course."

"Thank you." *Last night's ball* was one of Almack's regular Wednesday night subscription balls. It was also the anniversary of poor Freddy's death, and while she had long since left off wearing black for her late husband, she had not felt a busy social evening to be quite the thing, even after three years.

"You're welcome. Those of us who did attend, however, were appalled to notice a number of persons who should not have been there."

Good heavens. "What persons?"

Clementina Drummond-Burrell looked as though there were a bad smell in the room. "Mushrooms. Cits. Merchants, and a—a *fishmonger*!"

"A *very* wealthy one," Maria assured Annabel. "I doubt he actually sells the fish himself anymore. But still. . ." She shook her head.

"You are *très énervé* because he asked you to dance," Dorothea said with what could only be called malicious glee. "Were you afraid he still smelt of fish?"

Clementina scowled. Her preternaturally acute senses would probably have detected if the man had even *thought* about fish that evening. "You're just annoyed because his wife got her gown from *your* mantua-maker."

"Now, ladies—" Sally began.

"A fishmonger?" Annabel interrupted, to head off any further quarreling. "But how?"

"That's what we're here to find out. This may seem like a small matter, but you all must understand its potential import." Sally looked at each of them, her expression somber. "Much is at stake here."

Annabel nodded. The Wednesday night balls at Almack's in King Street were *the* most exclusive social events of the London season. Only those of superior birth and breeding were given the vouchers that permitted them to purchase tickets, and the vouchers were only bestowed by the Lady Patronesses—the ladies now assembled in this room. Almack's reputation as "the Marriage Mart," the place where the sons and daughters of the upper classes could meet and conduct courtships under the protective gaze of their mamas and of the Lady Patronesses, was an important one. No one wanted their gently-bred offspring to fall for someone not of their sphere, so this matter of strangers at a ball was a serious one: Almack's very *raison d'être* was being threatened. Without its reputation there would be no point to Almack's, and Almack's Lady Patronesses would not be needed and unable to use the cover of Almack's to fulfill their other mission—the guarding of London from supernatural dangers.

"You are very right, Sally, but I don't understand," Maria said. "None of us gave vouchers to these people—"

"Are we certain of that?" Georgiana Bathurst interrupted. Annabel winced at her acid tone; perhaps her sciatica was troubling her again. Being able to change one's body to take the shape of any animal seemed to lead to a tendency to rheumatism. Or it might just have been Georgiana being Georgiana.

"They certainly weren't on the voucher list," Sally replied, almost as acidly. "I checked. Would you care to corroborate?" She indicated a thick pile of paper on the table in front of her. Georgiana grimaced and shook her head.

"They weren't at the ball last week." Emily sipped her coffee thoughtfully. "So that means something happened over this past week to enable them to get vouchers and purchase their tickets."

"What do you mean, 'something happened?'"

Georgiana snapped.

"Well, isn't it obvious? Someone must be forging vouchers."

There was a momentary stunned silence.

"Forging vouchers?" Maria Sefton finally said. "But. . . but that's *wicked*!"

Dorothea groaned and leaned her forehead in her hand. A few of her curls writhed in protest.

"Indeed, Maria. But that is what appears to have occurred." Sally glanced at Mr. Almack—or the chair his incorporeal form occupied—and nodded. "Annabel, I believe you're probably the best person to take this on. Your shadow-shaping will no doubt prove useful in an investigation where stealth will doubtless be required."

"Me?" Annabel's voice squeaked. Surely one of the older, more experienced ladies should lead an investigation of such importance. "That is, thank you, Sally. I shall do my best."

"I'm sure you will. Frances would be a good choice to assist you." Frances was a spinster in her thirties, eldest daughter of the Duke of Carrick, and devoted to her King Charles spaniels and to reading three-volume novels—and anything else that came her way; she could hold an object and sense its origins or who had last touched it. Annabel caught her eye; Frances nodded her acquiescence.

"Very good," Sally said. "Then we will meet again Monday, an hour earlier than usual. That is all for today. Thank you for coming on such short notice. Annabel, a word before you go?"

Annabel waited while the other ladies gathered their wraps and left the room. Sally probably wanted to have an encouraging chat to prepare her for her first investigation. But Sally's face when she turned to her was anything but encouraging. "Please be seated, Annabel. I wanted to explain why I gave you this investigation."

"I am aware it is a great honor to lead my first," Annabel said cautiously.

"Of course it is," Sally agreed. "But it's not just that. Forging vouchers strikes at the very heart of Almack's. If this isn't stopped, its reputation might be irretrievably ruined. Customarily a more senior lady might have been expected to take this investigation. I might have myself, except for one thing."

"Yes?"

Sally fixed her with an unwavering look. "According to Mr. Willis, all the questionable vouchers have been signed by you."

"I b-beg your pardon?" Annabel swallowed hard. *Her* name. On the vouchers. Someone had used *her name*— "You can't think—you don't really believe I would—"

Sally reached out and touched her hand. "No, Annabel, I don't. I should have said that straight away. I know you well enough to be perfectly certain that you would never do such a thing. And that's why I want you to investigate this. You should be allowed to clear your own name—hopefully before next Wednesday's ball."

Annabel took a deep breath, and then another. "Why did Mr. Willis give tickets to whoever came for them if he suspected the authenticity of the vouchers that were presented to him?" she asked, her voice mostly steady.

"He didn't have any doubts at the time. It was only when I spoke to him this morning that he recalled anything out of the ordinary—and that was merely that some of the footmen who came to purchase the tickets wore unfamiliar livery. When he thought about it further, he realized that all the unfamiliar footmen bore vouchers signed by you. I think that in the future we must supply him with a voucher list to check names against." She sighed. "*More* paperwork."

Now that the initial shock was past, it was easier to think. "If they all had my name on them, that suggests they came from the same source."

"And probably a not very experienced criminal one," Sally added. "A cleverer person would have used more than one of our names to avoid notice."

"Yes." Annabel swallowed. "But why me?"

"That is the interesting question. Do you have any notion why someone would have chosen to use *your* name on their forged vouchers?"

"I haven't the faintest—oh, *no*. . . " Annabel closed her eyes. Because suddenly she was sure she knew *precisely* why her name had been used on the forged vouchers.

Early last week, she had been out paying calls and ordering new shirts for her sons, who would be home shortly for the Easter holiday from their first year at Eton. Her unflappable butler Hanscomb had, as usual, opened the door for her on her return.

"Good afternoon, madam. Lady Andromeda Colerain called and is presently leaving you a note in the library," he said, helping her off with her pelisse.

"Lady Andromeda? Thank you, Hanscomb. I'll go directly up to her."

Annabel had not seen her old friend in some weeks. They had made their come-outs together; Andie, though lovely, accomplished, and a considerable heiress, had remained unmarried, much to the despair of her doting parents. She was a dear, but her taste in men could only be described as execrable. Was something wrong? If she were paying a purely social call, she would not have cajoled Hanscomb into letting her write a note.

"Andie!" she exclaimed as she entered the library. "It's lovely to see you."

Andie looked up from Annabel's desk, where she was frowning over a heavily blotted piece of Annabel's notepaper. "I hope you don't mind—Hanscomb said I might leave you a note. This pen is quite dreadful, you know. I've already spoilt half a dozen sheets."

Annabel sighed inwardly. Her stock of writing paper had been sadly diminished since becoming a Lady Patroness; she had hoped to not have to reorder it *quite* so soon. "You never could trim a pen properly. Leave it alone and come tell me what your urgent matter is about. Do you know, I've scarcely seen you this spring." She went to the sofa near the fireplace and sat down, patting the cushion next to her.

Andie obediently rose. "I know. I've been so wrapped up in—in—oh, I have been desperate to speak with you, but Mama barely lets me out of the house these days. You're the *only* one I can confide in."

Oh dear. "Your mother loves you deeply.

Whatever it is you have to confide, can you not do so in her?"

"Of course not! She and Papa never understand."

On the contrary, they understood all too well. "Very well, who is it this time?"

"Who is who?" Andie was all affronted dignity.

"Your latest *beau idéal.*"

Andie's hauteur dissolved like a lump of sugar in hot tea. "Oh, Annabel, you *always* know—that's why I love you. He's—I've never met anyone like him before."

"Good Lord—you haven't gone and fallen in love with a rat-catcher, have you?"

"How could you say such a thing?"

Annabel sighed. "You'd never met anyone like the man who trained fighting cocks, or the wild animal keeper at Astley's Amphitheatre, or the draper's assistant who hung your mother's new drawing room curtains, or the mesmerist you met Godknows-where." She ticked them off her fingers. "That leaves us a rat-catcher, a publican, or a prizefighter."

A radiant smile broke across Andie's lovely face, and she took Annabel's hand and squeezed it. "Oh, darling—how did you guess? Yes, my Tom's a boxer—and a very, very good one, I am given to understand. My brother Miles says his purses are almost as high as Molineaux's."

Annabel closed her mouth, which had dropped open in astonishment. The fighting cock trainer had been bad, but this was worse. Far worse. "Where in heaven's name did you meet him?"

"Walking with Miles in Hyde Park—he knows

the most *interesting* people—and it was love at first sight! I can't wait for you to meet him—he's *so* big and strong and manly and has the dearest little crooked nose. He says it's been broken at least six times—can you imagine? Once—was it the fifth time?—it was broken by Cribb himself. Tom's so proud of that—why are you looking at me that way?"

Andie's parents might want to have a talk with her brother about the company he kept. "Your father's the Earl of Allston. You can't marry a boxer."

Her soft brown eyes filled with tears. "But I love him!"

"You loved the other ones too, if you recall."

"No, I didn't. Those were just—just the fleeting fancies of an impressionable child. But I'm twenty-six now—it can't be that." She clutched Annabel's hand harder.

Oh, Andie. Under her friend's starry-eyed radiance Annabel could feel the bewilderment of an over-indulged girl who was waking up to the fact that her girlhood had passed and that she had little idea of how to be a woman. This would take delicate handling. "How can I help you, dear?" she asked gently.

Andie's smile came out from behind the rain-clouds. "I *knew* I could rely on you. Annabel, can't you get Tom a voucher for Almack's? If Mama and her friends can see what a fine figure of a man he is— I'm *sure* he'll blend right in. He wears the prettiest waistcoats—they're always pink because his mother's name was Rose. Isn't that sweet of him? If only his hair were a little longer to cover that cauliflower ear of his," she added in a less confident tone. "But no one will notice a little thing like that. And if he smiles with his mouth closed, they won't notice the missing tooth. They'll see that he's—he's—one of nature's gentlemen, just like that Gentleman Jackson my brothers are mad about."

Annabel refrained from retorting that Gentleman Jackson was enough of a gentleman to not try to insert himself where he would not be wanted. "Andie, you cannot be serious."

"I am very serious!"

Patience, Annabel. She's not in her right mind just now. "But it isn't just up to me, you know," she said aloud. "All the Lady Patronesses have to agree to give someone a voucher. And I'm afraid that most of them simply won't be able to accept a prize-fighter at Almack's, no matter how gentlemanly he is."

Andie frowned. "It's not fair. If a man is honest and upright, he should not be barred from *anywhere*. And Tom has vowed that he won't do any house-breaking ever again—he promised me that he only served as look-out the last time. Oh, Annabel, you will try, won't you?"

Dear heaven—far worse than the cock trainer. "No, Andie, I will not."

Andie's eyes filled with tears again. "But—"

Annabel took both her hands and held them tightly. "Andie, listen to me. We've been friends for years, and I love you dearly. But I will not do this. For one thing, it is impossible; your parents will never approve of your marrying a prize-fighter, no matter how much of a nature's gentleman he is—though I don't think nature's gentlemen serve as look-outs in robberies. And second, I will not cause my fellow Lady Patronesses to wonder if I've taken leave of my senses. Asking for a voucher for a prize-fighter with a dubious past? They'll fall over laughing. . . and never trust me again. I'm sorry, darling, but *no*."

Andie wrenched her hands from Annabel's. "I thought *you* of all people would understand. You're just as bad as Mama and my father!" She leapt to her feet and scowled at Annabel. "And I thought you were my *friend*."

"I am." She reminded herself that Andie had reacted in much the same way when she had refused to help her elope with the mesmerist. "That's why I won't help you."

"Oh, you—you *traitor*." Andie's voice positively throbbed. "You'll be sorry—you'll see! My Tom and I will dance at Almack's whether you like it or not!" She stormed from the room in a manner that would have drawn much applause at Covent Garden. Annabel heard her steps fleeing down the stairs, heard someone—Hanscomb, most likely—inquire if Lady Andromeda needed assistance, heard her inarticulate response and the sound of the front door closing with a bang.

She sat back against the cushions of the sofa and closed her eyes for a moment. It was easy to forget how tiring these grand emotional scenes could be—or was tire*some* the more apt description? Both, probably. In a moment she would go down and apologize to Hanscomb for subjecting him to Andie's—

Footsteps hurrying back up the stairs made her open her eyes and sit up. Hanscomb flew into the room, looking more agitated than she'd ever seen him. "Your ladyship—Lady Andromeda—she's been hurt!" he blurted.

"What?" Annabel was already off the sofa. "How?

"Just—now." The poor man could hardly catch his breath. "She ran—out the door — directly into the street—didn't even seem to notice the carriage—" He scurried after her down the stairs. "I think she—was crying."

Annabel flew down the last few stairs and out the door into Chesterfield Street.

Andie lay in the street, evidently knocked senseless. A few feet down the road the high phaeton that had been the cause of her injury was being held by a groom who was trying to calm the horses hitched to it. Three men knelt at her side; one of them held her wrist in a reassuringly professional manner. "Don't you dare try to lift her, you young idiot, until I can ascertain whether she has broken any bones," he was saying as Annabel joined them.

"Oh, surely not!" The man thus addressed sounded young, frightened, and Scottish—and was very handsome, with auburn curls and bright blue eyes.

"If you've gone and murthered our Lady Andromeda, m'lord will have your guts for garters." The third man, whom Annabel recognized as Andie's father's coachman, spoke with gloomy relish.

"Is she badly injured?" Annabel addressed the wrist-holder, who had finished taking Andie's pulse and was gently turning her head from side to side.

"Not badly from what I can tell from such a cursory examination, though she will want to spend several days in bed. Are you any relation to this young woman?" The physician—for surely he must be one—looked up at Annabel with cool gray eyes. He was younger than she had expected from his words and manner.

"She ain't no woman, she's a lady," the coachman muttered.

"She's my friend. She was paying a call and, er, grew upset over the course of our discussion." She looked down at Andie anxiously. "She—she has a great deal of sensibility."

"The poor bonny lassie," the handsome one said softly. "I didn't see her—I swear it, ma'am. She wasn't there—and then suddenly she was. It's my first time driving in London—I daresay I was distracted." He swallowed. "What can I do to help?"

"Get your ridiculous rig out of the road, for one thing," the physician snapped at him. "And you—you're her coachman? For God's sake, stop standing there like a highway milestone and help me lift her into your carriage so we can take her home." He rose, reached into his coat pocket, and handed Annabel a card. "I was paying a call on one of your neighbors, ma'am. It's fortunate I happened to be near."

Annabel glanced at the card—Doctor Cyrus Quant-Roper, of Harley Street. The name sounded familiar, but there was no time to try to remember why. "I'm glad you were, sir," she said. "I am Lady Fellbridge, and this is Lady Andromeda Colerain. Her father is Lord Allston." It was strange to be making introductions for an unconscious person.

She watched as the doctor and the coachman discussed the best way to lift Andie into the barouche, while the young man, who had helped his groom calm his horses and move the phaeton out of the road, hovered alongside. "May I ask who you are, sir?" she asked him pleasantly but pointedly.

"Oh!" The young man fumbled in his pocket. "I'm sorry, ma'am, I'm so upset that I can't think straight. I'm Stranraer."

He handed Annabel a card. She just had time to register the fact that it bore a ducal coronet when a low moan quickly drew her attention back to her injured friend. Andie was regarding them blearily. "What. . . where am I?"

The three men all started speaking at once. Annabel tried to shush them but it was the young duke who did the trick by bending over Andie and sweeping her into his arms. "It was all my fault, ma'am. But you'll be back in full bloom in no time, says the good doctor here."

Andie stared up at him as he carried her to the barouche and stepped right up into it before tenderly depositing her on the seat. "But who are you? How— oh, my head." She screwed her eyes shut and winced.

Annabel came forward. "Andie, let's get you home. We'll worry about introductions later."

"I will, of course, accompany you," Dr. Quant-Roper put in.

"And I," said the Duke of Stranraer.

In the end both men did, Stranraer following Andie and the doctor in his phaeton. Annabel would have gone as well, but Andie refused her company and would not even look at her.

Sally sat back in her chair after Annabel told her about Andie's accident. "Oh, dear. Do you think she might have taken blank vouchers from your desk while she was writing the note?"

"I fear that it's possible. I shall check to see if

there are any missing. She did have the opportunity, though, and when she's in love her judgment isn't. . . good. I've sent her several notes but she hasn't replied. When I wrote to her mother, Lady Allston's reply was polite but didn't say much more than that Andie was on the mend." Annabel tried not to let her hurt show in her voice. "All I can conclude is that she's still in love with her prize-fighter and doing a good job of 'making me sorry.'"

"Hmm. Yes, it certainly sounds as if you should keep that possibility in mind." Sally sighed. "If it *is* she, it will be a ticklish situation to deal with."

"It's a ticklish situation no matter what."

"Very true." Sally rose. "Well, see what you and Frances can discover. And good luck."

Chapter Two

Emily was waiting outside Almack's when Annabel emerged from her discussion with Sally. "Might I beg a ride home? I think my coachman was thoroughly drunk—at least he smelled that way—and I sent him home to sleep it off. I didn't dare peek at his thoughts to confirm—reading a drunkard gives me a headache." She looked at Annabel with gentle, understanding eyes. "How are you? Getting your first investigation practically on the anniversary of Freddy's death is a bit much."

Annabel did not put it past her friend to have sent her coachman home on purpose just to be able to keep her company. Emily was like that.

"Of course you may," she said, "but I'm very well. I've had three years to grow used to it, after all."

"Goodness, has it been three years already? Poor Freddy." Emily shook her head.

Poor Freddy indeed. Her late husband had had the poor judgment to break his collarbone and several ribs, not on a battlefield in Spain or even on the hunting field boldly riding to hounds, but falling out of a tree at Vauxhall, doing monkey imitations to amuse his drunk friends and a bevy of fashionable impures. He'd contracted pneumonia and died, a shining example of why one should not climb trees when one was forty-seven, on the stout side, and deep in one's cups. It had been positively humiliating to accept the condolences of his friends, some of whom found the whole thing quite hilarious. Theirs had not been a love match, but *still.* . .

After they were settled in Annabel's carriage, Emily leaned against the blue leather upholstery with a sigh. "I hope that's the last seven o'clock meeting we have. The boys are down from school now, aren't they? How are they?"

"Very well. They brought a friend to stay for the holiday. Quite as thick as thieves, the three of them." Annabel smiled at the thought of her sons. "They're home for a few more days, though Summer Half will start soon."

"Well, that's good. Once they're back at Eton, you can start having a proper good time. Three years, Annabel! Don't you think that's long enough to have been alone?"

"Have a proper good time? Why should I want to do that?"

Emily looked shocked. "You see? You poor dear, you don't even know what you're missing."

Annabel smiled. "I'm quizzing you, Emily. I'd love to have a 'proper good time,' but truly, I don't know what one is anymore. I've been too busy being both mother and father to the boys, plus trying to steer the estate away from the rocks."

Emily would not be put off. "You simply haven't

gone about it properly. Why haven't you asked me for help?"

Annabel pretended to be absorbed in the passing scenery, hoping that Emily would not peek at her thoughts. Just as she had, at eighteen Emily married a much older man. She had given Lord Cowper a son and heir, then moved on to amuse herself with a handsome Italian diplomat and now was madly in love with Harry "Cupid" Palmerston while her husband stayed happily in the country.

Well, Emily was a Melbourne, and all the Melbourne women did more or less as they pleased. Annabel, on the other hand, was a Shellingham, and Shellingham women mostly went in for good works amongst their tenantry and epic feats of embroidery.

Emily was still speaking. "What we need to do is find you the right man."

Thank goodness it was a cool enough morning to have put the top of the carriage up; her coachman would have found this discussion most fascinating. "I don't want to marry again—at least, not just for the sake of being married. I've already done that once, and once was enough."

"Who said anything about marriage? Give up your freedom now, just when life could be so very amusing? There's nothing better than being a lovely, titled widow in London. What you need is a *cher ami* to help you enjoy yourself. Hmm." Her dark eyes narrowed in thought. "What about Lord Keene? He's a veritable Adonis and can be very entertaining in private situations, from what I've heard. Those clever hands of his—"

Annabel couldn't help giggling at Emily's suggestive drawl. "Those clever hands of his have probably been busy in half the boudoirs of London. I don't really wish them to be busy in mine."

Emily shrugged. "You never know what you might be missing. Jane Alton says he can do the most extraordinary things with his—oh!" She sat up straighter. "What about Lord Ordway? I caught him thinking some very interesting thoughts about you at the Swanleys' ball a sennight ago. You were wearing a charming gown with a gold net overdress and your hair in a fillet *à la grecque*, and I thought he would try to ravish you on the spot. At least he wanted to."

"That old dress? Thank you, but it's been made over twice now." Emily understood how small her dress budget was. "Besides, Lord Ordway is married and has six children. He evidently has no need to look elsewhere for someone to ravish."

"On the contrary, I expect he needs it more than ever. Lady Ordway's in the family way again and as big as a house. They suspect triplets." She looked at Annabel, her head to one side. "You *are* singularly attractive, you know. I could never understand why Fellbridge chased his demi-reps about town when he had you. Men say they admire willowy figures, but I don't think they much care to actually get their hands on them. You've the perfect amount of upholstery to make any man itch to touch you."

Annabel grinned. "I'm fat, you mean."

"Not a bit. You've got those lovely rounded arms and that soft bosom that they just want to pillow their heads on. Not to mention naturally curly hair and good teeth." She pouted. "Perhaps we should stop being friends. I believe I quite hate you, now that I think about it."

Annabel laughed heartily. "Emily Cowper, you

are the most beautiful woman in London, not to mention the biggest goose, and I love you dearly for it," she said when she could finally talk. "But please, no Lord Ordway."

Emily sighed. "Very well, I give up. If it won't be Keene or Ordway, then what about *him*?" She nodded toward an approaching curricle, painted a smart glossy yellow and drawn by a handsome pair of bays.

Annabel's laughter evaporated. She knew that curricle—and its driver.

As the vehicle drew nearer, the man driving it with such quiet aplomb glanced over—and a slow smile curved his mouth. He lifted his beaver hat to them with a flourish.

Or rather, to *her*. Annabel met the man's eyes— they were not smiling now, but dark and intent on her—

And then he was past them, his bays trotting smartly toward St. James's Street.

Annabel released a breath she didn't recall holding. "Good lord, Emily—the Marquis of Quinceton? Never!"

Emily looked at her in surprise. "Why so vehement? Quin's extremely good-looking if you don't mind that dark, fallen angel type of masculine attractiveness, rich, unattached—"

"—has the Devil's own temper, the bitterest tongue in London, and a reputation that won't bear scrutiny. He was one of Freddy's boon companions, if you recall. In fact, he was there the night Freddy fell out of the tree at Vauxhall." Annabel hesitated. "And he. . . unnerves me. I hate the way he looks at me whenever we happen to meet, smiling like a hungry wolf—"

"Really? I've never noticed that. I must pay closer attention the next time you're in the same room. Maybe he saves it for delectable widows." Emily grinned, spreading her fingers into claws and wriggling them threateningly. "'All the better to eat you with, my dear,'" she intoned in a deep voice.

"I should prefer not to be eaten, thank you very much," Annabel said severely. "And you may send Lord Quinceton to perdition. I'm sure he'd fit in there perfectly."

She dropped Emily off at the Cowpers' house, just a few streets from her own, and sat back with a sigh as her coachman eased the landau into the flow of traffic. Just because Emily had her handsome Cupid to warm her bed, she thought every woman needed the same entertainment. *When you have a hammer, every problem looks like a nail,* Papa's comfortable voice said in her head, and she smiled. Her father had a maxim for every occasion. What one would he find for her? Something perhaps about the other man's grass being greener?

When she came to London last year after leaving off mourning, she'd thought that the city's metaphorical grass would be greener. So far, it hadn't lived up to its allure. Or maybe she was more a Shellingham than she knew. Not that she'd wanted to immure herself at Chalfont Abbey and take up tapestry-stitching and dispensing soup and advice to the deserving poor—though with finances in the state they were, she might have been better off if she had. Freddy, alas, had been hopeless at managing money and left his estate in disarray. While she was just able to get along, putting profits back into the Abbey lands so that her elder son would have something to inherit besides debts, there was little left over each quarter.

Therein lay the problem. She'd been so single-mindedly bringing up her sons and managing Freddy's estate that she had no idea what she wanted for *herself.*

Not a Lord Keene or a Lord Ordway, certainly. And as for Lord Quinceton—she shivered. To find her heart's companion, though—a man who would be both friend and lover as poor Freddy had never been inclined to be—oh, how wonderful that would be. However, looking for such a paragon took time and attention, and just now, she had her first investigation to lead for the Lady Patronesses. Surely that should provide purpose enough. And besides, it was *fun.*

All her fellow Lady Patronesses agreed that while running the Wednesday night subscription balls was something of a bore, it provided the perfect cover for their more interesting—and secret—work as the *ton's* protectors against supernatural wrong-doing. Annabel had been surprised to learn just how much there was of that when Sally Jersey and Maria Sefton recruited her the previous year. . . and to learn what her fellow members were capable of. She had felt a little daunted by half-Gorgon Dorothea and shape-shifter Georgiana, next to whose powers her own shadow-shaping seemed a little flat. But as it turned out, everyone's abilities were of use for some investigation or other—

"Lady Fellbridge!"

Startled, Annabel looked up. The carriage had just pulled up before her house. Standing on the pavement before her door was a stout man in a brown worsted suit and carefully tied cravat, clutching his hat and staring at her anxiously. When he saw that he'd caught her eye, he gave her an ingratiating smile and bowed low, then scuttled forward, bending his head and surreptitiously mopping his brow with a handkerchief as he did. "Your ladyship, please—a moment of your time—nay, a second—"

Annabel fought the urge to grab a shadow from within the carriage and wrap it around herself to vanish from view. This was the fourth one this week: some well-to-do businessman who'd made his fortune, no doubt hoping to beg or cajole an Almack's voucher for his wife and daughters. Usually the hopefuls were content to confine their pleas to long, flowery letters extolling her kindness and generosity, but this week they all seemed to have decided to take the direct approach. It was a hazard of her position as a Lady Patroness; they'd all had to deal with them. Emily said she'd had a couple at her house that very morning.

"I'm very sorry, sir, but I have urgent business within," she said, not unkindly, as her footman opened the carriage door and handed her out.

"But your ladyship!" There was a desperate note in his voice. "They said that you—I can afford it, I assure you. . ."

Her step slowed. Afford what? And who were "they?" Might this have something to do with the vouchers forged in her name? She turned to ask him what he meant, but her footman had interposed his six feet of liveried muscle between them. "You heard her ladyship," he growled. "Be off with you." Before she could intervene, the man had scurried away.

Annabel tried not to show her chagrin; John

had only been doing his job. "Thank you," she said, and hurried up the stairs and through the door held open by Hanscomb, her butler.

"We are suffering quite a plague of those lately, madam," Hanscomb commented, helping her off with her pelisse.

"I know. It's very tiresome, though I can't help feeling a little sorry for them." This one—or another—would surely be back, and then she could question him. She took off her hat and gloves with a sigh, then brightened as a peal of laughter drifted down from the upper reaches of the house. "Where are the boys?" she asked, turning to the stairs.

"Lord Fellbridge and Masters Chalfont and Blackburn are in the library, I believe."

"Thank you." Annabel paused on the first step. "I am expecting Lady Frances Dalrymple to call today. After she arrives, I shan't be home to anyone else." The custom was for the assistant on an investigation to call on the principal to discuss plans of attack; it was a novel sensation to be the one receiving the call, rather than paying it.

"Very good, madam. Shall I bring refreshments?"

"Yes, and then we shan't want to be disturbed." A shout, followed by another gust of laughter, drew both her attention and her steps upward. She paused in the library's open doorway and smiled at the tableau before her.

Will, the eight-year-old ninth Earl of Fellbridge, stood at the table by the window with his hands clapped over his mouth, his face red from the effort of suppressing what was evidently strong mirth. His younger twin, Martin, less restrained, lay on the floor laughing helplessly. They were absurdly like Freddy, possessing his large frame and handsome Roman nose and slight tendency to fleshiness which she tried to counteract by making sure they got as much fresh air and exercise as possible. They had her clear, pale-blue eyes, though, and her mother insisted they had her smile.

The third occupant of the room sat at the table by which Will stood, smiling down at a piece of paper. The twins' friend, Augustus Blackburn, was a small, rotund, and rather homely child who was saved from complete unattractiveness by his meltingly sweet brown eyes with long eyelashes and his exquisite manners. According to Martin, Gus had latched onto them like a drowning man to a log after they had rescued him from a pair of bored second-form boys intent on using him as a punching bag. No first-form boys, and very few second-formers, cared to go up against the sturdily-built Chalfont twins.

He's a Colleger—a scholarship boy—and has no mum, and his father's a tutor at Oxford and forgets about him sometimes, Will had written when asking if Gus could accompany them home for the half-term holiday. Annabel had agreed at once. Poor child, to be left to the mercy of a neglectful parent, even if that neglect wasn't malicious. How well would Freddy have cared for the boys if she'd been the one to die early?

"Do you think I got the mouth right? That's the hardest part," Gus was asking Will anxiously.

On the floor, Martin fell into fresh paroxysms of giggles. "Right? It's him to an inch!"

Will uncovered his mouth long enough to take another look, then gave up the struggle. "It *is* him to an inch, Gus," he gasped through his hilarity. "Only worse!"

"Well." Gus's smile widened into a grin. He reached for a pen, dipped it into the inkwell before him (Annabel was glad to see it was set well away from the edge of the table and Martin's flailing limbs) and wrote something carefully at the top of the paper.

"Oh ho! Did he sign it?" Martin demanded. "Capital!"

"Mama!" Will had spotted her. He tried to make his expression sober but failed miserably.

"'Morning, *O mater mea*." Martin looked up at her upside-down from the floor. "See? I'm learning something!"

"Good morning, Lady Fellbridge." Gus leapt to his feet and bowed.

"Good morning, Augustus. At least one of you has some manners."

"I said 'morning.'" Martin crossed his eyes and gave her a seraphic smile.

"Saying it whilst lying on the floor doesn't count." She came into the room, pausing to nudge Martin in the ribs with the toe of her slipper. He protested, giggling, and curled into a ball like a giddy hedgehog. "Something seems to be inspiring a great deal of amusement here."

"It's one of Gus's drawings." Will held the piece of paper out to her. "Look at this! Isn't it brilliant?"

"Oh, not really." The boy blushed and looked down at his feet.

Annabel took the paper and tried not to chuckle too openly. It was a caricature of a man in academic robes—clearly one of the boys' masters at school—

and though she had never met him she could appreciate how Gus had subtly exaggerated the man's features into ridiculousness, at the same time communicating something of his manner and character. A very sophisticated piece of work for a nine-year-old, to be sure.

"Not your favorite master, I take it?" she said, handing it back to him with a smile. She should probably remonstrate with them for mocking their elders, but her brothers' tales of some of their masters at school had impressed themselves all too well on her. She looked at Gus's hands; they were small and clumsy-looking, with stubby fingers—certainly not what one expected of such a clever artist. Appearances could deceive, couldn't they? "Well, make sure you keep these well-hidden when you're at school. I don't think Mr. Turtle—er, Tuttle, would make an appreciative audience."

"Don't worry, we do," Will assured her. "The bigger boys have stopped ragging Gus so much because they all want him to draw pictures of *their* masters." He nudged Gus. "Becket Major wants you to do one of his step-father because he's a rotter and Becket hates him. You'll have to make sure you get a good look at him come the Fourth of June when all the old boys will be around. He says he'll pay you, if it's good enough."

"Or *bad* enough," Martin corrected him. The three burst into giggles again.

The next evening, Friday, was a rout-party at

Clementina's—Annabel's favorite kind of social entertainment. One could play cards, or listen to the music that was usually provided, or just find a quiet (relatively speaking) corner and talk with friends, depending on one's mood. Talking was precisely what she hoped to do: to ask Georgiana (in person, that is; she had sent her a note yesterday as well) to help with the investigation, and see if anyone had heard how Andie was.

Clementina was receiving her guests in the tall, marble-paved hall of her house, her figure striking in a primrose Circassian gown against a backdrop of potted palms. Yellow had not perhaps been a felicitous choice; she looked pale and tired though it was barely half-past eight, and Annabel remembered that she was three months along, if not showing yet. No wonder she'd been a little short-tempered this morning.

"We're all your friends here," she murmured as they shook hands. "No one would take it amiss if you received sitting down, you know."

"*I* would," Clementina murmured in reply, then, to Annabel's surprise, burst out, "You're so lucky! I won't even be able to think about leading my first investigation till next season." Clementina had joined the Lady Patronesses last year as well, just before Annabel. But with a baby on the way, Sally would not risk putting her on any investigations.

"Next season will be here before you know it," she replied soothingly. Clementina didn't need to know precisely why she'd been given this investigation. "It seems to arrive more quickly every year."

"I hope so." Clementina assumed her usual calm, somewhat bland demeanor. "September can't get here quickly enough." She glanced down at her still gently-rounded abdomen. "This does horrid things to my sense of smell."

Annabel remembered how she couldn't bear certain scents when she was carrying the boys. "You should go to the country till then. Summer in London is hardly the place to be if you're feeling even more sensitive to odors." The Thames in July and August was enough to nauseate anyone; to Clementina, with her exquisitely keen senses, it would be torture. Perhaps that was a matter the Lady Patronesses should consider undertaking some season.

"The country isn't much better, believe me. And Peter doesn't want to leave his clubs. He has political aspirations and wants to stand for Parliament in a year or two, so he's busy laying the groundwork."

And spending ridiculous amounts of money at his tailor's. Annabel watched Clementina's husband across the hall, where he was huddled with some fellow dandies from Brooks's club. But Clementina could afford him; she'd been an enormously wealthy heiress. "Pray don't overtax yourself tonight. Or anytime this summer. You're needed. . . and we *do* care."

For a moment Clementina's expression was stiff. Then it softened, like wax in the sun. "Thank you, Annabel. I—I truly appreciate your concern."

Annabel smiled and left her to receive more guests. Poor Clementina. She'd learned to be distant and standoffish because being close to people could be so overwhelming to her senses. It was a form of self-defense. But it was also a shame that she should be a victim of her own abilities. Perhaps she'd learn to unbend a little with the Lady Patronesses if they were careful with her.

She made a circuit of the rooms. In one salon a violin, cello, and piano played a trio by Mr. Beethoven; in the dining room a noisy preponderance of the gentlemen present had gathered around the table at which a footman was serving punch.

In the salon on the other side of the hall, she found Frances Dalrymple and Maria Sefton in conversation on a sofa. "No Georgiana?" she asked, sitting down with them. "I was hoping she'd be here tonight."

"No, she had to be at her sister-in-law's card party. Frances was just telling me that you've already had your meeting," Maria said, vigorously waving her ivory-sticked fan before her. She was one of the older members of the Lady Patronesses and often complained of the heat. "What are your plans?"

Annabel was always taken aback when members like Maria or Dorothea chattered freely about the Lady Patronesses' matters in public. Once, in her earliest days as a member, she'd timidly remonstrated with Dorothea over it. Dorothea had laughed. "If you whisper and behave in a secretive fashion, everyone will try to listen to what you are saying. If you speak loudly and carelessly, they will pay you no attention whatsoever," she said—and on the whole, Annabel had to admit she was right. Nevertheless, it still felt alarming.

"We shall begin with keeping a close watch on the office on the mornings when Mr. Willis is selling tickets," she said, though in a voice quieter than Maria's. "We intend to ask Georgiana to help as well."

Her meeting with Frances, shortly after Sally left, had been brief and straightforward. They had decided they needed to get their hands on an actual voucher so that Frances could try to take a reading from it. More than one would be even better. The plan was to have Georgiana, in the shape of a bird, follow any footmen with dubious vouchers home. She could slip into houses through open windows and, if possible, steal the vouchers; if not, Annabel could conceal herself in a shadow and slip inside to accomplish the same task.

And once they had one or two, Frances would hopefully be able to wring some information from them, so long as the footman who'd last held them hadn't been thinking too hard of what bawdy house he'd visit on his next half-holiday or something similar. Annabel had decided to not tell Frances about Andie, lest it influence how she read any vouchers they might obtain; Frances was a hopeless romantic, and there was no telling what she might incorporate into her reading.

Maria fanned herself vigorously. "Georgiana! I don't envy you working with her, even though we are old friends. 'Pon rep, she's becoming more bad-tempered by the minute."

Frances nodded agreement. "I had noticed that but didn't want to say anything. Is it the sciatica? It wouldn't surprise me, under the circumstances. The last time she changed—a marmoset, wasn't it—"

Annabel reached out with one foot and delicately prodded Frances in the ankle, at the same time turning to look behind her. With her affinity for shadows, she'd felt something dark loom up behind their sofa sometime in the last minute, so it was with no great surprise (though a great deal of displeasure) that her gaze fell upon the Marquis of Quinceton, leaning casually on the sofa back and clearly—and shamelessly—eavesdropping.

"My lord," she said coldly. "Have you perhaps lost something? That is the only reason I can think of for you to be lurking behind us."

"The only reason? Why, Fellbridge! I had assumed you to possess more imagination than that."

Annabel bit back a retort. He'd started calling her "Fellbridge" last year when she'd returned to London after her mourning year in the country. It had been annoying then and hadn't stopped being so, though she'd learned to ignore it. Mostly. It was easier just to do her best to avoid the odious creature.

"Quin!" Frances squealed, scrambling to peer behind her. Annabel had not thought anyone over the age of twelve capable of making such a sound, much less a woman of at least five-and-thirty. "I did not know you would be here tonight!"

"Neither did I. Yet here I am." To Annabel's dismay the Marquis came around and managed to insinuate his tall form onto the seat next to her, close enough that if she moved, she would be forced to brush against him. "Since you seem to find my lurking objectionable, Fellbridge, I shall cease at once and listen openly and unashamedly to your charming conversation." His dark eyes sparkled at her with mischievous amusement. It was marginally better than the usual hungry wolf look he gave her, but only marginally.

Frances didn't seem to find him odious, however. She was positively *simpering* at the man. Annabel supposed that he might be considered handsome, with strong, chiseled features and an athletic physique—Freddy once said he was particularly fond of fencing and spent hours each week at Angelo's Academy in Bond Street—but she had always preferred fair men to dark.

Not to mention charming, polite ones to—to ones who didn't unabashedly eavesdrop on private conversations. What had he heard? Had any of them said anything of a too-sensitive nature? She sent Maria a desperate look across Frances, who was still smiling at Quinceton across *her*.

Maria laughed. "There, an honest man! We were just discussing the most shocking thing, Quin— someone is forging vouchers to Almack's!"

Annabel just managed not to wince and screw her face into a pained grimace. A quietly warning "Maria!" was all she dared say.

The Marquis laughed, sounding genuinely amused. "Forging vouchers to Elysium? And selling them, one presumes? Why did I never think of that? It would be a veritable goldmine!"

"Don't be silly, Quin. You've got plenty of money." Maria waggled her fan at him. "Now, this is serious. We actually had a fishmonger and his wife and daughter present themselves this past Wednesday—can you believe it?"

"A fishmonger? Clementina Drummond must have been delighted with that. Half London must be mobbing your forger's door—ah, there you go! To catch him, all you must do is look for the half-mile-long queue of hopeful brewers and cloth merchants outside some building in Seven Dials, and you'll have him."

"Oh, Quin." Frances laughed and tossed her head.

"That's not a bad idea," Maria said. "What do

you think, Annabel? It's your investigation."

Oh, confound Maria! What was she going to let slip next? "It appears that Lord Quinceton is fond of a joke," she said quellingly—she hoped.

It evidently wasn't quelling enough. "An investigation? How very business-like," he said, turning to her. "But I wouldn't expect anything less of you, Fellbridge. I hear you've put another fifty acres back under the plow and are expanding your merino flock at the Abbey."

"Who told you that?" she was startled into asking.

He shrugged. "My steward—God knows where he heard it. I didn't ask. Sound moves, at all events. You'll be able to sell that wool at a good profit, I'll wager." He still appeared to be vastly amused—but the hungry wolf expression was in his eyes again as he looked at her. She hastily looked away.

"Merinos are much cleverer than people give them credit for, you know," Maria said meditatively.

Annabel had had enough. "I shall look forward to meeting my new ones, then, when the time comes. Good evening," she said, rising. Quinceton made to rise as well, but she hurried away before he could say another word and took refuge in the salon amongst the music appreciators.

Honestly! Between his teasing and Maria's cheerful babbling about the forger... and what about the usually sensible Frances? She had turned into a— a blushing booby in the Marquis' company. Why, she was quite middle-aged! It was perfectly ridiculous.

And why should he have the least interest in what she was doing at Chalfont Abbey? It was unnerving. Besides, how she ran the estate was strictly between her and Will's trustees. They'd approved her actions; she didn't care about anyone else's opinion. *Odious* man!

She spent another hour circulating through Clementina's salons, chatting with acquaintances and picking up gossip—a valuable commodity to the Lady Patronesses—though she unfortunately didn't learn anything of use in her investigation. Nor was there any word about Andie—everyone presumed she was still recuperating from her shocking accident. Ah well. At least her efforts had removed her from the Marquis of Quinceton's vicinity. . . until, of course, she was in the front hall waiting for her carriage to be brought around.

He bore down on her purposefully; she could think of no excuse to flee or a way to melt into the shadow of Clementina's potted palms, for his eyes were fixed on her. Oh, why hadn't her carriage already come?

"Was there something you wished to say to me, my lord?" she inquired coolly when it became impossible to ignore the fact that he was standing directly in front of her.

He raised his eyebrows. "So prickly, Fellbridge. May I ask why?"

She blinked. "What?"

A smile quirked the corners of his mouth. "You appear to have taken me in great dislike since your return to London. I merely wondered why. I'm not aware of ever having done you an injury, but my memory could be at fault."

Annabel opened her mouth and closed it. He hadn't, of course—and she wanted to keep it that way. His reputation—and his association with the less reputable of Freddy's friends—made her as nervous as his hungry wolf stare did. She didn't *know* he was bad, but she didn't want to try to confirm it, either.

"I. . . I dislike the way you call me Fellbridge," she finally said. "I would prefer *Lady* Fellbridge, if you please."

"Really?" Drat it, why did everything seem to amuse the man? "I mean it as a compliment. Your son is too young to carry it meaningfully, and you're far more a man than Freddy ever was."

Annabel drew herself up. "You have a very peculiar notion of flattery, sir!"

"Saying that you show evidence of intelligent, decisive behavior would seem a compliment to me," he said calmly. "I cannot help if you choose to take it in a different spirit."

She bit back a retort. Brangling with him would accomplish nothing. "What did you wish to say to me, Lord Quinceton?" she demanded, forcing herself to meet his gaze.

Something flickered in his eyes, then was gone almost before she'd registered it. "Even the most decisive and intelligent of people occasionally need a helping hand. If I can be of assistance as you hunt down your voucher forger, I am at your service." Before she could recover from her shock sufficiently to make a coherent reply, he had bowed and left.

Annabel got into her carriage a few moments later, grateful for the footman who prevented her in her distraction from climbing into the wrong one. What had that been all about? Why should the Marquis of Quinceton wish to pay the slightest attention to her affairs?

And what had he meant by paying her a *compliment*? Granted, it wasn't the usual kind of tribute a man offered a woman. If he'd called her beautiful, she would have laughed and forgotten about it within an hour, once the initial discomposure had worn off. But this was different. She shivered, remembering his words and his eyes as he uttered them.

And then she shivered again as the memory of more of his words that evening rose to mind. Why had he said that Clementina in particular must have been dismayed at the presence of a fishmonger at Almack's? Granted, she was known for being a stickler for proper form. . . but so were Sally and Dorothea. There could be no possibility—*surely* there wasn't—that he knew about Clementina's abilities. . . or could there be?

Good heavens, this would not do! She was permitting the man to completely derange her senses, for no very good reason. *This is ludicrous, Annabel!* she told herself firmly. *Put this nonsense out of your head at once!*

By the time her carriage had turned into Chesterfield Street, she had all but convinced herself that she was suffering from a bout of mental indigestion brought on by a surfeit of Quinceton. No more letting her imagination wander into such fevered paths, led on by the sinister—no, that was far too fevered, too—by the dubious marquis.

Her resolution to remain firmly anchored in sense and to avoid sensibility, however, lasted only until her coachman drew up before her house. John, one of her footmen, came hurrying out the front door.

"'Evening, my lady," he said, opening the door.

"Good even—" She paused, frowning. Beyond John's shoulder she was sure she saw someone—a very large, muscular man, judging by his shape and size—slip through the front door and dodge into the narrow alley between her house and the house next door. "Who's there?" she called sharply.

"Your ladyship?" John regarded her in puzzlement.

"I saw—I *thought* I saw someone leaving the house, behind you—you wouldn't have seen. . ." She accepted his hand and stepped from the landau, pausing to peer at the neighboring house; shadow-shaping had sharpened her ability to see into darkness. Was that a movement in the unlit stairwell down to the servants' area?

"Out the front door?" John sounded genuinely perplexed. "I can't think who it could have been. I was waiting in the hall for you to come home, and there wasn't anyone with me."

"Is there anything amiss, ma'am?" Her butler Hanscomb's imposing bulk appeared in the doorway, outlined in the light from the hall.

"I thought I saw someone come out of the house," she said, still staring into the darkness.

"I do not think it possible, ma'am," Hanscomb said, politely but definitely. "John has been in the hall since nine, and I myself locked the other entrances to the house hours ago. A trick of the light, perhaps."

"Of—of course." Annabel tore her gaze away from the house next door and ascended the stairs, Hanscomb drawing aside to let her pass. He waited for John to come in, then unostentatiously but firmly locked the door behind him.

"All secure, your ladyship. Just as it was before you arrived at home," he said with a reassuring nod.

Annabel tried to smile, and mostly succeeded. "Thank you, Hanscomb." She turned to the stairs and began to climb them, her back straight and her pace steady—but inside her mind was racing. She *had* seen someone emerging from the house—she was sure of it—and could not shake the impression she'd received, as it turned in the light from the doorway, that the large figure had been wearing a florid pink waistcoat.

Chapter Three

"I believe this might be one, ma'am," Mr. Willis murmured through stiff lips, inclining his head toward the open door of the tiny anteroom office where he and Annabel, swathed in a shadow, waited. "I've not seen that livery before."

Annabel rose from her chair and glanced at the footman in plain maroon livery approaching the door. "Very good," she murmured back, and reached up to tap once on the slightly open window where Georgiana Bathurst, in the guise of a pigeon, perched on the windowsill outside. "Just behave as you normally would, if you please, and we'll do the rest."

He reached up to tug at his cravat. "I shall endeavor to do my best, Lady Fellbridge."

Poor Mr. Willis. He knew, of course, about the Lady Patronesses' second, secret function within Almack's—how could he not, with his uncle-in-law still haunting the premises?—but being confronted with any evidence of their extraordinary talents always made the poor man very nervous indeed. Not that she blamed him; sitting in a small room for hours with an invisible woman would not have been easy for anyone.

It was early afternoon on Saturday. She and Georgiana (who'd received her note and come today, thank goodness) had been here since ten that morning, lying in wait—she in her shadows, Georgiana in her feathers—waiting for a forged voucher to be presented for the purchase of tickets to next Wednesday's ball. It had been a long morning for all of them—Georgiana kept shifting from foot to foot and cooing to herself in a discontented fashion, and Mr. Willis had sat in his chair gingerly, like one afflicted with piles. A slow but steady trickle of footmen and private secretaries had come into the office to purchase tickets, but none of them had had vouchers signed by her.

While Mr. Willis squirmed and Georgiana cooed, Annabel spent the morning thinking about the scene in front of her house the previous evening. Hanscomb, her footman, and her coachman all had denied seeing anything—or anyone—amiss, and she had no reason to disbelieve them. But she *knew* she had caught a glimpse of a tall, broad-shouldered man emerging from her house. . . and the fact that he had appeared to be wearing a flowered pink waistcoat strongly suggested that she had received a visit from Andie's prize-fighter—what was his name? Tom?

But how had he gotten into her house and, most importantly, why had he been there? Had Andie told him she was going to get him a voucher to Almack's from her old friend Lady Fellbridge? With Andie injured, had he decided to take matters into his own hands—especially since he had, according to Andie, experience with robbing houses? (*"Just as a lookout, Annabel!"* she could hear Andie's protest in her head.)

The sound of footsteps just outside the office brought her attention back to the moment. She inched closer to Mr. Willis, waiting.

The footman appeared and paused in the doorway. "This where the tickets for Almack's are sold?"

Mr. Willis nodded. "If you will show me your voucher, please?"

"Not my voucher." The footman grinned cheerfully and pulled it from a pocket. "Don't think you want the likes o' me dancing with the fine ladies here." He handed the voucher to Mr. Willis. "Three tickets, the missus said t'ask for."

Annabel touched Mr. Willis's shoulder and leaned over him to read it. As they had pre-arranged, he pretended to peer nearsightedly at the voucher then fumble for his spectacles, to give her a few extra seconds to examine it.

A sick, sinking feeling gripped her as she did. It looked like any Almack's voucher. . . and yes, there was what appeared to be her signature at lower right. But she had never written a voucher for a Mrs. Nehemiah Stubbs. Moreover, the handwriting of the name had a tentative quality to it, just as if someone had looked at her handwriting and tried to guess how she would form the letters. She tapped Mr. Willis's shoulder twice in their pre-arranged signal and stepped back, feeling slightly dizzy. It was definitely a forgery.

"Very well." Mr. Willis handed the voucher back and reached into a desk drawer. "That will be £1/10, if you please."

There had been some acrimonious discussion amongst her and Francis and Georgiana about what to do when they were actually confronted with a forged voucher. Georgiana had been all for immediate confiscation and summoning a Bow Street Runner; it had taken a great deal of patient explanation to convince her that such an action would make eventually discovering the identity of the forger much more difficult. In the meanwhile, Annabel had agreed to sign no more vouchers until they'd caught their man—or woman.

The footman dug a small, jingling pouch from his pocket. "There you go, sir. Waste o' good money, if y'ask me."

"I didn't," Mr. Willis said, and handed him the tickets. The footman grinned again, touched the edge of his hat, and sauntered out.

Annabel released a breath she hadn't known she was holding and leaned over to tap twice on the window. "Footman in maroon," she whispered. "He should just be leaving."

Georgiana made a pigeonish sound of assent and leapt into the air. Mr. Willis flinched and shifted in his chair to mitigate the movement. "What will happen now, if I may ask?"

"Lady Bathurst will endeavor to retrieve the voucher and bring it back here. If she's successful, we'll send for Lady Frances to come right away to do a reading on it, to try to identify the forger. If she can't get the voucher, we shall return on Monday morning and so on until we can get at least one to examine. Two or three would be even better." Annabel sat down again in the chair below the window with a sigh.

"You were able to obtain a clear look at it, then? It was definitely one of the bad ones? I tried to ensure you had time for a thorough examination." Mr. Willis opened the pouch, peeked inside, nodded, and tucked it into a drawer. "I thought it must be. The footmen who've brought in forged vouchers have obviously been from less distinguished households. You can tell by their training—"

"Talk to yourself a lot, do you?"

Annabel jumped, as did Mr. Willis. Another footman—a very young one—this time in bright blue livery, lounged in the doorway.

Mr. Willis recovered himself. "I generally choose the most intelligent person in the room to converse with, which often means I talk to myself. Have you business with me?"

"If you're the one what's got the tickets to Almack's, I do."

"I see. Very well, may I have the voucher, please?"

Annabel stood up quickly to peer over his shoulder. Of course; three hours of waiting, and now they had two forgeries in a row. Well, there was nothing else for it: with Georgiana gone, she would have to follow this one home and at least make note of the address if she couldn't gain easy access to the house. She would have no chance to warn Mr. Willis she was doing so; she had told him she would leave her hat on her chair if she had to follow a voucher, and turned to place it gently on the seat without rustling the ribbons and draped a separate shadow over it. Hopefully he would realize, when there was no response to his conversation, that she had gone in pursuit, though she wondered if he'd be brave enough to pat the chair to confirm her absence.

She waited while money and some cheeky words were exchanged—goodness, were all footmen so impertinent when not actually waiting on their employers?—and set forth after the young man, just slipping out the street door before he closed it. She snatched some of the building's shadow around her as extra protection, and took off after her quarry, who seemed to be headed for Duke Street.

Annabel had learned, over the last year of work for the Lady Patronesses, that there was a definite art to walking the streets of London whilst shadow-clad. The first rule was to stay close to a source of shadow, which meant keeping as close as she could to buildings or other large objects. Crossing the street could be problematic, but she usually endeavored to follow near enough to another pedestrian's shadow to not create a visible moving darkness. Beyond that, it was a matter of keeping pace with the people around her and watching for unexpected flailing arms or changes of direction.

Following someone was a more challenging prospect. This footman's livery was sufficiently conspicuous in color that it was easy to keep him in sight; less fortunately, he was a dawdler, frequently pausing to peer in shop windows or examine handsome carriage horses or ogle pretty girls on the street. That meant keeping out of the way of others while watching for him to start moving again. The day was clear and sunny, perfect spring weather, and the pavements were crowded with strolling, ambling Londoners who all seemed determined to collide with her. By the time they'd crossed Piccadilly, she was perspiring. Oh, please let him be heading directly home. . .

As it turned out, he wasn't. He made several stops: at a tobacconist's shop, an apothecary, and a lending library. Home eventually turned out to be on a small side street in Soho, in a respectable but not-quite-fashionable neighborhood. Annabel watched her blue footman clatter down the area stairs to the servants' entrance. The door below was wedged open to let in the soft spring air—thank goodness it was not raining! She tiptoed down the steps and peered inside.

A small but clean and well-organized kitchen met her gaze. A young kitchen maid stood at a table, kneading dough, while a comfortably fat woman with one plump bandaged foot up on a footstool sat nearby, directing her.

"More flour on yer hands, so the dough don't stick. Back at last, are you?" she was saying to the footman, who was picking at the remains of a chicken obviously waiting to be turned into soup. "Here, you leave that be. Miss 'enry's been down twice to see if you was back yet. Best get yourself upstairs afore the poor mite has a spasm."

The footman made a face at her and wiped his fingers on his backside, under his coat where the grease stains wouldn't show. Annabel restrained herself from scolding him; Martin had an unfortunate tendency to do the same thing. "She can wait another minute. I'm starvin'."

"She can, but she shouldn't have to. Begone with you, or we won't give you none of the bread an' cheese an' ale we was savin' for a snack in an 'arf-hour."

"Yes, mum. Yer a love." The footman stopped to

drop a smacking kiss on her cheek, winked at the giggling kitchen maid, and headed for an open doorway. Annabel flitted after him like a ghost.

A short, dark hallway led to a flight of stairs which the footman was already clattering up. Annabel left off her outdoor shadows and pulled on some softer indoor ones, following him as quickly as possible so that the noise of his heavy tread would cover any sounds she might make. The stairs went up for three more flights but he left them at the first landing, on what must be the ground floor of the house. She waited for him to go through the door, then opened it behind him just a crack and peered through it.

The footman was standing at a table in the front hall of the house, which was surprisingly elegantly furnished: the carpet was Turkish and the table at which the footman stood, depositing his packages, was in the Egyptian style so popular currently. She saw the small bundles from the tobacconist's, the apothecary—ah! There were the small pasteboard Almack's tickets, along with the voucher.

"Edmund—is that you?" a girl's voice called. Annabel drew back from the door, narrowing the crack through which she peeked, then after a minute widened it cautiously and looked again.

A very pretty girl, with brown ringlets and pink cheeks to match her pink muslin dress—Miss Henry, Annabel assumed—had danced into the hall. "Oh, it is! Did you get them? Was it all right?"

"Right and tight, miss," the footman said, in a much more respectful tone than Annabel had yet heard him use that day. "Here you are." He handed her the tickets.

"Oh!" The girl stared at them for a moment, then broke into a silvery laugh of pure delight. "Oh, thank you, Edmund! I must just go show them to Mama! Thank you! Oh, *how* can I endure until Wednesday? Wait until Papa sees! How I wish I could thank his friend for giving us one! Oh, I am so happy!" She lifted her skirts and hurried past the table and out of Annabel's sight, obviously on her way upstairs to find Mama.

The footman watched her go, grinning, then turned back to the door behind which Annabel hid. She gave a gasp and just managed to hurry down the stairs ahead of him, stepping away at the bottom while he continued toward the kitchen, obviously drawn by the promised bread and cheese and ale. Annabel wished she could sit down as well with a glass of ale, but her work was far from done. She waited until the conversation level in the kitchen indicated that all were occupied with their snack, and once more slipped up the stairs.

To her immense relief, the voucher still lay where the footman had left it among the packages on the Egyptian table. Annabel tucked it into her pocket, and after opening the front door and peering cautiously out, slipped out and closed it behind her. Ducking back behind the low wall that concealed the area steps, she dropped her shadow.

There! Assuming Georgiana had been successful as well, that gave them two vouchers for Frances to examine. All she had to do was find a hackney to return to King Street, because she was *not* going to walk all that way again, and—

And realized she'd left her reticule in Mr. Willis' office as well as her hat, so as to be able to walk more soundlessly while she followed the footman. Oh, botheration! She'd be footsore indeed by the time she made it back to Almack's but there was no help for it. Frances would be waiting for her.

She started to gather a handful of shadow, then let it slither through her fingers. Walking concealed would mean having to dodge and weave and pay close attention to everything around her, and just now she was too tired and furthermore wanted to think about what she had seen and what light it might cast on the identity of the forger. No one would know who she was in this neighborhood or care if she wore a hat or not. She stepped out from her hiding place, head held high, and started down the street.

As much as she disliked admitting it, Lord Quinceton was likely correct that whoever was forging vouchers was selling them: Miss Henry's innocent reference to Papa's friend who had given him a voucher was just the sort of well-meaning lie a doting father would tell his beloved daughter if he didn't want to upset her. But why would Andie have taken the at least two dozen vouchers that were missing from her desk? She'd only wanted *one* for her prize-fighter.

If she'd hastily grabbed a handful of vouchers while seated at Annabel's desk, just in case Annabel refused to give her one, giving away the remainder to all and sundry would be a fine revenge. But selling them? Andie's father, the Earl of Allston, was very comfortably off, and her mother had inherited a fortune from her nabob grandfather. Andie was not short of pin money.

But if her prize-fighter—Tom, was it?—with his admittedly shady past, had seen Andie's stack of vouchers, *he* might have decided that they should not go to waste. And if that had indeed been him sneaking out of her house last night—she drew in a sharp breath. Had he been looking for more?

Most her remaining anger and exasperation with Andie vanished. They had to find out if Tom the prize-fighter was the thief; if indeed he were, that would likely be a large enough lever to pry the pair of them apart. All she would have to do after that was keep Georgiana from taking away Andie's voucher by way of retaliation. Poor Lady Allston would be devastated if that happened—

"Fellbridge?"

Annabel glanced up—and suppressed a groan of irritation. Lord Quinceton had pulled up beside her in his beautifully lacquered curricle and was staring down at her in puzzled amusement. Oh, *why* hadn't she ignored her weariness and put a shadow back on at once when she'd realized she'd have to walk back to King Street?

"Good afternoon, Lord Quinceton," she said in a tone that would hopefully quash any further attempts to engage her attention and kept on walking.

He gave his reins the smallest twitch, and his team fell into a walk beside her. "This is an, ah, unexpected meeting."

"Yes, isn't it?" She forced a chilly affability into her voice. "However, I do not wish to detain you. . ."

"You aren't." He somehow managed to make his team's pace match hers, even as she lagged slower and slower. Drat him for being such a competent driver. "May I ask why you're walking down the street with neither a hat nor an attendant in sight?"

"You may ask," she said, quickening her steps

to see what would happen.

He kept pace with her, glancing from her to his horses and back, until she snapped, "But just because you might ask doesn't mean I'll answer!"

He laughed. "That's put me in my place! Come now, Fellbridge. I can only surmise that you're in some element of distress, or at least have been inconvenienced. Will you permit me to humbly offer what little succor I am able and accept a ride to—to wherever you're going?"

Annabel was oh-so-tempted to thank him frostily and decline. But he would doubtless persist in driving alongside her all the way to Almack's just to torment her. Besides, her feet were positively *beging* for relief. "If you will be so kind as to drop me in King Street, I would be much obliged," she ground out.

He raised one eyebrow but halted his team, called to a loitering boy to hold their heads, and leapt down to hand her up into the seat. "Not Chesterfield Street?" he asked when he'd resumed his place and tossed the boy a coin.

"I have business at Almack's."

"Retrieving your hat, perchance?"

"Yes," she said, barely biting out the syllable.

He drove in silence for some minutes. Annabel concentrated on the fact that her feet were no longer complaining and on estimating how long it would be before they would arrive in King Street. To her annoyance, the amount of carriage traffic seemed far heavier than usual, slowing their progress.

"How goes your investigation of voucher forgery?" he finally asked, glancing at her sideways.

She thought about pretending not to have

heard him, but he was fully capable of repeating the question at the top of his voice just to embarrass her. "I cannot begin to guess why this investigation—which exists solely in your imagination, I might add—should be of the least interest to you, Lord Quinceton."

He ignored the absurd contradiction in her statement. "No? And here I had always taken you for a person of superior perception. You disappoint me, Fellbridge." Before she could sputter her indignation, he went on. "Despite her occasional show of, ah, woolly-mindedness, I have always found Maria Sefton to be a clever enough woman. But perhaps she was mistaken when referring to an investigation yesterday evening."

"Indeed," Annabel said in as dampening a voice as possible.

"I am sure you are right," he said meekly—so meekly that she shot him a suspicious look. His gaze was fixed guilelessly on his horses, but the faintest hint of a smile about the corners of his mouth both enraged and silenced her. Oh, the infernal cheek of him!

Silence—blessed silence!—fell between them. Annabel had resumed calculating how much longer it would take for them to get to Almack's when Lord Quinceton spoke again. "The offer still stands, you know."

"I beg your pardon?"

"The offer of any assistance I might be able to render you."

Really, this was the outside of enough. "My lord, I should like to know what kind of assistance you possibly think you could render me."

"Very little, I'm sure." He paused, then added, "Though I am bringing you to King Street right now, I collect."

Annabel opened her mouth—and just in time closed it again. He *had* rescued her from a very tedious walk back to Almack's; she couldn't deny that. "Thank you, Lord Quinceton," she said stiffly. "I do appreciate that."

He smiled, but did not speak again. The rest of the drive took place in silence, a silence that made Annabel squirm. Why did the man have to take such delight in teasing her—and worse, why was he so *good* at it?

When they finally drew up in King Street, her feet were the only happy part of her. A footman came running out to help her alight.

"Thank you, sir," she said. Relief at being here, plus a hint of shame at her earlier churlishness, goaded her into showing a modicum of graciousness. "I trust I have not taken you too far out of your way."

"Oh, you have," he replied cheerfully. "But it was well worth it. I have wanted to take you driving this age but hadn't quite figured out how to convince you to accompany me."

And before she could formulate a response, he'd lifted his hat and driven smartly away.

"I sat on your hat," Frances greeted her apologetically when she walked into Mr. Willis's office a few moments later, once her ire had cooled. "I didn't know it was on the chair. I can't tell if it's ruined or not."

Of course she had. It was a fitting coda to the irksome journey she'd just made. Annabel brushed the concealing shadow from it. "It's just a little squashed on one side. Good enough to get me home with." Which she would reach if she had to drag herself there by her elbows. . . which she would do, if the only alternative was to accept a ride from that toad, Lord Quinceton—

She took a deep breath. Time to put him out of her mind. "Were you able to get the voucher?" she asked Georgiana.

Georgiana pointed at the desk where a voucher sat, one edge somewhat indented by being carried in a pigeon's beak. "And now, if my presence is no longer required, I would like to make my departure."

"Oh, of course. I'm so sorry if you've been waiting. It took me longer than I expected to get here, but now we have two." Georgiana's sciatica was probably bothering her again, poor thing. "Thank you so much for your help, Georgiana. I appreciate it deeply."

Georgiana gave her a short nod and swept out of the room.

"Well!" Frances said, as soon as she was out of earshot. "Could she have been any snippier? She barely said a word to me while we waited for you, Annabel."

"It doesn't matter," Annabel said. Suddenly she felt as tired as poor Georgiana undoubtedly was. It had been a long day—and it wasn't over yet. She took the Henrys' voucher from her pocket and set it down next to Georgiana's. "Let's see what you make of these."

Frances sat down at the desk, closed her eyes, and took a few deep breaths. She reached out before her and groped for one of the vouchers, laid it across her left palm, and ran the fingers of her right hand over it. Annabel extracted a small notepad and pencil from her reticule to take notes and watched her tensely.

"Oh," Frances said softly. "Someone was happy to receive this." She brushed her fingers across it again as if dusting off some unwanted residue, then rested her right palm against it so that the voucher was flat between her hands and brought it close to her chest. A small frown appeared between her eyebrows, as if she were trying to identify a distant voice.

"Great need," she murmured. "He very much needs the money. It won't do any harm, really, will it? And the money—he won't have to worry any more. He can go back, and not worry."

"*He?*" Annabel looked up quickly.

"I—I think so. He wants to go back where he belongs, with his friends." Frances's frown deepened. "And after that—" She sat for a minute longer, then set the voucher aside and felt for the other one. She held it too between her palms. "After that he can do what he really wants to do. Great need. . . " she murmured again, and relaxed against the back of the chair. "That's all I can get," she added in a more normal voice, opening her eyes and setting the voucher down. "There's no malice—just need for the money."

Annabel tapped her pencil, thinking. Frances seemed convinced that a man had done the forgeries. Did that mean Andie hadn't taken the vouchers? Or had she given them to her prize-fighter, who was selling them because he needed the money for some purpose? Did it involve carrying Andie off to live happily ever after in a quaint little cottage some-where? Andie would think it terribly romantic. . . for the first couple of hours. Annabel rather doubted Andie had ever set foot in a cottage—

But she couldn't worry about Andie's romantic escapades now. There was a thief and a forger to catch—and whether they were one and the same was a vexed question.

If Andie had stolen them from her desk, then she was likely giving them to someone else; Tom the prize-fighter was the likely recipient. Was he forging her name on them, perhaps with Andie's help? She could not be sure the man was lettered enough to do so. He might have sold them—or was in partnership with someone else—someone familiar with Almack's vouchers. . .

"Might the forger be someone who already has a voucher to Almack's that he used to copy from?" she asked Frances. That would explain it: Andie's prize-fighter could be working with or sold them to someone who could copy her signature and in turn sell them to fish-mongers and wine-merchants. She would have to sit down and make a list of the vouch-ers she'd approved in the past year, then show it to the rest of the Lady Patronesses to see if any of them had heard gossip about, say, a young man with excessive debts whose situation was becoming dire.

Frances rubbed her temples, thoroughly des-troying the coquettish curls clustered there. "I don't know. We ought to go through the voucher list and see if we can find anyone who answers to that description—Dorothea will know, if anyone will. Oh, my head. . ."

Poor Frances often got the head-ache after doing a reading. "I'll call on her tomorrow," Annabel said. "I do believe I've had enough for one day, too." She found Mr. Willis upstairs in the ballroom, supervising the washing of the windows, and asked him to hail a hackney to bring them home.

Though it was out of the way, she had Frances brought home first to Carrick House. It had been a productive day—Sally could not accuse her of procrastination!—even if she were exhausted now. If only Frances had been able to glean a little more information from the vouchers. . . but it was something to start with.

To her dismay, when the hackney pulled up before her house, a trio of what looked like honest, hard-working, successful merchant princes were standing on the pavement before it, eyeing each other uncertainly. Three of them! And this time there was no John-the-footman to keep them at bay to enable her to get into the house unaccosted. This was getting to be the outside of enough—she would *have* to remember to ask if the others were as plagued by voucher-seekers as she was when the Lady Patronesses met on Monday and discuss possible remedies. If only they had a witch among them, who could cast protective circles about each of their houses!

But what should she do in the meanwhile? Could she pretend to be her own lady's maid, and enter the house through the kitchen? Though it would shock her staff, desperate measures were sometimes required. . . but no. Her attire—even her hat, in its battered condition—was too distinctly that of a lady to allow her to attempt such a masquerade. She sighed, got out of the carriage on the street side to pay the driver, and prepared to run the gauntlet. Never had her front door seemed so far away as it did right now.

"Is that Lady Fellbridge?" one of them said as the hackney clopped away, revealing her.

"I think it's her," a second muttered. "Unless it's a caller. But what's she doing in a hack? Don't she have her own carriage?"

"No, it's her, all right," the third one said, in assured tones. "I saw a picture of her at the London Exhibition last year that the missus dragged me to. Your ladyship, if I might have a word—my friend Mr. Watkins said you were quite willing to deal—"

Annabel winced. So this *was* the reason she'd had so many hopeful voucher seekers on her doorstep: word had gotten out that vouchers could be had for a price from Lady Fellbridge. How deeply embarrassing—but here was her chance to try to learn something about the forger. She made her way partway up the stairs, not meeting anyone's eye, then paused. They clustered eagerly below her, hats doffed. "Lady Fellbridge—" began one.

"Might one of you be so kind as to tell me where you learned that I was selling vouchers?" she asked before they grew too importunate.

They turned and looked at each other, puzzled. "Why're you wanting to know that?" one asked. "Aren't you?"

"As a matter of fact, I am not—" she began, but her words were drowned by the cries of the men.

"For shame!" one said. "I saw the one you sold my friend—with your name on it, bold as brass!"

Annabel edged up a step. "It may have been my name, but—"

"It got my friend in at Almack's, so it's good enough for me!

"See here, your ladyship—my daughter'll be heartbroken if I don't come home with one!"

Would she have to beg? "Please—it is very important that I know who told you that I would sell you a voucher."

"Don't tell her," the first man said to his companions. "I'll wager she's having second thoughts and all and wants to get us in trouble."

The third climbed a step, reaching out a hand beseechingly, but stopped short of plucking at her sleeve, thank goodness. "Please, ma'am! I have the money with me right now." He held up a small purse and waved it at her, rather like one would show a bone to a dog. "Twice the usual amount!"

"Here, Borman, stop that!" The man with a friend named Watkins pushed down the other man's hand. "How'd you like it if some strange man 'costed your wife like that?"

"My wife ain't selling vouchers to Almack's, is she?"

Annabel hastily hopped up the last steps while the men argued below her. A small gray cat was sitting on the next-to-highest stair, regarding her disdainfully. "Excuse me, puss," she said, stepping over it. "This might be a dangerous place to sun yourself right now." She gave the doorknocker a sharp rap. Oh, where was Hanscomb?

The sound recalled the men to their original purpose. "Lady Fellbridge, please—"

Oh, bother! She was clearly not going to get any useful information from them. "Not now!" she called over her shoulder.

"When?"

"Shall we return tomorrow? What time?"

"Tomorrow, your ladyship?" Another of the men had actually begun to climb the stairs after her.

She didn't answer, but gave the doorknocker another desperate rap. The cat spat at her and ran away just as Hanscomb opened the door, and she nearly fell inside.

Chapter Four

On Monday morning, the Lady Patronesses met in their comfortable room in King Street. Annabel had not had a chance to apprise Sally of their findings; Martin had had one of his bilious attacks yesterday and she had remained at home to care for him, reading *Gulliver's Travels* to the three boys who had sprawled on his bed to listen.

Emily took the seat next to her. "Any luck?" she murmured.

"Some, I trust," Annabel just had time to whisper back before Sally cleared her throat and said, "Shall we begin? Annabel, have you a report for us?"

Annabel took a deep breath—but before she could begin, Georgiana Bathurst leaned forward. "Sally, if I may speak?"

Sally blinked and glanced at Annabel with raised eyebrows. Annabel returned her look with a lifting of her shoulders to show her puzzlement. What did Georgiana mean to say? Had she learned something new about the vouchers—something she hadn't had time to communicate to her and Frances?

"It is irregular not to permit the principal investigator to speak first—that is, assuming that what you have to say is relevant to the discussion for which we have gathered," Sally replied to Georgiana.

"Oh, it's quite relevant." Georgiana rose from her chair, smoothing her skirt complacently as she did. "You see, *I've* found the forger."

A few gasps were heard around the table. Annabel regarded Georgiana with confusion. "You have? Why didn't you tell me?"

Georgiana turned to look at her. Her expression hardened. "Don't play the innocent with me, Lady Fellbridge." The use of her title felt like a little slap. "You know very well who the forger is. In fact, I daresay you and she are intimate friends."

"But it's *not* a she," Frances protested. "I'm quite sure it's a he. I got a very masculine identity from both the vouchers."

"Georgiana, I don't have any idea of what you're talking about." Maria's usually placid brow was furrowed. "Can you stop being so cryptic? Is there a forger or not?"

"Was your friend in on it, too?" Georgiana ignored Maria and instead pointed at Emily, her finger shaking with the force of her emotion. "Is that how you got us thinking about forgers? Very clever of you, to be sure, but not clever enough."

"I am sorry. I was not aware that we would be enacting amateur theatricals at our meeting today," Dorothea drawled. "I shall be Cleopatra, yes?" She stroked one of her curls.

The room was engulfed in a flood of exclamations and expostulation. Sally tapped her pencil sharply on the table's edge, and when that had no effect, rose from her chair. *"If everyone will be so good as to refrain from speaking?"* When Sally used that tone of voice, she meant it. Everyone quieted, and she turned to Georgiana. "Very well. Georgiana, will you please speak plainly? Who is the forger?"

Georgiana moved her accusing finger from Emily's astonished countenance to Annabel's. *"There* is your forger! But there is no forgery going on. Why should she have to forge her own name in order to sell vouchers?"

This time, dead silence met Georgiana's words. Sally sat down and regarded her levelly. "That is a very serious accusation, Georgiana. I hope that you're ready to support it with incontrovertible evidence. And for heaven's sake, sit down, please."

Annabel fought back a growing impulse to seize a handful of shadow and hide. Was this really happening? Had Georgiana gone mad?

She realized her hands were clenched in her lap, the nails digging into the tender flesh of her palms. Emily reached under the table for one, holding it tight. A small, unmirthful laugh rose in her throat. Was Emily comforting her, or looking to read her mind for signs of guilt?

"Don't be such a gudgeon," Emily muttered from the corner of her mouth.

Georgiana took her time settling herself in her chair before fixing Annabel with a smug stare. "Lady Fellbridge asked me to help obtain some of these so-called forged vouchers. I joined her at Mr. Willis's office on Friday, and at her signal followed a footman who had just come in to purchase tickets. I was able to remove the voucher from the house in Hans Town where it had been taken and return with it to King Street, but Lady Fellbridge herself was out, supposedly in pursuit of another voucher. I had leisure to examine the voucher I had retrieved, and was struck by how skillful the forger was—I could not see that the signature differed in any way from Lady Fellbridge's."

"Are you *that* familiar with Annabel's handwriting?" Clementina asked.

Georgiana flushed at the skepticism dripping from her words. "Familiar enough to know it when I see it," she snapped. "Which made me ponder. We all know Lady Fellbridge's—"

Emily gave an exasperated groan. "This is quite ridiculous! Her name is Annabel. A. Na. Bel. Or had you forgotten?"

"Emily, please." Sally sounded tired. "Pray continue, Georgiana."

"Thank you." Georgiana gave Emily a superior look. "As I was saying, everyone knows that Lady Fellbridge's financial position is a precarious one. We all know she's pinching pennies in order to hold the estate together and send her sons to school. I began to wonder if she hadn't thought of a new way to raise some funds—by selling vouchers!"

"Oh, *really*." Dorothea looked bored. "You will have to do better than that if you want to convince us that Annabel is the guilty party. She's a Shellingham. She's no more capable of doing something like that than the Prince of Wales is of being faithful to—to anyone."

"Wait until you've heard the rest, Countess High and Mighty!" Georgiana shot back. Dorothea snorted and shook her head.

"So when she returned to King Street with some tale of having been detained while fetching her voucher, I left, pleading indisposition, and went to her house. I had a suspicion that I could make some interesting discoveries if I was patient enough. My patience was soon rewarded." She sat back and folded her hands, looking smug.

"If you don't finish explaining yourself, I shall *strike* you!" Emily cried.

"Emily, don't make me ask you to leave the room," Sally said sternly. 'Georgiana, I should be much obliged if you would forego the tension-increasing pauses and *just get on with it*."

"My apologies, Sally," Georgiana said primly. "I went to Lady Fellbridge's house and took the form of a cat, hoping to slip inside and examine her papers. My sciatica would not permit my taking a bird form again so soon."

"But how interesting," Dorothea murmured. "I had thought, stupid me, that sciatica was an illness of the lower limbs, not the upper."

Georgiana glared at Dorothea but went on. "Upon my arrival at her house, I found three men of unmistakably mercantile appearance waiting on the pavement outside her house. When Lady Fellbridge herself arrived in a hackney an hour later, they fell upon her, demanding the chance to speak with her. When one of them offered to give her money, and another referred to his daughter's heartbreak, it became abundantly clear what they were there for. For some reason she put them off, saying to come back the next day."

A cat! Annabel stared at her. There had been that little gray cat, sunning itself on her front steps after she'd dropped Frances off. . . and she certainly hadn't told those men to come back. They were the ones to say that; desperate as she'd been to escape them, she'd never have said that—had she?

"That proves nothing, Georgiana," Sally said.

"But this does. I went back to her house first thing on Sunday and waited all day, watching, and saw a very interesting transaction take place. About three in the afternoon, the men gathered again. . . and a small boy came quietly out of the house, looked about him in a most sneaking manner, and went down to talk to them. I saw him give each of them pieces of paper—voucher-sized pieces of paper, I might add—and in exchange, they each gave him small, heavy-looking purses. There!" she added, looking down her nose at Annabel. "What do you think of that, my lady Treachery? And shame on you, involving your innocent children in your crime! I call it reprehensible, and I hope their trustees will be informed that you are an unfit mother. Not that they're probably your husband's," she added, her lip curling. "The boy I saw looked nothing like Fellbridge—so short and dark—"

"Annabel's boys aren't short in the least degree," Emily interrupted, frowning. "And they're the image of Freddy. You must have been at the wrong house, *Lady* Bathurst."

Sally looked pained. "Don't you start that foolishness too," she muttered, then turned to Georgiana. "Emily is correct. Annabel's sons are the very image of their father."

Georgiana opened her mouth, then closed it. "I know what I saw," she finally said. "And I saw a boy come out of Lady Fellbridge's house to sell vouchers to those men. Maybe it was a servant boy, doing his mistress's bidding."

Annabel was still sitting stunned in her seat. Who, and what, had Georgiana seen? She employed no pages, and the only boy in her house who fit Georgiana's description was little Gus. But she'd been with the boys all day yesterday, keeping Martin quiet and entertained in his room until he finally drifted off to sleep in mid-afternoon, and then—

And then she'd sent Will and Gus away and closed her eyes for a few minutes there in the chair by Martin's bed, still tired from Saturday's exert-ions—

What was going on? Gus might well have gone outside in mid-afternoon to talk to those men. . . but why?

A fleeting memory drifted into mind, some-thing someone had recently said: *Look for the queue of hopeful brewers and cloth merchants outside some building in Seven Dials, and you'll find your forger*. Only it wasn't in Seven Dials, but Mayfair. And another memory: *He's a Colleger—a scholar-ship boy—and has no mum, and his father's a tutor at Oxford and forgets about him sometimes. . .*

She stood up abruptly. "Sally, may I be excused for a short while? You can hold the rest of the meeting without me, can't you? I think I might know what is going on."

Sally looked at her, eyebrows raised, then nodded. "Of course, Annabel," she said. "How long do you need?"

"Not much more than an hour, I hope."

"What?" Georgiana gasped. "You're going to *let her go*?"

"It seems that Annabel has uncovered some new information that she wishes to investigate," Sally replied calmly.

Annabel nodded. If she were right. . .

"But—but—" Georgiana leapt to her feet once again, positively sputtering. "What if she flees for the continent?"

"*Bon Dieu!*" Dorothea rolled her eyes. "Theatrics again."

Emily sighed. "Where do you think she's going to go? We're at war with France, remember?"

"At least call for a Bow Street Runner to watch her—"

"Georgiana, you know they don't operate in this part of London. And anyway, you're being quite ridiculous." Sally pursed her lips and blew a puff of air at her. It sent Georgiana firmly back into her chair and held her there.

To Annabel's relief her coachman was still outside the building with the landau, having a comfortable chat with Clementina's coachman. He started at her sudden reappearance.

"Will you take me home again, Thomas? I'm afraid I've forgotten something," she said, feigning unconcern as Mr. Willis handed her into the carriage. Once there, she closed her eyes and let out a long, shuddering sigh. Having to accuse Andie of the forgeries would have been dreadful. But she wasn't sure this would be any easier—

"Now, lassie, it isn't that bad, ye ken," a concerned voice said next to her.

Annabel jumped and bit back an exclamation. "Mr. Almack?"

"Aye, 'tis me, Lady Fellbridge. Ye looked as though a little company wouldn't come amiss."

She frowned. Was he here to check up on her? "Did Sally send you?"

The voice chuckled. "No, I sent myself. I just enjoy being in on the kill, so to speak, when I can. It's one of the few pleasures left to an old, and I might say incorporeal, man. And I thought ye might like the company."

"I do, thank you. You are very kind." She sighed again. "I'm not looking forward to this 'kill' in the least."

"Ach, you'll do it to a turn. Dinna worry."

"Thank you for—for not thinking it was me," she said after a moment's companionable silence.

"Now, lass, no one did except our Georgiana, and we all know she's a bit of a crank. Or maybe more than a bit," he added, pensively.

"I suppose the circumstances did look very suspicious," she said, trying to be fair.

He made a dismissive sound. "Naw. She's just a crabbity auld wumman. Too many young and pretty girls among the Lady Patronesses these days. You're making her feel her years."

Annabel raised an eyebrow. "At six-and-twenty, sir, I am not precisely a young girl."

"But ye canna say you aren't pretty, now can ye, Lady Fellbridge?"

"You may be dead, Mr. Almack, but you're still an incorrigible flirt!"

There was a smile in his voice. "Weel, one tries

to keep up."

She smiled too. "I imagine you've been in on any number of 'kills' over the years."

"Not as many as ye might think. I dinna like to get in your way—you ladies are the ones doing the work. Even before there were investigations," he added, reflectively.

"That sounds like a tale worth hearing."

"Och, lassie, that's all ancient history."

"Come, now, Mr. Almack." Annabel pretended to frown. "You cannot drop a tidbit like that and not follow through. Which ladies were doing *what* work?"

He was silent for a moment. "It was 1771," he finally said. "I'd opened the club the year before, and it was just starting to catch on with the class of people I'd hoped to attract, thanks mostly to the ladies I'd asked to serve as Lady Patronesses. One of my better ideas, if I do say so."

"But not your only good one."

He chuckled. "I do like a discerning woman. Weel, there was a prodigious lot o' gambling in it in those days—there was gambling everywhere, of course—so we always had to be vigilant for sharps and cheats. And two of my Lady Patronesses seemed to be especially good at noticing who was playing with marked cards or slipping an extra king into a deck. So I started to watch them, to see how they were doing it."

"And?"

"And? And after a bit, I thought I knew how they were doing it—but I wasn't sure I believed what I saw with my very own eyes."

He paused, tantalizingly, until Annabel said,

"What did you see? You are a dreadful quiz, sir!"

He laughed. "I am, aren't I? Verra well, I'll tell you what I saw. Lady Bulstrode always seemed to know whom to watch—because, as I later learned, she was reading minds. She would tell Mrs. Callors, who would contrive to trip and fall on someone with aces up his sleeves or otherwise create a disruption—whilst she made any questionable cards somehow vanish into her own sleeves. They told me later they did it because they couldna abide cheating, and especially not in an establishment to which they'd lent their names and reputations."

"Oh my goodness," Annabel said. She had seen Lady Bulstrode's and Mrs. Callors' portraits in the Lady Patronesses' meeting room in King Street, but hadn't known what their role had been. "What did you do?"

"Do? I did nothing, lass, but let them get on with their business. But the next time I needed to invite a new Lady Patroness to join us, I made a few verra discreet inquiries to see if I couldna find another lady with unusual abilities. Lady Bulstrode and Mrs. Callors helped me; by that time, we had reached an understanding. And so I got in the habit of choosing my Lady Patronesses not only for their social standing, but also for their other gifts."

"And you succeeded."

"Oh, aye. By the time I died, all my ladies were gifted. I canna help thinking it was one o' the best things I did. Few of them had known there were others in the world like them, so to have the companionship of several ladies of unusual abilities—it made a bond between them. I'd venture ye know something about that."

Annabel thought about her own loneliness growing up, wondering why no one else could shape little figures out of shadow and set them dancing across the nursery floor or win at hide-and-seek even when standing in the middle of a room. It had been a revelation when Sally and Maria had called on her to invite her to be a Lady Patroness—and Sally had breathed a gust of wind that fetched a passing sparrow into the room, which Maria proceeded to have a conversation with. She learnt that she *wasn't* the only oddity in the world—and that her oddity could be used to do good.

"I do know, sir. And I thank you," she said.

"No, I thank *you,*" he said, very seriously. "My ladies are all very dear to me; it's why I decided to stay on after I died. That, and not wantin' to miss anything interesting." He paused. "*You* were interesting. I remember watching you when you first came to Almack's as a girl. I'd seen ladies who could make themselves invisible, but never one who did what you did with shadows. You did a fair bit of eavesdropping, as I recall."

Annabel laughed a little shamefacedly. "My friends were wild to know what the chaperones and Lady Patronesses were saying about them and their prospects, so I found out for them. It also could be quite useful when young men with bad breath and sweaty hands tried to engage me to dance. Being a ghost gave you your own powers, didn't it?" she added, after a moment. "That's how you saw what I could do."

"Aye, I'm always on the watch for future recruits," he agreed. "It's part of why I decided to add to the Lady Patronesses' duties back in '89. That and being worrited that all the fuss and bother in France might make its way over here, in one way or another, and it did. You ladies were in the perfect place to guard your sphere of society. Bow Street Runners are all verra good if you're after a thief from the East End or someone of that ilk. But they just won't do if your quarry is a French Comte wanting to steal jewels or indulge in a little blackmail to finance a Bourbon insurgency. Crime, alas, is not limited to the lower orders. That is why you ladies were *needed*." He chuckled again, but not so mirthfully. "And we need you still. The Prince of Wales and his brothers don't exactly set a good example for the rest of society, and France is even worse a problem today than it was in '89."

"It is indeed." Annabel thought about her brother Robert, in Portugal somewhere with the army. It was comforting to think that she and the other Lady Patronesses were helping to keep London safe while he and others fought to contain that madman, Napoleon.

The carriage slowed, and she saw to her surprise that they were already in Chesterfield Street. Mr. Almack had done a neat job of keeping her distracted—for which she was very grateful.

To her relief, no line of supplicants in search of vouchers waited outside her door. So far, so good— until she remembered who had made the comment about looking for a queue outside the house of the forger. But thinking about the Marquis of Quinceton would not do anything toward preserving her equanimity right now—and calm was what she needed.

"Er. . . you understand, sir, that while I welcome your presence, it would probably be best if you remained in the background," she said to Mr. Almack, just before the groom opened the carriage door.

"Of course, lass. I'll keep mum. But I'll be there if I'm needed."

"Thank you." Annabel straightened her shoulders as she climbed the stairs to her door. What a ghost could do to help, she didn't know. But the moral support was comforting, anyway.

Hanscomb looked surprised as he let her in. "Is all well, ma'am?"

"Just a slight change of plans, Hanscomb. No thank you, I shall keep my pelisse on—I am only here for a little while. Do you know where Master Gus is?"

"All three boys are in the conservatory, ma'am."

It might have been better if Gus were there alone, but she would manage. However. . . "Er, you should probably know that there's a reason we have had so many—importunate persons near the house of late. They will likely stop coming very soon."

"Very good, ma'am."

"Very good indeed. They were beginning to rattle me." She gave a rueful chuckle as she pulled off her gloves. "Do you know, I was *sure* I saw someone sneaking out of the house the other night as I arrived home from Mrs. Drummond-Burrell's rout? I'm sure now it was just my imagination playing hob."

"Indeed, ma'am."

Was it still her imagination, or had a peculiar expression crossed her butler's face? He gave a small cough. "Ah. . . might I request the favor of a word at your next convenience?"

"Of course, Hanscomb."

He bowed. Annabel paused before a mirror to

check her hat until Hanscomb had withdrawn. "This way, Mr. Almack," she murmured, and felt a hint of a cool breeze brush past her.

The conservatory was a large one, built by Freddy's father who'd had a passion for rare plants and been as bad as his son at managing money. She found Will and Martin near the entrance, their lead soldiers set up in battle formation amid a grove of potted ferns.

"We're fighting in India, Mum," Will explained. "Only Martin keeps pretending to be a flock of tigers and eating the rear-guard."

"I don't think tigers come in flocks, darling. Where's Gus?"

"Drawing an orchid." Martin jerked his head toward the back of the warm, humid room, then turned back to the soldiers. "RAWR! MORE MEAT!" he growled.

Annabel made her way to the far end of the room, where a small table and chairs were set up for the purpose of admiring choice specimens as they came into bloom. Gus was perched on a chair, his sketchpad open and a box of watercolors beside him. He was squinting intently at a large orchid in a pot.

"My goodness, you *are* a talented artist," she said, taking the chair next to him. "First the carica-tures of your masters, and now this."

Gus's head jerked in surprise, but his hand never wavered. "Lady Fellbridge!" He stuck his brush in a glass of water and leapt to his feet to make her a proper bow. "Oh, not really I'm not. But I mean to be, someday."

"A great painter, like Mr. Lawrence?"

He sat down and took up his brush again, his

lip curled in mild scorn. "That would be boring, painting portraits of stupid people all the time. I want to go on expeditions all over the world and paint what I see. Like Mr. Sydney Parkinson who sailed with Captain Cook, only *I* shan't die of dysentery on the way."

Annabel regarded him with mild surprise. So the heart of an intrepid explorer beat in this small, rather unprepossessing boy's breast? Well, perhaps it wasn't so surprising, if he'd had the courage to do what she suspected—

She opened her reticule and took out the voucher she'd taken from the Henrys' house. "I wondered. . . might this be your handiwork as well?"

Gus looked up, brush suspended in mid-air. His eyes widened when he saw the voucher, and a flood of color suffused his round face. "Oh," he said, and set down his brush again. "You found out."

"Yes, I found out," she said gently. "Why, Gus?"

Tears filled his eyes, but he blinked them back. "I needed the money, ma'am."

This time, it was Annabel's turn to blink. "For what?"

"For everything." He looked down at his hands, limp in his lap.

"Everything?" she prompted, when he did not continue.

"Everything," he finally said. "My father—he's not a rich man, and he doesn't make very much money being a tutor at Oxford. When he does, he forgets sometimes and spends it on books. There— there isn't usually much left for anything else."

"Oh." Annabel resisted the urge to fold him in a hug. Dealing with money woes was difficult enough for an adult, as she well knew. But for a young boy who couldn't rely on his only parent to keep them afloat... "And?" she asked gently.

"And Eton isn't cheap, even though I'm a colleger." He swallowed hard. "I have to pay for any classes besides Latin and Greek, and books and supplies and all that. And if I'm going to be a naturalist painter one day, I need to be able to go to university and put money aside for my first exploring trip—they're more likely to hire you if you can at least bring your own supplies. You have to bring *a lot* of paper and paints if you're going to be away from a stationer's shop for three years," he added, looking up at her earnestly.

"I would imagine you do. Go on," she encouraged. "I'm not one of Martin's tigers. I shan't bite."

"So..." He sighed and dropped his gaze to his hands again. "So a day or two after I got here, I went out with Will and Martin. We were going to the park, but a man stopped us and asked us if we would tell you that he was prepared to—to 'reimburse you handsomely,' is what he said, if only you'd give him a voucher. I didn't know what he meant, but Will and Martin ran away, and I ran with them. After we were in the park, I asked them what the man had wanted, and they told me about Almack's and your being an important lady there who helped decide who could go and who couldn't and wrote vouchers for the ones who could go and I... I got thinking."

He hesitated, scanning her face as if trying decide what to say. She gave him an encouraging nod. He sighed and continued.

"It sounded like a lot of people wanted to get into Almack's who couldn't—people who would be willing to pay a lot of money to get in—and maybe I could get some of that money. I figured that no one would notice if a few extra people showed up—assemblies are usually dreadfully crowded, aren't they?—and I could perhaps make enough money to pay for the term—they weren't going to let me back to school for the Summer Half if we couldn't pay up front, you know." The words came faster and faster, and this time the tears spilled over. "I'm very sorry, ma'am, but I—I waited till you were out that night and Will and Martin were asleep, and went into your desk. I found some vouchers there and a letter you'd started but not finished, and I practiced and practiced till I got it as right as I could—your writing, I mean. And then I waited, and the next time I saw that man outside the house again I went out and talked to him and asked him how much he'd pay for one, and he asked how much I wanted and I said twenty guineas. He looked surprised—I figured out after that I'd asked for too little—and he gave me the money on the spot and I told him to come back the next day, first thing, and I'd bring him the voucher. And I did." He gulped.

Annabel sat back. Of course. It was blindingly simple, now that she thought about it. . . and wasn't the simplest answer often the right one? But who would suspect a little boy—? "He wasn't the only one, though," she said aloud.

"Oh, no. The day after that, there was another man. He said his friend had told him to come. I was smarter that time. I asked for fifty guineas. He wanted to argue with me about the price—I guess his friend had told him it would be less—but I said that it was fifty guineas or nothing. He agreed."

"And then he told his friend?"

Gus nodded. "Two friends, actually. After that, there were at least a few every day. I couldn't always get out to talk to them if Will and Martin and I were busy or if Hanscomb or someone were near the door, but they kept coming back anyway until I could."

Annabel steeled herself. "How much money have you made?"

He took a breath. "Seven hundred and twenty guineas."

She was able to school her face into neutrality, but it was a near-run thing. Seven hundred and twenty guineas! That would last him for most of the rest of his years at school, if he were careful with expenses.

"I *do* need to buy a new coat, at all events," he said quickly, as if he'd read her thoughts. "This one don't fit so well anymore."

"I daresay you'll have to buy a new coat every year. Boys have a bad habit of growing," she said with mock severity.

He grinned sheepishly, but the smile quickly faded. "Do I have to give it all back?" he asked in a small voice.

That was a very good question. Strictly speaking, of course he should. That was what Georgiana would expect at the very least—if not having him immediately transported on a prison ship. On the other hand. . . "Gus, the vouchers you wrote—none of them were for the entire season, were they?"

He looked confused. "No—do you write them for a whole season? The one I—I copied from had a place for the date, so I thought they were for just one ball."

"So the last ones you wrote were for this week's ball, and no later?"

He nodded.

"And you don't know where the people you wrote the vouchers for live, do you?"

"They didn't tell me," he said simply.

"Ach, there's no way we'll be able to get those back and return the money," a quiet Scottish voice murmured into her ear. "And making a scene at the door on Wednesday night denying anyone entry won't do either if we want to avoid talk. Much as it pains me, they paid for those vouchers and they'll get to use 'em. The lad can keep the money."

"I concur, sir," she said under her breath, then pretended to cough slightly. "Very well," she said more loudly. "Gus, listen to me. You have an unusual talent, and I hope you become the most famous painter ever. But you mustn't *ever* do anything like this again. It was neither fair to Almack's to circumvent its rules—not to mention possibly ruining my honor and credibility amongst my friends—nor to profit from the desperation of others. It was very wrong, you know—all of it."

He looked horrorstruck. "I didn't think of that— that I could be hurting your honor, I mean. It's just that when that man asked me how much I wanted— it was as if. . . all I could think of was that I could stop worrying, at least a little." He rose from his chair, placed his plump, deceptively clumsy-looking hand over his heart, and bowed. "I do most awf'ly beg your pardon, Lady Fellbridge, and I promise I won't ever do it again."

She rose too. "I accept your apology and your promise, Master Blackburn. Now, as a budding naturalist, would you mind setting Martin straight on the hunting habits of tigers, before his flock wipes out Will's brigade?"

Gus groaned. "It's not a *brigade*, Lady Fellbridge—it's a company!" He scurried away to join the boys.

Annabel chuckled, then sat back in her chair with a sigh. "Appearances *can* be deceiving, can't they?" she murmured, as much to herself as to her invisible companion. "Who would have thought a podgy little boy like that could be capable of such mischief?"

"I wonder ye can ask such a question, with two little boys of your own," Mr. Almack replied. "But aye, appearances can deceive. It's a good lesson to remember, in our line of work."

They were silent, listening to the boys' vociferous play. The tigers were evidently winning. "Have I done the right thing, Mr. Almack?" she murmured at last. "I should hate to think this might be Gus's first step on the road to a life of crime."

"On the contrary, ye might have shown the lad that our actions often have more consequences than we expect, and that what seems like an unimportant trifle can turn out to be something much more serious. I think ye've done the right thing, Lady Fellbridge."

"I hope so, sir." She rose. "And now, I expect we had better return to King Street and tell them the investigation is completed, before Georgiana sends the Household Cavalry after me."

Mr. Almack chuckled. "I'll get back to King Street on my own, then, and make sure she doesn't. Your servant, ma'am." With a swift swirl of cool air, he was gone.

Annabel tiptoed out of the conservatory. How would Georgiana react to her news? Would she accept that Gus had been the culprit? Suddenly she understood why Mr. Almack had accompanied her: there was no possibility that Georgiana could accuse *him* of lying.

To her surprise, Hanscomb was hovering in the hall by the door. She remembered his request for a word—but surely he didn't expect to have it now, unless— "Is there anything amiss?" she said to him, pausing to pull on her gloves. "I must go back to King Street, and may have to remain there a little later than usual." No telling what loose ends they would have to tie up, now that this investigation had been completed.

"Er, my lady. . ."

Good heavens. Hanscomb—her steady, unflappable butler—was *fidgeting*. "Yes?"

His face wore an expression that on anyone else might have indicated mild discomposure. But Annabel knew him well enough to perceive that the poor man was deeply anguished. "Ma'am," he stammered, "I—I assure you that I—that is, you shall have my resignation upon the instant—"

This was beginning to sound serious. Hanscomb had never in the least the type of servant who gratuitously threatened resignation. "What is it, Hanscomb? Are you unwell?"

"I am in perfect health, my lady." A note of desperation edged his voice. He paused to master his emotion, then fixed her with an agonized but resolute look. "But I—" He swallowed. "I fear that I have not been. . . entirely honest with you, and quite rightly deserve to be sacked."

Annabel regarded him in amazement. "I do wish you would tell me what you are talking about, rather than making such cryptic—not to mention overwrought—statements."

Hanscomb ducked his head. "One moment, please, ma'am." He went to the door of the tiny chamber used to keep guests' outer garments when they called or dined, opened it, and said something, then turned back to Annabel. "Ma'am, please permit me to present"—he almost gulped—"my nephew."

A mountain of a man stepped from the coat room, his shoulders barely clearing the narrow doorframe. Annabel took in his cauliflower ear, his small but undeniably crooked nose, and most of all his pink waistcoat (this morning embroidered with delicate rosebuds), and was not sure whether to sink to the floor in horror or to burst into hysterical laughter. She settled for clutching the edge of the console behind her. "Y-your nephew. . . Tom, I believe?"

"Tom Porteous, ma'am." The mountain made a creditable bow, shooting a swift glance as he rose at Hanscomb, who gave the slightest nod in return.

"How—how pleasant." Drat it, why were there no chairs in the hall? Just now she would welcome one. A dozen questions had boiled up in her mind— this young man's relations with Andie and whether she had seen him sneaking out of the house fore- most among them—but she could not decide on which to ask first.

Hanscomb evidently guessed her dilemma. "Thomas is my younger sister Rose's son, ma'am. She married without my parents' blessing and has been cut off from the family ever since. As they are now gone, I thought it the proper thing to effect a reconciliation."

Tom grinned. "Uncle 'Orace—*H*orace," he enunciated carefully, "is brushin' up my manners for me now that I'm done fightin'—er, competing in the ring."

Annabel was conscious of a distinct sinking feeling. Was he done fighting and "brushing up" his manners in preparation for an appearance at Almack's, with Andie on his arm? Hadn't Andie told him that no voucher for him would be forthcoming? "That is. . . most kind of your uncle," she said faintly.

Tom grinned and opened his mouth to speak, but Hanscomb gave him a quelling look. "It is Thomas's intention to set up an establishment like Mr. Jackson's," he said. "He has saved a sufficient amount from his purses to enable him to finance such a venture. I suggested that in order to attract a better class of clientele, he should learn to present himself in a straightforward and manly yet genteel manner."

Like Mr. Jackson's. . . did that mean that he was not interested in appearing at Almack's?

"I got the straightforward and manly part down pat," Tom put in. "The genteel bit is what keeps giving me a leveler."

"You are proving to be an apt pupil," Hanscomb said. Tom's visage took on a hue to rival his waistcoat. "But I fear I permitted pride in my pupil's progress to cloud my judgment, ma'am," he added, turning to her. "I suggested he come for a lesson Friday evening while you were out. We had gone to sit in the conservatory where we would be undisturbed so that I could drill him on forms of address for the peerage, and lost track of the time." It was his turn to redden. "I have abused your trust by introducing strangers into your house without your leave. I should not have tried to sneak him out of the house that evening as you arrived home and confessed at once, but in the heat of the moment I found that I could not think at such short notice how to do so, and panicked. It was not how I should have—"

By this time Annabel's shock had subsided enough for rational thought to resume. Gus's confession had solved the mystery of the vouchers missing from her desk; still, she was grateful to have this loose end tied up as well. Or at least partially tied up: what about Andie and her passion for this unexpectedly personable ex-prize-fighter?

She waited for Hanscomb's apology to wind down, then nodded to him gravely. "I accept your apology, though I truly don't feel your transgression was as grave as you think it was."

"Thank you most sincerely, ma'am." Hanscomb seemed visibly relieved. He made her a low bow, then shot a look at his nephew, who hastily followed suit.

"But—er, Tom, I must ask you," Annabel said. "Does Lady Andromeda support your plans to open a boxing establishment?"

The twinkle in Tom's eyes dimmed. "I don't rightly know, your ladyship. I ain't—I *haven't* seen Andie in a couple weeks, nor even got a word of a note from her. I—well, I s'pose it was like to happen sooner or later that she'd understand we were no more like than chalk an' cheese. But she was always kind to me, and I can't do aught but wish her all the best."

He spoke with a simple grace that moved Annabel; he *was* one of nature's gentlemen, wasn't he? "Hanscomb, I hope you will continue your lessons with your nephew; you certainly have my blessing to do so. And when my sons are older, Mr. Porteous, I hope that you will consent to take them on as pupils at your establishment."

This time, both uncle and nephew turned waistcoat-pink with pleasure.

Chapter Five

After Annabel returned to King Street and revealed the identity of the forger and the circumstances around his crime, Sally took over as only Sally could. She approved their actions and warmly congratulated Annabel on the successful completion of her first investigation, firmly quashed Georgiana's demands to hand Gus over to the magistrates, and drew up a plan to minimize the possible damage to Almack's reputation at that coming Wednesday's ball.

So it wasn't until Tuesday afternoon that Annabel had a quiet moment to lock herself in the library with a sustaining glass of Mama's elderflower cordial and the latest letter from her steward at Chalfont Abbey.

She hadn't got much past the first few paragraphs when there was a discreet knock on the door and Hanscomb appeared, wearing a bemused expression. "Madam, I understand that you did not wish to be disturbed, but Lady Andromeda Colerain is below and wishes most vociferously to see you. I thought that—"

"Andie's here?" Annabel almost dropped her cordial. "Goodness, yes! Send her up!"

When Andie *still* hadn't replied to any of her notes, Annabel had been sure she'd lost her friend forever. She'd felt even worse about it when Gus, not Andie, had turned out to be the author of the voucher contretemps.

But maybe Andie had forgiven her for being practical and clear-headed. And since it appeared that she'd forgotten all about her prize-fighter, Annabel couldn't help wondering if her forgiveness mightn't have something to do with a certain auburn-haired young Scotsman—the handsome young Duke of Stranraer who had, literally, swept her off her feet (well, backside, if one was being strictly accurate) after almost running her down. Oh, what a satisfactory solution to this problem—and the general problem of Andie Colerain—that would be!

"Annabel, darling!" Andie breezed into the room, bearing an enormous bouquet of daffodils. She shoved them toward Annabel, then embraced her around them. "How *are* you?"

Annabel detached herself and went to hand the crushed flowers to Hanscomb, who vanished back into the passage. "I'm very well—the more pertinent question is how are *you*? I've been so worried."

"Oh, I've never been better!" She picked up Annabel's cordial, sniffed at it, and made a face before setting it down. "Oh, dear. A letter from your bailiff? You only drink that stuff when he writes you."

"It's very fortifying. But Andie, the accident— your head—"

Andie waved her hand vaguely. "The merest bump. I was quite well almost directly. I do beg your pardon for not responding to any of your notes, but I've been so very busy." Her smile was both arch and dreamy at the same time.

Only a girl head-over-heels with an attractive duke would smile like that. "Ah, I wondered."

"You did? No, I shouldn't be surprised—you always know, dearest Annabel." She sat down on the sofa and beamed up at her. "We're engaged, you know. And Mama and Papa are completely delighted."

"Andie!" Annabel sat down next to her and hugged her. "I'm so happy for you!"

"You should be. I'm very happy myself." Her eyes shone softly. "Annabel, he's just perfect. I've never met anyone like him."

"I would imagine not." There weren't many handsome young Scottish dukes running loose in London, after all.

"He was such a darling while my head was hurt—no one could have been kinder or more solicitous." She sighed happily.

Annabel remembered the way Stranraer had lifted her into the barouche and sighed too. It *was* romantic, wasn't it?

"He came every single day until I was better—sometimes twice a day!" Andie continued.

"Of course he did!"

"And by the time I was better, I knew—we both knew—that we loved each other!"

"Andie, darling, I am so happy for you! When is the wedding?"

"Oh, as soon as possible. That's part of why I

haven't been to see you—I've been having my trous-seau made." She blushed. "All my nightgowns are to be blue silk, because he likes me in blue."

Annabel didn't reply but pressed her friend's hand. This could not have turned out better. "Your parents will miss you sorely, though."

"Why should they? It's the oddest thing—his family's home is only about ten miles from Allstonleigh. In fact, Papa and Cyrus's papa both hunt with the Quorn and know each other slightly. Isn't that wonderful?"

Annabel blinked. It was not surprising for a Scottish duke to have a hunting box in Leicester. But Andie had said *know*, not knew; how could Stranraer's father be alive if he were the duke? "I meant when you go to Scotland."

"Oh, we'll only be there a few weeks." Andie shrugged. "He can't be away from London too long, of course. His patients would miss him."

"His *what*?"

Andie looked at her strangely. "His patients. They're devoted to him, even if he's rather young for a physician. I think it's his bedside manner—he's so firm and masterful." She blushed again.

Their entire conversation rearranged itself in Annabel's mind. "Andie, you're marrying the *doctor*? Not the duke?"

"Duke? What duke?" Andie's brow creased in confusion for a few seconds before clearing. "Oh, the one who ran me down? He was a darling boy—I did like his hair. But how could I find a boy like that more attractive than a man like Cyrus?" She laughed. "Oh my goodness, you thought I was engaged to *him*?"

Annabel was still floundering. "But—but—I

didn't think your parents would—um—approve."

Andie drew herself up. "A physician is a gentle-man, is he not? And besides, Cyrus is the younger son of Lord Horley. Why shouldn't they approve of my marrying a viscount's son?"

Lord Horley—the Quant-Ropers! *That* was why the name had sounded familiar; Lord Horley was a friend of her father's. Compared to a prize-fighter, he would look like the most eligible suitor in the world. Lord and Lady Allston were wise—and probably breathing a deep sigh of relief. "I am certain they must approve very much," Annabel said truthfully.

Andie prattled on for a good hour about her Cyrus and all their plans for their new London house that Papa was buying them and the entertaining they would do, for "it was very important for a physician to maintain good social connections." Annabel list-ened and exclaimed yes and no at the proper junctures but couldn't keep her thoughts from wan-dering just a bit. When confronted with a handsome duke who obviously found her attractive, it was Andie all over, who'd barely known a day's illness in her life, to fall in love with so exotic a creature as a physician. At least *this* alliance was not an object-ionable one.

After she embraced Annabel before taking her leave, Andie regarded her thoughtfully, head to one side. "You truly thought I'd fallen in love with Stranraer, didn't you?"

Annabel met her eyes. "I did—or at least I'd hoped so."

Andie nodded. "Hmm. Maybe you *don't* always know."

"No, I expect I don't," Annabel sighed.

If Wednesday evening's ball at Almack's seemed much thinner of company than usual, with fewer Lady Patronesses in attendance as well, it was because. . . well, it *was*.

Sally's damage control plan had sent the Lady Patronesses hastily improvising social events for Wednesday evening in order to lure away as many of their friends—Almack's usual denizens—as possible, leaving the ballroom to the purchasers of Gus's forged vouchers. Sally, Emily, and Clementina were all giving impromptu dinners which would run mysteriously late, not permitting their guests to arrive at Almack's before the witching hour of eleven when the doors were barred to late arrivals. Dorothea had managed to procure the services of Madame Barrantini for a private concert at her house and inveigled much of the diplomatic corps to it. Even Georgiana had been persuaded (though browbeaten perhaps might been the more accurate word) into giving a last-minute whist party, leaving Annabel, Frances, and Maria to hold the fort at King Street.

Holding the fort was not a comfortable experience, Annabel soon found. She overheard much grumbling from some attendees: "Is this all?" one stout matron in diamonds and feathers complained to another. "Why, there's no one here but who we might see at a Pantheon ball. Where's all the lords for our Lizzie to dance with? Don't know what you might think, but *I* think this Almack's is just a great humbug!"

Annabel maintained a serene countenance

through the flash of annoyance the words caused her. But a few minutes later a man—she was sure he was part of the group that had accosted her that dreadful day when Georgiana had been lurking in cat form on her front steps—approached her, to her dismay.

"That wasn't you selling the vouchers, was it?" he said without preamble. His blue eyes—which were surrounded by deep laugh lines—did not hold even a hint of a smile.

What could she say to him but the truth? "No. It was a—a regrettable incident that won't happen again."

He nodded. "Thought as much, when we came in and saw who was here—and who wasn't. Got everyone safely out of the way before we came, eh?"

Annabel felt herself redden. "I—"

"I can't say as I blame you, 'specially since this wasn't any of your doing. It was the lad, I take it? No, you don't need to answer that. I expect he's learnt his lesson." He fell silent, staring out at the half-empty ballroom. "You've a family, I take it?"

"Yes, but it wasn't—"

"Don't matter if it was a son of yours responsible for this, though I could have guessed it wasn't. No, what I wanted to say was, if you have young 'uns, and if you're any sort of parent, then those young 'uns are the most important thing in the world to you. Am I right?"

Annabel thought of William's solemn air, his consciousness of the responsibility of being the Earl of Fellbridge. . . until his younger twin's *joie de vivre* reminded him that they were, after all, eight years old. "Yes," she said fervently. "Yes, you are."

He nodded. "Then you'll know that if there's

something in your power that will give them a step up, an advantage in life—or p'raps just make 'em happy—well, you'll go after it, won't you?" He didn't wait for her response—he probably knew that none was required—and went on. "I have three sons, ma'am. They're good boys, and already keen to follow me into my business. I have a daughter, too. She's got as good a head on her shoulders as her brothers, but there isn't much call in the world for her to use it. I can't give her a factory to run or a sales book to fill with orders. But I can try to give her a chance to better herself in a different way. Can you blame me for trying to get her in here, when the means seemed within my grasp?" He stepped back, bowed, and walked away.

The one part of the evening Annabel did enjoy was seeing Miss Henry look radiantly happy, dancing in almost every set. At one point she caught the girl's eye and gave her a smile and a nod, and was afraid the child would faint: Oh, to be nodded to by a Lady Patroness of Almack's! For a moment, Annabel felt bad: when Miss Henry's father tried to come to her house for another voucher, he and all the other supplicants would be deflected by the pair of stout footman Mr. Willis had sent over to stand guard at her doorstep, driving away all but legitimate callers. But at least the girl would have had her one enchanted evening at Almack's to tell her friends and someday her daughters about, the night when a Lady Patroness had smiled at her. Would Almack's ever change, and anyone who could afford the price of a ticket be allowed in? Maybe, someday. . . but then Almack's would not be needed.

She sighed and went to join Maria and Frances.

"It seems to be going as well as possible," she said in a low voice.

Maria nodded. "I've asked Mr. Willis to set his watch ahead a quarter-hour, so that it will turn eleven sooner. And I do believe that the first violin is going to be taken ill at precisely twenty minutes to twelve, and the music will be forced to end early. If we're lucky, we'll be home not long after midnight."

"When do the boys return to school?" Frances asked. To her credit, she had taken no umbrage at not having been involved in the final resolution of the investigation. "The poor little thing," she'd said, when Annabel had explained about Gus to her afterward. "Two of us would have frightened him to bits. You did exactly the right thing."

"Saturday. Term starts on Monday." Back at home, Gus was frantically busy with his paint-box, hiding away in the conservatory and getting the twins to warn her off. Martin said he was working on a surprise for her, but Will had tackled his brother into protesting silence before he could completely spoil the secret.

"At least little Augustus *will* be returning to school," Frances said, kindly.

"Yes," Maria agreed. "And everything will once again be in regular train—oh, good evening, Quin!"

Annabel just managed not to groan. Why, oh why, had Lord Quinceton decided to make one of his occasional appearances at Almack's *tonight* of all evenings?

"Quin!" Frances's voice rose an octave.

"Good evening, Lady Sefton. Lady Frances. Fellbridge." Lord Quinceton bowed, shooting Annabel a quick amused glance as he joined them, as if he'd guessed at the tight hold she'd placed on herself. "An, ah, unusual crowd tonight. May I ask if you caught your forger, Fellbridge?"

"She certainly did, Quin—it was quite neatly done, too," Maria said. "And you won't believe who it was!"

"Oh? Someone I know?"

"No, I shouldn't think so. It was a mere schoolboy, the friend of Annabel's sons who came home on holiday with them! The poor thing is an amazing artist and very clever besides, but just desperate for cash—they were going to give him the boot from Eton if he could not pay for his extra lessons. It was most diverting! Can you imagine—he's the last one in the world you'd have suspected!" She leaned closer to Annabel. "Mind you, I think we should keep in touch with the child," she muttered. "Skills such as his might be useful to us some day. You never know."

"Indeed." Annabel tried not to shrivel in embarrassment. In fact, Sally had already called at the house for a demonstration of Gus's abilities and had given him her card, "just in case."

Lord Quinceton broke into a low laugh. "Oh, poor Fellbridge! Nursing a viper in your bosom!" His eyes dropped to her chest, then back up to meet hers. "Lucky viper," he murmured, pitching his voice so that only she could hear.

Oh, the infernal gall of the man! Annabel went in an instant from mortification to cold fury. "I know very well how to deal with snakes of all description, Lord Quinceton," she said, meeting his hungry wolf gaze squarely. "It generally involves crushing their obnoxious little heads under my heel."

An appreciative grin stretched across his face,

and he raised his hand, sketching a fencing salute to her, then turned away.

"Quin, wait!" Frances fluttered after him.

"My goodness." Maria watched Frances's departure with ill-disguised surprise. "Is she still dangling after him after all these years?"

"What? Frances?" Annabel stared after her as well. "I thought she had more sense than that."

"Oh, didn't you know? Frances has been simply nutty over Quin ever since her come-out—what, fifteen years ago? Yes, at least fifteen." Maria shook her head. "He's never given her the least encouragement, but she keeps on trying to fascinate him, poor girl."

Annabel shuddered. "I can think of any number of men more worth dangling after than Lord Quinceton."

Maria brightened. "Can you? Oh, good! Dorothea was saying just the other day that we really need to find you a *cher ami* to keep you company now that you're well out of mourning. What about Lord Keene? He's quite the charmer, so I hear!"

Author's Note

Mr. Lawrence, Sydney Parkinson, and Captain Cook

In those pre-photography days, Young Gus Blackburn's desire to be an artist-naturalist was a perfectly reasonable one: how else would the discoveries of explorers be recorded accurately and scientifically unless a trained artist came along? His hero, a young Scottish artist named Sydney Parkinson (1745-1771), was recruited by Joseph Banks to accompany him on Captain Cook's first Pacific voyage in 1768 and produced over a thousand exquisitely careful (and beautiful) drawings of flora and fauna before, most unfortunately, dying of dysentery while the mission was en route to Capetown from Java.

Sir Thomas Lawrence (1769-1830) was in no danger of dying of an exotic tropical disease; in 1810 he was acknowledged as one of England's foremost portraitists and had just received the patronage of no lesser a person than the Prince Regent. He would paint well-known portraits of many well-known people, including members of the royal family, and was sent abroad to paint many European leaders after Napoleon's defeat.

Marquis or Marquess?

Observant history-geekish readers may have noticed that I refer to Lord Quinceton as the marquis of that name, rather than marquess as is used today. "Marquess" didn't actually become the received spelling in England until around 1840, when the English nobility of that title decided as a group to adopt that form of the word. Debrett's still used marquis in its early 19th century edition, so 1810 was in the period of transition for the word. I have chosen to go with "marquis" as that is the spelling used in a letter by Caroline Lamb from 1809 in a collection of the Bessborough family's correspondence.

Boxing

Boxing was one of the most popular sports of the early nineteenth century, both as a spectator sport (with a lot of wagering happening!) and as a participatory one. Boxing fans would accumulate from all over the country to see fights featuring the stars of the day like Tom Cribb, Bill Richmond, and Tom Molineaux engage in bouts—indeed, one of the greatest boxing events of the era happened in December 1810 between Cribb, the English champion, and Molineaux, a former slave from Virginia—one of those epic fights that old men would, years later (when deep in their cups), claim to have witnessed. Upper class men could take sparring lessons from "Gentleman" John Jackson, a former champion who opened a boxing studio in Bond Street (next to Angelo's Fencing Academy) and earned his nickname from his excellent manners and comportment. There's a rich body of boxing slang that crept into usage among sporting types; Georgette Heyer made extensive use of it in her novels.

Astley's Amphitheatre

Formerly located on Westminster Bridge Road in Lambeth (it was demolished in 1893), Astley's Amphitheatre was an indoor performance venue that drew delighted visitors starting in 1773 and continued popular through the Regency with its equestrian show and, a little later, circus performances (the diameter of its stage in fact became the model for all future circus rings—forty-two feet.) It offered the sort of boisterous entertainment that the ton rarely admitted visiting, but secretly loved.

Was a physician a gentleman?

Regency-era medicine was quite different from what we know today—and I'm not talking only about scientific knowledge. There were three main classes of providers of medical care; at the bottom was the apothecary, who compounded medicines and might be consulted for simple complaints or by those who could not afford the services of anyone higher up the medical hierarchy. Next up was the surgeon, who took care of matters like broken bones, amputations, the treatment of skin and eye issues, and serious physical exams. Apothecaries and surgeons received their training through apprenticeships; socially, they were lumped in with tradesmen.

Physicians, on the other hand, were (like clergymen and barristers) considered to be gentle-men and were university trained. Aside perhaps from taking a pulse or examining the state of a patient's urine, they did no hands-on work: rather, they listened to a patient's description of symptoms then prescribed medicines ("physic") for an apothecary to make. Many physicians were horrified by the introduction of the stethoscope in 1816 and refused to use it because it was a tool—and use of tools implied physical labor, which a gentle-man certainly never engaged in.

Be very glad you live in the twenty-first century.

The Lady Patronesses

Both social historians of the early 19th century and Regency romance authors have long mourned the fact that there are no reliable accounts of exactly who the Lady Patronesses of Almack's were at any given time. Captain Gronow's memoirs of the era (and his list of Lady Patronesses) are not really regarded as reliable, as they were written several decades after the events they depict. I mourned too, until I realized that not knowing meant I could use whomever I wanted to (within reason) in these stories.

So I did.

I chose the Lady Patronesses whom I found most interesting and gave them abilities suggested by contemporary accounts of their personalities: Sally "Silence" Jersey, known for being a chatterbox, just had to have the ability to shape wind, for example, and the portraits of Dorothea Lieven with her dark curls clustered about her temples immediately suggested the gorgon ancestry I gave her. Not all the Lady Patronesses I present here are historical figures—neither Annabel Fellbridge nor Frances Dalrymple existed, obviously—but the rest were known members of that most exclusive sisterhood. To help readers keep track of all these ladies and their names and titles, I've included a dramatis personae of the historical characters.

Why yes, as a matter of fact, I *am* having fun.

One thing that struck me as I researched the Lady Patronesses was how young many of them were—in their early to mid-twenties. I think it's easy to assume that anyone holding a position of such social authority must have been at least middle-aged, and that the Lady Patronesses were a group of fearsomely haughty *grandes dames*, but they most emphatically were not.

The Marriage Mart

Modern readers may find the entire concept of Almack's to be troubling: a place where people of a certain group could meet other members of that group in order to look for marriage partners, with the guarantee that no persons from outside their group would be allowed admission.

But Almack's wasn't just about pure snobbishness or an us-against-them mentality. The thing to keep in mind is that through this era, marriage was as much a business transaction as it was a personal one. Families considered what other families they wanted to ally themselves with through the marriages of their sons and daughters for reasons of outright monetary gain as well as for less tangible but still enormously important assets like social, economic or political influence. You might decide that you wanted your son to marry the daughter of a family whose political support you sought for your career, or who might bring as part of her dowry land or other assets you coveted. And while marriages for love were becoming more the norm over the course of the century, can you blame parents who were stuck in the older mind-set for valuing a place that offered pre-approved company for their romantical sons or daughters, so that they might fall in love with the "right" sort of person and make everyone happy?

Vouchers

Curiously, in the course of my research I was unable to find out precisely how ticket sales for individual Almack's balls were handled. So I made one up that seemed to make historical and social sense as well as work well for my story. If anyone has documentary evidence on how ticket sales for the Wednesday night subscription balls were actually managed, I would love to know about it. You can reach me via email at marissa@marissadoyle.com. . . and as always, I welcome reader questions and comments, so please feel free to contact me at that address.

THE
VANISHING
VOLUME

Chapter One

London, late April 1810
A Monday Morning

On Monday morning Annabel, Lady Fell-bridge, left for the weekly meeting of Almack's Lady Patronesses a little early in order to accomplish an important errand. She was slowly clopping around the corner onto Old Bond Street (or rather, her carriage was) when she noticed a familiar figure on the pavement hurrying in the same direction.

"Pull up, please, Thomas," she called to her coachman, then more loudly, "Frances! May I offer you a ride?"

Lady Frances Dalrymple, one of Annabel's fellow Lady Patronesses, looked up and smiled. "Annabel! Thank you, but I've a stop to make before I go on to King Street." She held up a book. "I must just run into Hookham's."

Annabel held up her own book. "So must I."

Frances' smile widened. "Ah ha! *The Fifty Shades*?"

"What else? Climb in!"

As the groom helped Frances up, Annabel glanced at the blue sky above the buildings around them. Sometimes, being in London on a warm day in late April just seemed *wrong*. "Back at home, my narcissus beds are probably in their glory," she observed with a small sigh.

"Back at *my* home, the flowerbeds—not that we have many because my father doesn't approve of them—might still be under six inches of snow. Of course, that's Scotland for you," Frances added philosophically.

"Why doesn't your father approve of flower-beds?"

"Flowers make him sneeze. And. . ." Frances hunched her shoulders. "Flowerbeds would mean hiring more gardeners than are needed to just keep the grass scythed and the kitchen gardens growing."

"Ah." Annabel could sympathize with that. Only the knowledge that their families would likely starve if she didn't keep the gardeners at Chalfont employed had prevented her from reducing the out-door staff.

"But I know what you mean," Frances continued hurriedly. "Spring does seem rather wasted on the Season, doesn't it? Then again, if we were in the country, neither of us would likely have a circulating library close by. I do hope they have two copies of the third volume available," she added, patting her book.

"So do I, or one of us will have to call the other out. Pistols at dawn on Hampstead Heath and every-thing." Annabel chuckled. "Except that our seconds will be too busy themselves, fighting over who gets to read it first."

It had been more than a week since her sons Will and Martin and their friend Gus had returned to Eton, and to keep from missing them too much, Annabel had plunged into an orgy of novel-reading in her free time, visiting Hookham's Circulating Library almost every other day. Emily Cowper had told her she simply *had* to read E.C. Spruce's latest, *The Fifty Shades of Udolpho*, which had come out just a few weeks before and had taken the reading public of London by storm.

"Have you read *The Fifty Shades* yet?" had replaced "good morning" as a greeting among her acquaintances. Conversations everywhere, from chance encounters in the street to dinners in the houses of the *Ton*, revolved around whether the lovers Ermentrudina and Osberto would be able to escape the horde of dread phantoms—the "Fifty Shades" of the title—that plagued the ruinous Apennine castle in which they had taken refuge whilst fleeing Ermentrudina's sinister suitor, Count Atroccio, and her equally sinister stepmother, the Marchesa dell'Obesa. Annabel had devoured those first two volumes in two days, and was now bent on the devouring the third, as was Frances. . . hence the threat of pistols at dawn if only one copy were available.

As they drew up in front of Hookham's Circulating Library, Frances glanced at the watch at her waist. "We should just have time before the meeting starts. . . and wasn't I clever, being on the right side of the street just as your carriage went by? Because now I can get out and into Hookham's first!"

Annabel laughed. "'O, thou fiend! O, I am undone!'" she quoted. They were the last words of volume two, uttered by Ermentrudina as the Count bundled her into an antique coach at the height of a furious tempest, while the Marchesa lured Osberto into a death-like stupor with her seductive but poisonous perfume.

"Do you think he'll *ravish* her?" Frances asked anxiously as they entered the shop.

"Who? Osberto? I'm not sure he'd be capable at the moment—"

Frances giggled. "No, silly! The Count and Ermentrudina."

"Oh. I shouldn't think so. An old, badly sprung traveling carriage is hardly a conducive setting for a ravishment. On the other hand, the use of the word 'undone' does make one wonder about the state of Ermentrudina's stays. . . But this *is* E.C. Spruce, so who knows?"

They approached the counter, where a harried-looking young man was talking to another sub-scriber, an older woman in a velvet turban adorned with down-sweeping lavender-dyed ostrich feathers. "What do you mean, you don't have it?" the lady was saying, her plumes quivering with the force of her indignation.

"I'm sorry, your ladyship, but they're all out. Several are overdue, in fact. If you wish, I shall add your name to our list to be informed as soon as a copy is available—"

"But you do not understand—I cannot wait that long!" her ladyship cried. "Or rather, it's. . . it's my elderly mother. Yes, my dearest mama. She is on her deathbed, you see, and only my reading *The Fifty*

Shades of Udolpho to her can soothe her dying sufferings! Will you condemn poor mama to such a fate? I must have a copy *now*!"

The clerk looked appropriately sympathetic, but Annabel noticed the way his lips twitched before he mastered his expression. "Madam, were it in my power, I should provide it to you immediately. But I cannot give you what I do not have. I am certain a copy will come in later—or tomorrow. Perhaps these ladies—?" He looked at Annabel and Frances hopefully.

They shook their heads. "Volume two," Frances said, raising her book.

"Ah." He turned back to the woman. "In the meanwhile, perhaps your mother might enjoy a nice book of sermons? In such extremity, they might prove a comfort—"

The woman drew herself up. "If you will not have mercy on a dying woman, perhaps another library will." She turned and swept toward the door, barely allowing her footman time to open it for her and get out of her way.

"Oh, dear," Frances said, coming up to the counter after she was gone. "We could not help overhearing—"

The clerk struggled manfully for a moment, then grinned. "That was the best reason I've heard today. A dying mother. . ." He shook his head, then looked at them suspiciously. "You aren't here for the third volume of *The Fifty Shades of Udolpho*, are you?"

"Er, I'm afraid we are."

"But we promise that neither of us has a dying mother," Annabel added quickly. "Are you truly out of the third volume?"

He raised his eyes to the ceiling. "You've no idea. All our copies are out. Overdue, too, most of them. I guess that third volume must be an out-and-outer. I can take your names, same as I said to Lady Lyer."

Frances sighed. "I suppose so." She laid her copy of the second volume on the counter next to Annabel's. "And I was so looking forward to reading it this evening! I said no to a rout at my cousin's house tonight because of it."

"I have Marjorie Banks Gilbert's latest one here," the clerk said, picking a book from a shelf behind him and holding it out to her invitingly. "Came out just last Thursday—*The Noble Barbarian*. She's supposed to be every bit as good as E.C. Spruce."

Frances looked at it sadly and shook her head. "No, thank you. We really must be going, Annabel, if we don't want to be late."

"I should be happy to bring you to Earle's or Booth's Circulating Libraries after the meeting, if you like," Annabel said as they regained the carriage. "Or we could stop at Hatchard's or Ridgway's and purchase it."

Frances brightened. "If it wouldn't be too much trouble. . . and if we end up at Hatchard's, I will buy a copy and you shall be the first to read it when I am done. Which will probably be by tomorrow noon. Oh, where *do* you think the Count will take Ermentrudina?"

Dorothea Lieven was alighting from her carriage in King Street just as they arrived. She waited for them, and they ascended to the Lady

Patronesses' meeting room together. Clementina, Emily, and Maria were already there, excitedly chattering at one end of the table. Annabel was pleased to see that Clementina looked much more animated than she had over the last weeks; perhaps she had left behind the difficult third month of her pregnancy.

"But will the perfume prove fatal to poor Osberto?" Maria was asking plaintively.

Clementina shook her head. "I rather doubt it, or the third volume won't be very long, will it?"

"Yes, and what about that? Why hasn't the Marchesa been poisoned by her own perfume?"

"Is it not obvious? She has been ingesting it in small amounts to build up her tolerance to it," Dorothea interjected, peeling off her gloves.

"Dorothea!" Frances exclaimed. "You've read *The Fifty Shades* too?"

Dorothea assumed her haughtiest expression. "Of course not. I do not have time to waste on foolish novels. I am bored to tears with the subject, but I have heard so much talk about it that I cannot help but know. It would merely seem to be the logical thing to do, that is all."

"We shan't ever know unless those of you who've got your hands on the third volume make haste to finish it and return it to Hookham's." Annabel sat down next to Emily and prodded her elbow in mock impatience. Emily had crowed to her at a ball on Saturday evening about having secured the third volume from the circulating library. "Well, how was it? Don't you dare say you were too busy yesterday to read it!"

Emily turned bright pink. "I wasn't, but. . .

actually, I—er. . . I *haven't* read it."

Annabel groaned. "If you're not careful, you'll be drummed out of town. Very well, you'd better lock your doors and spend the rest of the day buried in it."

"I can't." Emily looked as though she were about to burst into tears. "It's gone."

"What? What do you mean, gone?"

"I planned to spend all morning in bed yesterday, reading it. It was on my bedside table, even. But when I woke up, it wasn't there!"

"Did your maid borrow it?"

"She swears she didn't. Everyone in the house swears they didn't touch it. And now darling Harry's cross with me because it turns out he was reading my copy when I wasn't watching, and he wants to know what happens, too." Harry was "Cupid", her lover Lord Palmerston.

"Then it fell behind the bed." Dorothea gestured impatiently. "Make him crawl under it and look."

"He did. He practically tore my room apart."

"Now, that is odd," Maria put in. "I can't find my copy, either. I was certain I'd left it in my morning room, but it wasn't there or anywhere else I looked."

"Oh, how very droll—I've mislaid mine as well," Clementina said. But her expression was thoughtful, not amused.

"But you haven't heard the all of it," Emily said. "I felt so badly about losing Hookham's copy that I went to Hatchard's this morning before coming here to buy a replacement, and they don't have any copies. None at all."

"Well, it *is* hugely popular," Frances said, with a disappointed look at Annabel. "I suppose we can cross them off our list."

"No—they had several copies yesterday when the shop closed. This morning, none. They're all gone!"

"Sold out that quickly? My goodness!" Maria marveled.

"But that's it—they *didn't* sell. Last night they were there, and this morning, they weren't. They've just. . . disappeared."

"It is far more likely some enterprising clerk took them to sell himself," Dorothea put in, but Emily shook her head.

"I said as much to the head clerk, but he was quite certain that wasn't the case. He was the last to leave the shop last night, and the books were all still there. And don't say *he* took them, because he did not—I looked. Besides, the poor man was distraught."

Annabel nodded. Emily very rarely used her thought-reading abilities so directly, but this was clearly a special case.

"Oh, dear. Who was distraught?" Sally Jersey had breezed in, followed by a footman carrying the usual baskets for the sorting of voucher petitions. He placed them on the table, bowed, and left.

"The head clerk at Hatchard's," Emily replied. "All their copies of the last volume of *The Fifty Shades of Udol*—"

"No, don't tell me!" Sally clapped her hands over her ears. "I just started it yesterday! And besides, we need to get to work. There are a ridiculous number of voucher requests for us to go through—leftovers from poor Annabel's adventure, I expect."

"Frances and I are going to stop by a few more

circulating libraries and bookstores after the meeting," Annabel murmured to Emily as they took their seats. "Would you like to come?"

Emily's face cleared. "Would I!"

To Annabel's surprise and growing confusion, their stops by "a few more" circulating libraries and bookstores ended up taking the rest of the day.

At every circulating library they visited—Haldane's, Booth's, Dangerfield's, and even Cheesewright's in Cheapside—the story was the same: all copies of the third volume of *The Fifty Shades of Udolpho* were out to subscribers. Several were overdue, but that wasn't unusual for such a popular new book.

What *was* unusual was what the booksellers had to say—the same story, every one of them: their stocks of the third volume of *The Fifty Shades of Udolpho* seemed to have melted away in the night, like non-Scottish spring snow.

"Might it be thievery?" Annabel asked the head clerk at Ridgway's. "The story *is* hugely popular."

"That's the thing, your ladyship," the clerk said. "If that were the reason, why haven't the first two volumes disappeared as well?" He bit his lip, then continued. "It's uncanny, is what it is. There were ten copies of the third volume in the shop on Saturday morning. By the end of the day, they were gone. . . but we'd only sold five of them. The rest had just vanished."

"What do you make of that?" Frances asked

when they were back in Annabel's carriage.

"He was telling the truth," Emily said firmly. "There's something very odd going on here." She turned to Annabel. "Let's go to Allardyce's in Oxford Street. I will be very interested to hear what they have to say about this."

"That's an excellent suggestion!" Frances agreed.

Annabel nodded and relayed the request to her coachman. Allardyce's Bookshop had been in business for a very long time. . . and the Allardyce family had been known as accomplished witches and wizards for just as long. If anyone might have an idea about mysterious goings-on to do with a book, it would be them.

Young Mr. Allardyce was in the shop that day, looking harassed. But he greeted them with his usual politeness, waving aside his clerk to serve them himself. "In what way may I assist you, Lady Cowper?" he asked Emily.

"*The Fifty Shades of Udolpho,*" she said without preamble.

"Certainly. We have the first two volumes right here—"

"We would like to talk to you about the third volume."

"Ah." He nodded thoughtfully. "If it would not be inconvenient, perhaps we could discuss this in my office?"

"That would probably be for the best," Emily agreed, and they followed him past the counter to a small room which held a desk and table piled with books and papers. A small girl in a starched white apron, no more than five, sat at the table, tracing a map of Africa in a large atlas.

"May I present my daughter?" Mr. Allardyce said. "Melusine, why don't you go upstairs and see if Mama needs help with your brother?"

"She sent me down here because he's being a fussy little pustule and I wanted to turn him into an earthworm. Earthworms don't squall and pull my hair," she added, scowling.

"Earthworms are also slimy and wiggly," Mr. Allardyce said severely. "And having one for a brother might prove embarrassing in later years. Now, up."

The little girl sighed and closed the atlas. "I still wish we'd got a kitten instead of a brother," she said, and fixed Emily with a stern look. "Do *you* have brothers?"

"Yes, and they get much nicer when they're older," Emily said.

Melusine looked unconvinced but left the room after dropping them a curtsy at her father's urging. Mr. Allardyce sighed and pulled out chairs for them.

"*Could* she turn him into an earthworm?" Frances asked, wide-eyed.

"No. But that wouldn't stop her from trying. She's very advanced for her age." He couldn't quite conceal the note of pride in his voice. "Now, *The Fifty Shades*. Is this a formal investigation by the Lady Patronesses?"

"Er, no. At least not yet." Emily told him about their conversations with the booksellers and library clerks, as well as her own experience with the disappearing book. "We wanted to know if you might know anything about it."

"I wish I did," he said, ruefully. "Having your

stock mysteriously disappear is a shopman's worst nightmare. But this isn't ordinary theft."

Emily glanced at Annabel. "We'd come to that conclusion as well. The question is, why are they disappearing from stores and libraries and even private homes?"

"There's an important piece of information there: books are not being destroyed on the spot—there has been no evidence of burning or dissolution, no?"

Emily shook her head.

"Then someone—or something—must be physically removing them," Mr. Allardyce said somberly. "Stealing them, to be blunt."

"Something. . . not natural?" Frances asked in hushed tones.

"It may be entirely natural—most spiritous beings are. But certainly nothing human."

"But why should a—a 'spiritous being' wish to take all the copies of volume three of a popular novel?" Frances asked plaintively.

"Oh, everyone's a critic these days," Emily joked, but her eyes didn't smile. "Or perhaps it's Fordyce's ghost, jealous that novels are outselling his sermons."

"I don't believe it's a ghost," Mr. Allardyce said. "They're not corporeal enough to carry off large numbers of books."

Obviously, he hadn't met Mr. Almack; Annabel wouldn't have put it past the genial old ghost to do pretty much anything he wanted to do. "So if it's capable of stealing books, then it must have some kind of body," she said.

Emily brightened. "Well, there we go. If it has a

body, then it must be possible to capture it."

Frances looked unconvinced. "I suppose it might, but how?"

"We'll lay a trap for it," Emily said breezily. "Put a copy of the third volume in a locked room, hide behind the draperies, and wait for it to appear. Simplest thing in the world!"

"Assuming we can find a copy of the third volume to use as bait," Annabel added.

Emily deflated slightly. "Oh. Yes, there's that."

"Very well," Annabel said when they'd regained the carriage after exchanging promises with Mr. Allardyce to keep each other informed of anything concerning *The Fifty Shades of Udolpho*. "I doubt we're going to find a copy in any bookstore or library, though I suppose we could continue to search. What should we do now?"

"Do you think it's worth going to the printer?" Frances asked.

"That's a good idea," Emily said. "If anyone's going to have a copy, it will be them. Where is the Aphrodite Press again? Leadenhall Street?"

"Yes. Thomas, Leadenhall Street," Annabel called, and relaxed into the seat. The Aphrodite Press specialized in the sensational. They had been the premier printer of gothic novels for years, and E.C. Spruce was their most popular author. Surely they had some inkling of what was happening with *The Fifty Shades* and would want to know its cause. . . and maybe, if the press were so kind as to lend them a copy, she could sneak just a peek into it, enough to see where the Count was taking Ermentrudina—

"Georgiana seemed better this morning," Frances ventured.

Emily grimaced. "No, she did not. She was just as horrid as ever to poor Annabel. Some people just can't abide being proved wrong."

Annabel sighed. Georgiana still refused to even look at her, almost two weeks after she had wrongly accused Annabel of forging Almack's vouchers. "Surely she will get over it soon," she said hopefully.

"I rather doubt it. Sally may have to have a word with her." Emily waved a hand, dismissing Georgiana and her grudge. "Now, what shall we say at Aphrodite? Certainly nothing about 'spiritous beings' stealing books, or they shall think we're trying to write our own novel."

As it turned out, they didn't have to say much of anything. Impressed by the confluence of no fewer than three members of the aristocracy before his desk, the harassed-looking secretary showed them into the office of the press's principal himself, Mr. Hannibal Erastus Warburton, and handed him their cards.

Mr. Warburton was a small man of middle age but possessed of enormous vitality, as if a much larger person had been squeezed into his diminutive frame. He glanced at their cards and his eyebrows rose. "My dear ladies, I am—no, honored is not strong enough a word! But it will have to suffice in its insufficiency."

He rose from behind an enormous desk littered with stacks of loose manuscripts, unbound books, and countless letters, and bowed deeply, one hand on his breast. "What, if it pleases you, may I do for such august—and charming—ladies?" His twinkling blue gaze caressed Emily's delicate features, then slid appreciatively over Annabel's figure. "Rest assured that whatever it is, I will do my utmost to complete it to your satisfaction."

Frances looked taken aback at his effusiveness. They had agreed to leave speaking with Mr. Warburton to her, since visiting him had been her excellent idea. It would also give Emily a chance to take a quick look at his thoughts in case he was engaged in some shady dealings with *The Fifty Shades*. "Um. . . well. . . that is, we wanted to talk to you about a book—"

"Ah, a book! I am always delighted to discuss books. They are my life, my dear madam. Now, what book would you care to discuss?"

Emily came to Frances's rescue. "Sir, we have just spent most of the day visiting bookshops and circulating libraries, trying to find a copy of the third volume of *The Fifty Shades of Udolpho*. We could not find a single one."

To their surprise, Mr. Warburton clapped his hands in glee. "Isn't it splendid?"

Emily sputtered slightly. "S-splendid?"

"Yes!"

Annabel tried next. "Sir, are you aware that it even seems to be vanishing from private homes?"

"I know!" he said happily. "Any copies still left in my warehouse have gone too, and it's the best thing that could have happened! Do you know what has occurred as a result? Sales of volume one and two have soared! Everyone has heard about the vanishing book and wants to know what it's all about. Even persons who rarely read novels are clamoring to purchase all three volumes of *The Fifty Shades*, just so they can say their copy has disappeared too, and isn't it terribly mysterious? It gives them a *frisson* far more exciting than the book itself. I wish I'd thought of it. It's genius, sheer *genius*, I say!"

Annabel realized she was staring openmouthed at the little man who was almost bouncing in his high leather chair.

Frances leaned forward, plainly shocked. "But don't you want to know who's doing this?"

"Yes, so that I might shake his hand! I could not have thought of a better advertisement if I'd tried!"

"But—but people want to know what happens in the third volume!"

"Pshaw!" Mr. Warburton waved a hand. "It's exactly like any other E.C. Spruce novel. Justice and love win the day, at the end."

"But we need to know *how*!" Frances sounded close to tears.

Emily patted her hand. "Mr. Warburton, would you have any objection to our investigating the cause of this—this strange phenomenon?"

He rubbed his chin and looked at her warily. "And putting a stop to it, I suppose?"

"Oh, come now, sir," Emily said severely. "There *are* a great many people wanting to read that third volume. And the circulating libraries and bookshops will become very cross if the books they've purchased from you to stock their shelves continue to disappear."

"Hmm." Mr. Warburton looked thoughtful. "That's true. I suppose I can't afford to make them angry." He sighed. "Very well, ladies. If it would give you pleasure to figure out the cause of the disappearing third volume, then by all means do so."

"Thank you." Emily beamed at him. "Now, would you happen to have any copies left of the third volume? We'll need one to lure the thief."

He shook his head. "There's a second printing in the works right now, but it will be days before the books are bound and ready."

"Oh." Both Emily and Frances looked so disappointed that Annabel was sure they'd had the same thought as she about sneaking a look.

"Perhaps we could ask Mr. Spruce," Annabel said. "Could you give us his direction, sir?"

Mr. Warburton sighed again. "Oh dear. I do hate to have to say no, my dear countess, but my authors are very jealous of their privacy. Mr. Spruce in particular does not wish his whereabouts to be known. Imagine how difficult it would be to write if adoring readers constantly showed up on one's doorstep! If you wish, I could forward a note with your request and allow him to respond as he sees fit."

"That's better than nothing, I suppose," Emily said as Mr. Warburton passed a sheet of paper, pen, and ink across the desk. Annabel wrote a quick note explaining their mission and included her card, and watched while Mr. Warburton folded and sealed it.

"There," she said. "Now I suppose we must wait."

"Just as Ermentrudina waits in the gown of antique, spidery lace the Count compels her to wear, at the top of the crumbling tower in Book Three," Mr. Warburton said, raising his eyes to the ceiling.

"*What tower?*" all three of them demanded, in unison.

He smiled at them. "Ah. That would be telling."

"Now what?" Frances asked when they were once again in Annabel's carriage.

"Home. I've had enough of this for one day." Emily discreetly yawned.

"And I was so looking forward to volume three tonight," Frances mourned.

"We could stop at Hookham's once more and find you something else to read," Annabel said. Poor Frances looked as if she'd lost her best friend. "It's scarcely out of the way. Didn't the clerk there recommend a book for you?"

Frances wrinkled her nose. "I've never cared for Marjorie Banks Gilbert's books. She's far too overwrought."

"More overwrought than *The Fifty Shades of Udolpho*?" Emily's eyes were wide.

"Yes—but for all the drama, they just don't have. . . I don't know. Heart, I suppose one could call it. They're like a bad opera, when you want to snicker at the star-crossed lovers rather than cry with them." She sighed. "I'll just have to reread volumes one and two and hope that E.C. Spruce writes back to Annabel *soon*."

Chapter Two

On Wednesday afternoon, Annabel and Emily braved the threat of an April shower to ride in Hyde Park during the fashionable five o'clock promenade hour. The gray skies had kept all but the most dedicated equestrians away, which suited Annabel quite well. She liked having room to *ride* and not just amble along the way many ladies did, being decorative in their riding habits. Riding was the only acceptable form of exercise possible in London—no brisk walks across fields and down country lanes. No wonder Grandmother Shelling-ham had loathed it here.

"No word from Mr. Spruce, I assume?" Emily asked as they walked their horses side by side down the Ladies' Mile after a refreshing canter. The lowering gray skies made the tender young green of the spring foliage in the park seem to glow with an inner light.

"No, but I don't think we should despair yet. He might well either live at a distance from London and hasn't received it yet, or perhaps lives not too far and just received it today."

"Or lives right in town and won't speak with us," Emily added gloomily. "I'll bet E.C. Spruce hates people and is a complete hermit. Why else all the need for privacy?"

"If E.C. Spruce hated people, I doubt he would be able to write such passionate books about them—oh, bother!" Annabel would have liked to use a much stronger word than that, for the Marquis of Quinceton was approaching on a large black hack, destroying the peace of the afternoon. Could she cast a shadow about her before he noticed? Of course, a seemingly riderless horse walking alongside Emily would look highly suspicious—

"Drat what?" Emily's famously dreamy, come-hither eyes were also, regrettably, somewhat short-sighted.

"It's Lord Quinceton, coming toward us—there, on your right."

"Oh, good. Now I can see for myself this 'hungry wolf' business you were so emphatic about the other day." She raised her voice. "Quin! Here! Do come and settle an argument for us!"

"Emily! Did you have to do that?" Annabel muttered. She hadn't seen Lord Quinceton since that evening at Almack's when he'd twitted her so outrageously about Gus, and would have been quite happy to remain deprived of his company.

"Oh, hush." Emily gave the marquis a broad welcoming smile as he trotted up, lifted his hat in greeting and turned his horse to join them. "Well, Quin, what do you think? I was just telling Annabel that I thought E.C. Spruce—you know, the author—

must be an utter misanthrope because he won't see anyone, but Annabel says he cannot be because no one who writes romantical books like his could hate people."

Annabel waited for him to leap into agreement with Emily and use it as an excuse to tease her. But to her surprise he hesitated, then said, "As I may claim an acquaintance with him, I must agree with Fellbridge. E. C. Spruce may prefer his privacy, but he is not a misanthrope."

"You *know* E.C. Spruce?" Emily said, thunderstruck. "Good God, Quin, why didn't you say so?"

"I believe I just did," he said, with a hint of his usual ironic smile.

Emily flapped an impatient hand at him, making her mare dance skittishly. "That's not what I meant. We need to talk to him."

"So I heard."

"You did? From whom?"

"From Lady Frances, when I dined with Glenrick last night." Lord Glenrick was Frances' brother, and heir to the Carrick dukedom. "She waxed quite eloquent on the subject—something about his books disappearing and needing to consult Spruce on the issue. I could not decide whether to take her seriously or not. One never can, with her," he added—rather callously, Annabel thought. Yes, Frances could be vague at times and silly at others, but there wasn't a dearer person in London. How dare he speak disparagingly of her, even if she did dangle after him so obviously!

"It's quite true, I assure you," Emily said. "The third volume of Mr. Spruce's *The Fifty Shades of Udolpho* has vanished from London—yes, completely vanished! And I am not hoaxing you," she exclaimed as he lifted an eyebrow. "We intend to do something about it, but we need a copy of the book to do so and hoped Mr. Spruce might still have one."

"Have you spoken with the printer?" He looked highly amused.

"Yes, we saw him on Monday. He didn't have any copies either and wouldn't give us Mr. Spruce's direction. Annabel wrote a note that he said he would forward to Mr. Spruce, but we're not sure we trust him to do so."

Annabel felt—positively *felt*—Lord Quinceton's gaze come to rest on her. "Another investigation, Fellbridge?" he asked. "You do endeavor to be kept busy, don't you?"

When would the man stop calling her that? She swallowed back a sharp retort. "It is not an investigation, my lord. We are merely—er, curious. And I should think that Mr. Spruce must be concerned about the disappearance of his books."

"If he even knows. As you have learned, he guards his privacy closely."

"Yes, but this could hurt his reputation," she said, resolutely forgetting Mr. Warburton's strange delight at the situation on Monday. "We would be distressed to see any harm accrue to so well-regarded an author."

"Hmm." He rode beside them in silence for a few minutes. Emily caught Annabel's eye and raised her brows hopefully. Annabel nodded. If he could arrange a meeting for them with Mr. Spruce, or at least write them a letter of introduction—

"Very well. I have no pressing engagements tomorrow," he said abruptly. "Would that suit you?"

Emily gawked at him. "What?"

"You wish to speak to Mr. Spruce. I can accompany you to his house tomorrow and present you," he said, in the manner of one speaking to a small child. "Is that not what you wanted?"

"Oh! Yes, of course it is. It was just a little unexpected. Thank you, Quin! Only—" Emily bit her lip and cast a sideways look at Annabel. "Only, I simply *can't* tomorrow—I have several engagements myself. Annabel will have to go."

"*What*?" Annabel's first impulse was to shove Emily off her horse. How *could* she? Emily knew full well how she felt about the marquis—

"Fellbridge? Will that do?" Lord Quinceton's voice was definitely mocking, but there was a curious glint in his eye. "I will come for you at noon."

It took all her willpower not to wither him with a glance and a coolly uttered *Not if you held a gun to my head.* "Thank you, my lord, that will suit me." She hesitated, then couldn't resist adding, "Though I do admit, sir, to some surprise that you should be acquainted with a figure of literary merit."

"Annabel," Emily muttered warningly.

"Are you fond of his books, Fellbridge?"

"I would hardly be concerning myself with this matter and going with you to call on him if I weren't."

"I see. Although I confess to not having read his books, I assure you that I am his friend." He paused. "Though from what I understand of his work, I would scarce call it *literary*. Still, some people seem to enjoy that sort of thing."

Annabel felt hot color flood her cheeks.

Emily snickered. "Oh, Annabel, you asked for that one."

Lord Quinceton was grinning openly. "Yes, she did. My apologies, Fellbridge. But you do have an unerring tendency to bring out the worst in me."

"Restraint is a Christian virtue, my lord," she said through gritted teeth.

"And one I've never been particularly well-acquainted with. Noon, then?"

She didn't trust herself to speak, but nodded.

He smiled and lifted his hat to them, then nudged the bay into a canter and was gone.

"Emily, I'm going to *murder* you!" Annabel said when he was out of earshot. "How could you do that to me?"

"Why, what did I do?" Emily said, her voice high and innocent.

"You suddenly found yourself extremely busy tomorrow and left me to go with him. You know I can't abide the man! I'll wager a guinea he doesn't know Mr. Spruce in the least and is just making a game of us."

"Annabel." Emily dropped her teasing tone. "Now you're being *silly*. Quin was being perfectly amiable—at least, as amiable as he knows how to be—until you went needling him. You deserved that set-down, and honestly, we're lucky he didn't tell us to go to the devil. If we want to be able to learn anything about why *The Fifty Shades* is disappearing everywhere, it would behoove you to not behave like a six-year-old when Quin comes for you tomorrow. And yes, he really does know Mr. Spruce. I peeked."

Annabel bit back a defensive retort. Very well, perhaps she had been the littlest bit childish in her reaction—just a *little*—but. . . "Thank you for looking. But I still don't like him, because I don't trust him.

Something he said in passing a week or so back about Clementina makes me wonder if he doesn't know more than he ought to about the Lady Patronesses."

Emily pursed her lips. "All the more reason, then, to be pleasant to him so you can find out what he might know. Men will bare their souls to pretty women, given the least bit of encouragement."

The remainder of their ride was unusually silent.

Emily was still distinctly chilly toward her that evening at Almack's, which seemed odd to Annabel: her friend almost never bore grudges. But apart from that, Almack's seemed to be back to normal after the voucher upheaval of two weeks before. Young girls in their white or pale pink or yellow gowns, along with their hopeful mamas carefully surveying the room for eligible dance (and matrimonial) partners, lined the ballroom. Not for the first time, Annabel sighed with relief that she was no longer of their number: sometimes, being young was such an *ordeal*.

She bowed and nodded to friends and acquaintances, had a word with Mr. Willis near the door, and was on her way to the seats reserved for the Lady Patronesses when she spotted Frances a short distance away, conversing with an unfamiliar man, and went over to them. Frances would be delighted to hear that progress had been made on finding out what was going on with *The Fifty Shades*.

"Annabel!" Frances seemed pleased to see her. "May I present my brother, Glenrick? Alex, this is my good friend, Lady Fellbridge."

She curtsied in response to his bow. Now that she was closer, she could see the family resemblance between him and Frances—the same straight, light brown hair, long noses, and compact build. He was younger than Frances, she knew—perhaps a few years older than she was herself.

"How pleasant to see you at Almack's, sir," she said. "I don't recall your visiting before."

He pretended to stagger, as if from a blow. "Not in the past year or two, but you once gave me two dances in this very room, before you were married. I am devastated that I made so little impression on you."

Gracious—*had* they met? She didn't recall having done so. . . and considering she'd written down the name of every eligible gentleman she had danced with during her Season in her diary, along with their salient features (alas, put on the fire when she married, for it would have made amusing reading today), she was certain she would have remembered dancing with the heir to a dukedom. "Then you must forgive me. I expect I did dance with you, but I was a shockingly green young lady in my first Season and had a regrettable tendency to forget most of the people I met. And after my marriage I was not often in town."

"I hope that you will not be so quick to forget me this time, madam. I am sorry we never met after your marriage. We are kinsmen, you know: your husband and I were cousins on our mothers' sides."

"Oh, I didn't know that. Freddy never said." There was a great many things Freddy hadn't told her; this was evidently another one.

"Yes," Lord Glenrick said with a little sigh. "So very sad, his loss. But I am glad that you have returned to London. Frances has said many flattering things about you. I see that she has not exaggerated."

"I never exaggerate, Alex! I've told you that at least a thousand times!" Frances tapped his arm with her fan. "Do you see what I must suffer with, Annabel?"

"Perhaps Lady Fellbridge would be kind enough to take me off your hands for an hour or two. Would you care to drive in the park tomorrow afternoon with me? Do say yes, to oblige my sister." He smiled mischievously. "You can see what a good brother I am to her!"

"Yes, when it suits your own inclinations!" Frances retorted.

Annabel laughed. "I would be very happy to take you off Frances' hands tomorrow, but I already have an engagement and don't know what time I shall return." She turned to Frances. "That is what I came to tell you—I am being taken to pay a call on— er, on that author we have been discussing."

Her discretion was unnecessary. "Mr. Spruce! You found him?" Frances clutched at her arm. "Oh Annabel, you're so clever! How did you do it?"

"I can't take any credit for it. It seems Lord Quinceton actually knows the man and offered to bring me."

As soon as the words were out of her mouth, she regretted them. All the pleased excitement drained from Frances' face, and her shoulders drooped. "*Quin's* taking you to see him? But why didn't he tell *me* that he knows Mr. Spruce when we dined last night?"

"Perhaps because I had not yet decided to inflict any of you upon him?" Lord Quinceton's voice drawled.

Lord Quinceton! For the first time she could recall, Annabel was glad to see him. "Good evening, sir," she said, turning and finding herself actually smiling at him.

"Quin! Why didn't you tell me you know Mr. Spruce, you bad creature!" Frances' scold sounded more like a caress.

"You didn't ask me. 'Evening, Glenrick. Your servant, ladies." He bowed.

Lord Glenrick laughed. "You *are* a hand, Quinceton."

"Quite possibly. Fellbridge, I have been sent to find you." He held out his arm to her.

Glenrick raised an eyebrow. "Must you take *Lady* Fellbridge away when I am trying very hard to engage her to go driving with me?" He smiled at her. "As much as I like you, Quin, you are very much *de trop* just now."

"Of course not," Lord Quinceton said cordially, "if *you* would do me the favor of explaining to Sally Jersey why I was unable to bring one of her Lady Patronesses over to consult with her."

"Oh, I didn't know Sally was here. You must excuse me, Lord Glenrick. Frances, we'll talk later." Annabel hesitated, then took Lord Quinceton's arm.

"I shall call on you very soon, Lady Fellbridge, and claim you for that drive. Depend on it!" Glenrick bowed and smiled warmly at her. But the marquis was already steering her away.

They left the ballroom and entered the card room. Annabel glanced around, puzzled; Sally usually preferred to establish herself in the ballroom, which was much livelier. "Is she here?"

"Hmm? Who?" Lord Quinceton sounded abstracted.

"Lady Jersey, of course." She frowned and stopped walking. "Or did she really send you to find me?"

"Oh. No." With a seeming effort, he turned his attention to her. "Invoking Sally Jersey's name seemed the most likely way to extract you from the unsavory company you were keeping."

"Unsavory!" Annabel's voice had risen, and one or two of the card players glanced up at her. She pressed her lips together and kept silent till they had reached a less populous corner. "Pray, what do you mean by calling Lord Glenrick unsavory? Did you not dine with him just last evening?"

"Yes. But just because I am proof against him doesn't mean you are. Keep away from Glenrick, Fellbridge. He's not—" he hesitated. "He's not a person it would add to your consequence to know."

"I know it." She sighed theatrically. "These ducal heirs can be so tiresomely encroaching."

He didn't smile. "Some of them, yes."

She stared. "You are serious! How is he encroaching, if you please?"

"He's making a nuisance of himself, trying to live in my pocket."

"If it would not be impertinent to inquire—why should Glenrick toad-eat a—forgive me—a mere marquis?"

"It is somewhat mysterious to me, I admit."

She took a breath, willing herself into calm. He was joking. He had to be. But he was also taking her to see Mr. Spruce tomorrow; she would not jeopardize that by tearing at him, just as Emily had cautioned. "I cannot perceive why I should find Lord Glenrick in the least alarming. I liked him. And his sister is a dear friend of mine. But—but I shall make note of what you say."

"I suppose that's the most I can ask for."

As if he had the right to ask for anything from her! She looked up at him quickly; his face was stern and set, without the usual sardonic curve to his lips.

Very strange.

Mr. Spruce, as it happened, lived in Hampstead. Annabel thought she handled the not-inconsiderable journey with Lord Quinceton as well as could be hoped for.

He came for her promptly at noon, helped her into his handsome curricle with a quiet compliment on her appearance that to her surprise did not set her teeth on edge, and set his pair of match bays northward. It was a fine day and the streets were thronged, so Annabel gladly remained silent and let him concentrate on driving. It gave her further opportunity to think about their encounter the night before.

What had he meant by warning her off Lord Glenrick? She had liked the man, liked his easy manners and his gentle badinage with his sister. And liked his polite but frank admiration. He wasn't a philanderer like the married Lord Ordway or a male *cocotte* like Lord Keene. She would have been delighted to go driving with him today if she had not been engaged to see Mr. Spruce and would still welcome his paying a call on her. . . but not with the same unalloyed pleasure in the wake of Lord Quinceton's warning. Obviously he must know something about the man—but what? And why would it cause him to warn *her*, whom he must have noticed did not hold him in the greatest like? Did she dare bring it up today, where it would be difficult for him to evade her question?

"There's really no need to maintain strict silence, Fellbridge. I am capable of making polite conversation, though you might not credit it," he said after some twenty minutes.

Annabel felt herself flush and wished she could wrap herself in a nice, dark shadow. "I—I did not wish to distract you while the roads were so busy."

"You put me in mind of a schoolroom miss on her best behavior." His voice was full of restrained amusement. "Believe it or not, Fellbridge, I am also capable of conversing politely and driving at the same time."

Oh, dear. "I am sorry. My husband. . . he disliked chatter when he drove. I would seem to be out of practice."

More silence. Finally he said, "I am quite amenable to being practiced upon."

"Yes. . . I, er. . ." Oh, heavens, what should she say? All at once she felt like the schoolroom miss he'd likened her to: her mind had gone horribly, whitely blank. It wasn't very polite of him to tease her this way, but when had conventional politeness ever stopped him? "I have been. . . surprised to see you at Almack's so often, sir."

"I happen to find the company this spring unusually stimulating," he replied promptly.

"Er, indeed." What was she supposed to say to that? Unless—was—was he referring to *her* company? It seemed a distinct possibility; he must find needling her an excellent source of entertainment. *Now* of course would be the perfect time to ask him about Lord Glenrick, but she simply couldn't. Then inspiration struck. "Have you known Mr. Spruce a long time?"

"A number of years. Incidentally, Emily Cowper was not very clear about the nature of the problem we are consulting him about. His books are disappearing, you say."

Oh, dear. Well, it was bound to come up sooner or later. "Not all of them. Just the third volume of his most recent book—but yes."

"Is someone buying them up? Stealing them?"

"No, not buying them. I suppose it would be considered theft. They're vanishing." She braced herself.

"Vanishing." His voice was politely incredulous. She was grateful for the "polite" part.

"Yes. Emily's copy was in her bedchamber Saturday night and gone Sunday morning. She isn't the only one. Booksellers say that they're disappearing from their shops between one minute and the next."

"*Literally* vanishing." This time he turned to look at her.

"Yes."

He was silent for several minutes. "If it were anyone but you, Fellbridge, I would assume I was being hoaxed," he finally said.

Another compliment? He would put her quite out of countenance shortly. "It's no hoax, Lord Quinceton."

"No. That's the damnable thing."

He remained silent until they pulled up before a sturdy, square house, built across a lane from the edge of Hampstead Heath. A glimpse of a neatly-kept garden behind it was just visible, but before it was the bleak, empty wilderness. Annabel wondered if Mr. Spruce's desk looked out over the heath; it would be a most useful source of inspiration for his novels.

A groom came running from the side of the house to take the horses, and Lord Quinceton helped Annabel alight. He did not release her hand but led her up the shallow steps to the front door and plied the knocker.

The door was opened by a dignified, white-haired housekeeper wearing a starched white cap. When she saw the marquis, her sober expression was quickly replaced by a broad smile.

"Your lordship!" She opened the door wider to admit them. "My word, what a pleasant surprise!"

"Good afternoon, Mrs. Barnes. Is Mr. Spruce at home? I should like him to meet Lady Fellbridge." Lord Quinceton advanced into the front hall, square like the house itself and furnished with neat propriety.

The housekeeper dropped Annabel a quick curtsy. "Your ladyship," she murmured, then looked back to the marquis. There was a small hesitation in her manner, but she nodded. "Certainly, sir. Will you wait in the Small Parlor, please?"

"Thank you. How are Master James and the

little ones faring at school?"

"Oh, famously, my lord. Master James was cramming for his examinations when he was home at Easter. He still has his heart set on Cambridge," Mrs. Barnes said, leading them into a small, comfortable room. "Master John and Master Geoffrey are going on well. Master Geoffrey has decided that there will be a place for him on the Rugby Eleven someday."

"As soon as he's taller than the wicket," Lord Quinceton said with a chuckle.

She smiled. "Oh, don't let him hear you say that, sir, or he'll be forced to knock you down." She swept aside the curtains and opened the windows to let in the soft afternoon air, then left them.

Lord Quinceton approached a chair by the empty hearth, removing his hat and gloves. "What is it, Fellbridge? You have a certain look on your face."

Annabel sat down on the sofa opposite him. "I didn't understand that Mr. Spruce was your *friend*," she said, reluctantly. "I assumed you were merely acquaintances." It was strange to think of him having friends, people with whom he was on comfortable, even confidential, terms. She was far too used to viewing him in an adversarial light to admit that such a thing might be possible.

"His youngest son is my godson. Why? Am I not permitted friends?" he asked, coming uncomfortably close to echoing her thoughts. "Some people enjoy my company, you may be astonished to hear."

Annabel felt her cheeks grow warm, but before she was able to frame a response, the door opened. A small woman, perhaps in her mid-thirties and dressed in a quietly elegant gray silk dress, entered the room; she put Annabel in mind of a robin, with her dark hair, fresh complexion, and air of friendly curiosity.

"Geoffrey!" She crossed the room toward him, her hands outstretched. "Why did you not send word you were coming? It's been a ridiculous amount of time since your last visit. The boys were sorry not to see you over their holidays."

Lord Quinceton had risen and took her hands, smiled down at her, and bent to kiss her cheek. "I'm sorry I didn't have the chance to see them, Eliza. Mrs. Barnes tells me my namesake has gone cricket-mad. Are you all well?"

"Yes, thank you. And 'mad' is precisely the word. I feared for my windows the entire time he was home." She half-turned so that she could meet Annabel's eyes. "Please excuse us, ma'am. My lord Quinceton is for all intents a member of the family."

Annabel rose. "No excuses required, Mrs. Spruce. How do you do?"

The woman hesitated and looked up at Lord Quinceton. He cleared his throat, and Annabel saw a distinctly mischievous twinkle enter his eye. "Actually, Fellbridge, that's not quite it. May I make E.C. Spruce known to you?

Chapter Three

Annabel knew she was staring. How could she not? *"You're* E.C. Spruce?"

The woman turned back to fix Lord Quinceton with a reproachful look. "You didn't tell her, did you?"

"I always leave it to you to decide to whom you wish to reveal your secret, my dear," he said, openly grinning now.

She snorted. "When *will* you grow up, Geoffrey? You're as bad as the boys." She turned and made Annabel a small curtsy. "I am sorry this overgrown rascal didn't tell you the truth, Lady Fellbridge—he knows that I trust him not to disclose it to people who don't need to know. I received your note from Mr. Warburton, by the way—I'm glad Geoffrey brought you to me, even if he did make a prank out of it. Please, let us sit down and discuss it. Mrs. Barnes will bring us some refreshments shortly." She sat down on the sofa and smiled up at Annabel.

Annabel sat down, trying to reconcile the mental picture she'd formed of E.C. Spruce. "He" was a woman! What was her relationship with Lord Quinceton? Were they—but no, that wasn't any of her business, and she put it firmly out of her mind. "Thank you, Mrs.—er, I beg your pardon, what should I call you?"

"My true name is Eliza Denton. Spruce is a *nom de plume*, as you might have guessed. Since I am trying to preserve some degree of anonymity for the sake of my children, it seemed the best course to follow. I am a widow, Lady Fellbridge, and turned to writing to support myself, at that reprobate's suggestion." She nodded toward Lord Quinceton. "He has been kind enough to watch over us since my James's death."

"Mrs. Denton—" Annabel paused and scowled at the marquis. "I'm *so* glad you're enjoying yourself."

"I always enjoy myself in your company, Fellbridge," he replied promptly.

Mrs. Denton looked between the two of them, opened her mouth, then seemed to change her mind. "You were about to say, ma'am?" she said to Annabel.

"Yes. . ." She took a deep mental breath and put aside all the things she intended to say to Lord Quinceton on their drive home. It would be a miracle if there were any paint left on his curricle when she was through with him. "Has Mr. Warburton acquainted you with what is happening with the third volume of *The Fifty Shades of Udolpho*?"

She frowned. "I believe he tried to, but his communication was not very clear. It's no wonder the man is a printer; he would never succeed as a writer." She shook her head. "He said something about the books. . . disappearing?"

"I'm afraid that's precisely it." Annabel told her about the experiences of her fellow Lady Patronesses and the booksellers they had spoken to.

Mrs. Denton stared at her in wonderment. "I must confess, Lady Fellbridge, that if I had not heard it first from Mr. Warburton, I should be hard-pressed to believe what you say." She rose from her seat and took a few quick, nervous paces up and down the room. "What do you say to this?" she demanded, pausing before Lord Quinceton.

"Only what you did—that I should not have believed it from anyone's lips but Fellbridge's," he said.

She looked amused. "That wasn't quite what I said, but it is close enough."

There was a knock on the door, and Mrs. Barnes entered bearing a large tray laden with tea and cakes. Mrs. Denton sat down to pour, and when the housekeeper had passed the cups and plates and left them, said, "What else, Geoffrey?"

He sipped his tea meditatively. "My first thought is, who are your enemies?"

"My enemies, or E.C. Spruce's? I can't say I have any that I know of, unless you count Major Struthers next door, whose cherry trees the boys have been known to raid. And as for Mr. Spruce—well, he isn't real, so how can he have an enemy?" Mrs. Denton laughed lightly, but it sounded forced.

"E.C. Spruce might have many enemies. People who don't approve of his books. Jealous rival authors. Competing printers. You can't count them out, Eliza, just because you write behind another name."

"That is true." She sighed. "If you listen to Hannibal Warburton, this is the best thing that could have happened, and sales for the three volumes are treble my last book's. But I don't like it. My readers may find it a novelty now, but they will eventually become annoyed if they cannot read the volume they've paid for. And beyond that, it *feels* malicious. I would dearly like to know how it is happening. How can books just vanish?"

Annabel set down her teacup. "Mrs. Denton, my friends and I had occasion to speak with a bookseller in town who has a great deal of knowledge about matters of this type, and—"

"Matters of what type, Fellbridge?" Lord Quinceton interrupted.

"Hush." Mrs. Denton frowned at him. "Pray go on, Lady Fellbridge. What did the bookseller say?"

Oh, why could they not have sent Lord Quinceton from the room on some errand? She was too aware of his eyes fixed on her; the last thing she wanted was for him to begin to suspect anything about the Lady Patronesses. . . or *her*. "It is his opinion that the disappearances are the work of something not quite of this world. He suggests it might be some, er, 'spiritous being,' as the only thing that might account for books disappearing from locked bookshops. He could not guess at the origin of such a creature, but if it is capable of taking books, it must be able to assume a corporeal form. And if it does, then it can be caught. My friends and I would like to attempt to do so."

"You?" Mrs. Denton looked dubious. "But how?

What do you know of such things?"

It was time to tread carefully. "I don't believe we *know* anything. But we would like to try. The rub is that we'll need a copy of the third volume as bait and can't find one anywhere in London. We hoped that you would have one we might borrow. Is it not the custom for printers to send authors a copy of their work upon publication?"

Mrs. Denton smiled, a little grimly. "Mr. Warburton very kindly sends me *two* copies. But as I have a mother, two aunts, and two sisters, my copies are quickly claimed."

"I see." Annabel tried not to let her disappointment show.

"Wait, Eliza," Lord Quinceton said into the following silence. "Don't you have a manuscript copy?"

"Well, yes," Mrs. Denton said. "I always have my copyist make two, just in case anything happens to the one I send to Mr. Warburton."

"Do you think that would serve to bait your trap, Fellbridge?"

"I don't know," Annabel said. "But it's worth a try."

"Geoffrey!" Mrs. Denton exclaimed. "Do you mean to say you *want* Lady Fellbridge to attempt this? What if... oh, I don't know! It sounds too much like one of my own foolish stories. And it makes me very uncomfortable to think of you putting yourself into any difficulty—much less danger—over my problem."

"Don't let Fellbridge's appearance deceive you." The teasing note was back in his voice. "Under that delightfully feminine exterior, she's as tough as a pair of old boots."

Mrs. Denton frowned at him. "Quin, *really*."

"At some time, sir, I am sure you will grow weary of quizzing me. I can only hope that day will come sooner rather than later," Annabel said severely. At least now that she had made Mrs. Denton's acquaintance, she was no longer forced to be conciliating toward him.

"I will never tire of that, Fellbridge. Never."

"Geoffrey," Mrs. Denton said, drawing herself up. "Go away. I would like to speak sensibly with Lady Fellbridge, and you are not helping matters. Go inspect my stables if you will. I hired a new groom a fortnight ago and I am sure you would enjoy terrifying the poor man. You may return in a half-hour."

To Annabel's surprise, he meekly stood up. After the parlour door closed behind him and they heard his tread cross the hall toward the front door, Mrs. Denton sighed. "My word, he *is* fractious today. Every bit as bad as the boys after two days of rain."

"Isn't he always?" Annabel was surprised into asking.

"Oh, no. He is the kindest of friends. I don't mind telling you that he. . . well, he saved our lives. When James died of a malignant fever, I did not know what I should do. My youngest—his godson—was still in swaddling clothes, and there was very little money beyond a small income from James's mother's family, which just paid for my oldest son's schooling and kept us from starving. James had been a successful barrister, on the rise within his chambers, but that income obviously ceased. Geoffrey helped me sell our London house and move here, stood in as uncle to the boys, and suggested I try my hand at writing. He more or less supported us while I wrote my first book. I had sold a few poems and essays to magazines, you see, and liked the work, but it never occurred to me that I could keep us with it. But he was right, as he usually is. When he isn't being fractious."

"I have that effect on him, he tells me," Annabel said. This was an unexpected side of Lord Quinceton, one that she was not sure she could reconcile with the rest of him that she knew. The carousing partner of Freddy—not to mention her own tormentor—was also a comforter of widows and orphans.

"I had noticed that." Mrs. Denton was frowning slightly. She shook herself and turned back to Annabel. "My dear Lady Fellbridge, I thank you for your concern, but I cannot let you pursue this matter of my book."

Annabel took a breath. If Mrs. Denton had taken a chance on trusting her, then she would take a chance on trusting Mrs. Denton. "When I said that my friends and I had no knowledge of such things as might be taking your books, I wasn't being entirely truthful. Or rather, we don't know the precise nature of the book thief, but we feel ourselves sufficiently competent in various ways to be able to deal with whatever it might be." When Mrs. Denton looked at her skeptically, she bent and reached under the sofa for a handful of shadow, shook it out, and dropped it over the tea table before them. It vanished.

Mrs. Denton stared at the spot where it had been. "My table is gone," she said in a small voice.

"Not really. It's just hidden." Annabel pulled the covering shadow off and let it slide off her fingers and dissipate, then waited.

"I... see," Mrs. Denton finally said. Her countenance had grown pale, but she did not seem in danger of losing her composure. "Are all your friends capable of such—such..." She seemed unsure of how to finish her sentence.

"Not *this,* precisely, but they have their own abilities. It's why we think we'll be at least a match for whatever is stealing your books." At least, they would if Clementina and Dorothea agreed to help.

"Is this why Geoffrey brought you to me? Does he know that you—"

"Oh gracious, no! I will be very much obliged if you would keep my secret from him and everyone. It isn't knowledge that I and my friends would wish anyone else to know."

"I can understand that." Mrs. Denton sat back and stared at her. "Does your husband know?"

"My husband is dead—I am also a widow—but no, he didn't know."

"A widow!"

"These past three years. It seems you and I have much in common—I too have sons in school."

Mrs. Denton appeared taken aback. "You must have been a very young bride, to have sons at school!" She paused. "Do you miss your husband?"

Annabel hesitated. It was a surprising question and from anyone else might have seemed rude. But Mrs. Denton was in the very same circumstances as she and seemed genuinely interested to know. Besides, she was an author; they could probably be forgiven some eccentricities.

"I... to some degree, yes," she said slowly. "It is awkward to be a widow, as you well know, and means I must do things I would not have to if my husband were alive to take care of them." Not that Freddy had been very good at them, but Mrs. Denton didn't need to know that. "But it was not a love match."

Mrs. Denton sat back in her seat. "I am sorry," she said.

But it sounded like a rote response. Mrs. Denton gazed at her fixedly for so long a time, her thoughts obviously elsewhere, that finally Annabel laughed nervously. "I hope you are not considering how I might fit into your next story."

Mrs. Denton started. "Goodness, no! I was just thinking. . . that is, I. . . Thank you, Lady Fellbridge. In light of. . . of what you have shown me, I can't imagine anyone else who might be able to solve this mystery. Will you pardon my leaving you for a few minutes while I get the manuscript for you?"

She jumped up and hurried to the door. Annabel heard her speak briefly to someone in the hall, and a moment later Lord Quinceton came in, looking bemused.

"Did the stable-hand meet with your approval?" she asked.

"I beg your pardon?" He blinked. "Oh. Mostly. Where did Eliza go?" He resumed his seat.

"To get the manuscript."

He nodded. Annabel rose and went to the window, pretending to be absorbed by the view, in hopes that he would not find it necessary to make conversation with her.

Her hopes were vain. "You were the only one I could have brought here, you know," he said suddenly. "I would never have trusted anyone else with Eliza's secret."

"All part and parcel of your considering me an

honorary man, I assume," she said drily.

He seemed to consider that. "Quite possibly. Though there aren't many men I would have trusted, either. They're almost the worse gossips." A pause. "When do you plan to beard your ghost?"

"I don't expect that it is a ghost, and I am not certain. Why do you ask?"

"Because I intend to be there with you when you do."

What! She half-turned from the window to fix him with a cold look. "I don't recall inviting you, sir."

"I'm inviting myself."

She clung to her temper with an effort. "No."

"Why not?"

"Because it isn't any of your business."

"It became my business as soon as you accepted my invitation to call upon my friend, to whom I feel no small degree of obligation," he said calmly.

Oh, bother the man! There was enough truth to that to make it difficult to put him off. "Very well. I acknowledge that you may have some interest in this matter—"

"Thank you. Very handsomely said."

"—but I am sure your delicate sense of honor will permit you to understand when I say that I am not the only one who will be 'bearding this ghost,' as you put it, and I cannot speak for how *my* friends might receive your. . . involvement."

His eyes gleamed. "Secrets, Fellbridge?"

"Everyone has them, including, I am sure, you."

He laughed. "Oh, I have dozens. I just didn't expect *you* to have any." His expression sobered. "I don't jest, in any event. I don't care for your doing whatever it is you're going to do unprotected."

She took refuge in lightness. "Unprotected! Why, Lord Quinceton! And here I thought that you regarded me as a fellow man and awake on all suits! Could it be that you haven't been entirely truthful?"

He actually had the grace to color slightly. "Fellbridge—"

"Just so. And what, pray, makes you presume that we will be unprotected? Just because you won't be there to—"

The door opened, interrupting her. "Here it is," Mrs. Denton proclaimed, brandishing a thick stack of pages bound with a red ribbon. She halted just past the threshold and looked from Annabel to the marquis. "Oh. I beg your pardon. . ."

The atmosphere in the room *was* perhaps a trifle charged. . . but whose fault was that? Annabel ignored Lord Quinceton and left the window. "There's no need to do that, Mrs. Denton." She eyed the manuscript. "Thank you for trusting me with it. We will do our best to keep it safe, of course, but you understand it might not be possible—"

"If it should have to be sacrificed, it will be no great loss. Mr. Warburton still has the printing plates." Mrs. Denton crossed the room to Annabel and handed it to her. "Thank you, Lady Fellbridge. I will be much in your debt if you and your friends can find the author of this malfeasance and stop it."

"It will be our pleasure to do so." She held out her hand and Mrs. Denton took it. They smiled at each other, and Annabel knew that they could trust each other with their respective secrets.

The following day found curious preparations being carried out in Annabel's library. The curtains had been drawn against the early afternoon light and the room carefully arranged. The manuscript pages Mrs. Denton had given her lay on a table in the middle of the room; all other furniture had been drawn to the edges, leaving a clear space around the table. A candle in a low stick had been lit and placed on the table next to the manuscript. The servants had been warned not to come near the library for the rest of the day, and the room was still, apart from the restless flicker of the candle's flame.

Annabel had been in a fever of worry lest the manuscript disappear overnight and had sent urgent notes as soon as she arrived home from Mrs. Denton's to Clementina Drummond-Burrell and Dorothea Lieven, summoning them to her house the next day. She had slept badly, waking frequently to check that the manuscript—wrapped in a thick shadow and tucked under her pillow—was still there. Fortunately, it did not disappear, and as fortunately, Clementina and Dorothea both arrived at the appointed hour.

"Did you read it?" Clementina demanded as soon as Annabel had removed the concealing shadow and showed it to them.

Annabel laughed. "I didn't even think to! I was so worried about it vanishing and planning what we would do today that I didn't take one look."

"You are either very disciplined or very silly." Dorothea picked up the manuscript and casually riffled through it. "Oh!" she murmured, pausing at a page. Her gaze traveled greedily over it.

"Probably the latter—why, wait a minute,

Dorothea! I thought you said you hadn't read *The Fifty Shades!*"

Dorothea blushed and set the pages down hastily. Annabel looked at Clementina, which was probably the wrong thing to do: they both burst into giggles.

"What else was I to do, when all the rest of London was agog over it?" Dorothea said with an injured air. "Conversation would have become very one-sided if I had not."

"I am amazed you were able to convince Mr. Spruce to give it to you. Why don't you think it vanished from his house?" Clementina asked when they had finished teasing Dorothea.

"I don't know. I wondered about that, while I wasn't sleeping last night. Perhaps because it is not an actual book but a manuscript?"

"I hope that doesn't mean it won't work to tempt our thief."

"I know." If that were the case, it would be a very long afternoon. "But I did conceal it quite thoroughly in a shadow last night. And maybe whatever is taking the books has so far confined its actions to London? Mr. Spruce is in Hampstead." That wasn't revealing too much, she hoped.

"In that case, then we ought to complete our preparations now that it *is* in London and not concealed," Dorothea said.

"Yes." Annabel ushered them to three chairs set a few feet from the table and, when they were all seated, cast a shadow over them. "Can you still see and hear well enough, Clementina?" she asked anxiously.

"Yes, though it is a peculiar sensation."

Clementina tried to touch the shadow, but her fingers slid through it.

Annabel smoothed it down again. "Dorothea? Are you ready?"

"I will not know until something arrives. It will be but the work of a moment to cast aside this shadow, yes?"

"Yes."

"Hmm." Dorothea hunched her shoulders. "I warn you that I cannot be sure that I will be able to deal with whatever it is."

"I understand that."

"If it is human, *pouf!*" She gestured. "I will fell him like that. But we are not knowing the nature of this thief, that it *is* human."

"No."

Dorothea sighed. "I will do my poor best. But I am not the least bit sanguine. And so. . .we wait."

"I trust it won't take too long," Clementina murmured after a few minutes. "Staring at a copy of the third volume of *The Fifty Shades* and not being able to read it may kill me."

Annabel patted her hand. She hoped she hadn't done ill by inviting Clementina to participate in this due to her interesting condition, but Clementina's exquisite senses would hopefully give them a little extra warning when—*if*—whatever was taking the books should appear. Nor was she sure that Dorothea's gaze—her mother had been a gorgon— would stun the thief as it might a human one. . . but it had been the best plan she and Emily had been able to dream up on short notice. She sat back and prepared to wait.

What would the Marquis of Quinceton say if he

knew what they were up to right now? Their ride home yesterday from Mrs. Denton's house had been a quiet one; he had not repeated his request to help "beard the ghost," but it was clear even without possessing Emily's powers that he was thinking about it. When he'd dropped her at her house, he only said, "I will call tomorrow."

Well, if he did, he would find that she was not "at home," which would serve him right for attempting to be so high-handed. What right did he think he had to "protect" her. . . as if he could? Oh, it would have been *so* satisfying to have staggered him by swathing herself in a shadow right there in Mrs. Denton's parlor and asking him if he still thought his presence was necessary to keep them safe. His dark eyes would have widened, and he—

"Ssh." Dorothea touched her arm. "What is it, Annabel? You are restive."

"Nothing. I beg your pardon." She forced herself to relax. Gloating over the marquis' hypothetical astonishment would have to wait until later.

They sat. Clementina shifted in her seat and sighed occasionally, and Annabel hoped she would not grow too uncomfortable. The tick of the clock on the chimneypiece above the fireplace seemed to grow louder with every passing minute. The rumble and clatter of an occasional carriage passing in the street outside was the only other sound, and Annabel found herself listening for the rhythm of horses' hooves to provide counterpoint to the clock—

Clementina's hand tightened on her arm. "There's something," she barely whispered.

A fraction of a second later a small *phht!* of displaced air broke the silence, setting the candle flickering wildly. Annabel stared at the table through the veil of shadow and just managed not to gasp aloud. Something not quite human-sized—or shaped—was crouching on the table next to the manuscript, where nothing had been a moment before. She saw small, claw-like hands reach for the manuscript and yanked on the shadow hard, pulling it from over all of their heads.

"I should not do that, if I were you," Dorothea said, standing up. The thing on the table squeaked in surprise as it turned to stare at her. . . and fell to the floor, immobilized.

Chapter Four

"There. Did I not tell you it would work perfectly?" Dorothea stepped forward and peered down at the thing on the floor. "*Bog na nebe*! What *is* it?"

Clementina hurried to the windows and threw open the curtains, then opened the windows themselves. "What is that *smell*?" she added, in a choked voice.

A distinct odor of brimstone drifted up from the thing on the floor. Annabel joined Dorothea to stare down at it, and Clementina looked over their shoulders.

For one thing, it was blue—a rich, vibrant, midsummer-sky blue—and its back appeared to be covered in thick, quill-like gray feathers, like a strange blend of hedgehog and bird. Its face was small and furious, with a long, thin nose on which perched a pair of spectacles, and black, pupil-less eyes that squinted up at them blearily. It had delicate goat's hooves and furred legs like a satyr's, small, three-fingered hands with long talons, and a long, slender tail, like a cat's.

"*Mon Dieu*, but it is ugly!" Dorothea announced. "What shall we do with it?"

Annabel saw one of the odd little hands twitch. "Dorothea, will you please take charge of the book?" If the—*thing* should suddenly come out of its parlay-sis, she didn't want it snatching the manuscript and disappearing back to wherever it had come from.

Dorothea picked up the pages and held them tight to her breast. "You shall not have them, sir. . . or—" She looked up at Annabel. "You don't suppose it's female, do you?"

"If that's the female, I would hate to know what the male smells like." Clementina shuddered delicately.

"It squealed like a little girl," Dorothea commented. "Just before it fell over."

The creature stiffened and, with a prodigious effort, pushed itself to a sitting position. "I did not!" it squeaked, then cleared its throat and muttered, "Didn't," in a somewhat deeper tone.

"Did," Dorothea said.

"May we ask who you are and why you're here?" Annabel asked, before matters could degenerate.

The blue thing looked up at her, eyes narrowed. "Why should I tell you? And anyway, you already know why I'm here." It stared sullenly at the pages clasped in Dorothea's arms. "And I thought I'd taken care of them all."

"I think you mostly had—at least the ones in London."

The thing relaxed. "Thought so. That's all the deal was for—London. *He's* trying to change the terms on me and make it all of England, but that won't fly. A contract is a contract." It folded its arms and stuck out its chin.

Annabel thought quickly. A strange, obviously supernatural being. . . a contract. . . the scent of brimstone. . . "You're a demon, aren't you?"

It smirked. "You're a downy mort, aren't you?"

Clementina giggled through the handkerchief pressed over her nose and mouth. "It talks like my housemaids, when they think I can't hear them."

"And you're under contract to someone to steal every single copy of a certain book from London," Annabel went on.

"Volume three of *The Fifty Shades of Udolpho*," the little demon agreed. "To remove utterly from every house, bookshop, and circulating library in London."

"How banal." Dorothea shook her head. "Someone with the soul of an under-clerk hired you to do this."

"His soul ain't much," the thing agreed, a little touchily, "but a demon has to take what it can get these days." It sighed and looked up at Annabel. "The name's Titivillus if you really want to know. The patron demon of scribes, they call me. See?" It turned slightly and displayed its feathered back. "Diabolical quills. Guaranteed minimum of six errors per paragraph, including the most embarrassing spelling mistakes possible, designed to create the maximum distortion in meaning and tone when you write with one of these. *And* they never need sharpening. Want one?"

"Er, no, thank you. How do you do, Titivillus?" It seemed safer to be polite to the creature, at least for now. "Would you care to get up off the floor so that we may converse more easily?"

Titivillus pushed its spectacles further up its nose and regarded her cautiously. "You just want to talk?"

"Yes."

It rose to its feet, somewhat unsteadily, and peered over the edge of the table. "Don't see a pentagram up there. You ain't meaning to try to trap me and make me do something?"

"Why should we want to remain in your company longer than we have to?" Clementina muttered.

"No, we truly just want to talk."

"You won't let her do whatever she did to me again, will you?" It looked sideways at Dorothea. "She's got gorgon eyes, I swear."

"Yes, I do," Dorothea agreed imperturbably. One or two of her curls stirred. "At least, half gorgon on my mother's side or you would have been turned into a particularly homely piece of garden statuary by now. If you will behave yourself and answer whatever questions Lady Fellbridge puts to you, I will restrain myself from helping you to achieve that condition."

Titivillus put a hand to its head. "Thanks for nothin'. My noggin's going to ache for a week. What do you want to know?"

Annabel pulled one of the chairs closer to the table and sat down. "We would like to know who asked you to take the books and why."

It dropped its hand and glared at her. "He didn't *ask*, the rotter—he forced me! No one's ever dared do that to Titivillus before—summoning me like any common demon!"

Annabel remembered Emily's statement about men baring their souls to pretty women who listened. Perhaps it would be true of demons too. "That must have been a dreadful shock," she said sympathetically.

The demon put on an injured air. "It was. There I was, minding my own business, giving a poet the itch so he couldn't make his rhymes come out—not that he needed much help from me, he was that bad—and the next minute, I was stuck in *his* study, my face ground into the middle of his study carpet." It thought for a moment. "His housekeeper needs a good beating. It smelled bad."

"How could you tell?" Dorothea muttered.

"And once he had summoned you, you were bound to do what he asked? That scarcely seems fair."

Titivillus nodded. "I know. It's about time something was done about that, but it's the usual procedure—if a demon gets summoned without its consent and is trapped by the summoner, we're forced to sign a contract to do whatever he wishes in order to get free."

"Quite unjust!" Annabel said soothingly.

"You know what? You're not so bad." The demon grabbed the edge of the table and hoisted itself up onto it, perching on the edge with its little goat feet dangling. "I'll wager you'd never pull such a paltry trick on a poor demon like Marjoribanks did."

Marjoribanks? Why did that name sound familiar? She glanced up at her companions. Clementina looked blank, but Dorothea had a thoughtful look on her face. "Marjoribanks," she repeated slowly.

Annabel turned back to Titivillus. "I should

think we wouldn't! How can we help you?"

"Get my contract and rip it up," it responded promptly. "I'm busy enough as it is keeping up with my regular work—messing up typesetters and tipping over trays of type. I don't need an author wasting my valuable time with his fussing and jealousy." It sniggered. "Wait till his next book comes out! I'll put more misprints in it than Hell has cinders."

Ah, another clue. . . so this Mr. Marjoribanks was an author too. It appeared that Lord Quinceton had been on the right track when he posited that another author was behind the disappearances. Not that she had any intention of telling him so. "He wanted you to steal all the copies of the third volume? That hardly seems a worthy task for someone of your abilities."

Clementina coughed slightly.

"It certainly isn't!" The demon put on a distinctly aggrieved expression. "Treating *me*, the great Titivillus, like a packhorse to pick up books for him! And only the third volume of the blasted book! I've read it a dozen times now—professional interest, you know, had to check the error rate. But I have no idea why Ermentrudina decides to do such a shocking thing with Count Atroccio in the second to last chapter. She mentions something that had happened earlier driving her to do it, but I don't know what it is. The very thought of her giving him her—"

"No!" Both Dorothea and Clementina clapped their hands over their ears.

Annabel just managed not to do the same. "Haven't you read the first two volumes?"

"No." Titivillus sighed. "I can't while I'm under

contract. I'm tied to this book. So I have no idea why all these terrible things happen in volume three, like Osberto's permitting the Marchesa to do *that* to him after he declared he would rather throw himself from the highest cliff!"

Dorothea actually moaned.

Annabel leaned forward. "If we were to find a way to let you know what happened in the first two volumes, would you tell us who holds your contract?"

Titivillus's tail, which before had lain limply on the table, straightened. "I certainly would!" It smiled, revealing pointy teeth. "No one's read to me since I was hatched, practically."

"You want it *read* to you?"

It gazed at her soulfully. "How else can you tell me what happens in the story?"

Annabel looked up at Dorothea. "Er...would you be willing—"

"I have a *very* bad reading voice," Dorothea said firmly.

"I'll do it," Clementina said from behind her handkerchief.

Annabel gestured at her nose with elaborate casualness. "Are you, ah, *certain*?"

She hesitated, then nodded. "So long as we are by an open window, I think I can manage it. It's the least I can do. And I think Dorothea may be more useful to you in dealing with whomever it is who—"

"It's Gilbert Marjoribanks," Titivillus supplied helpfully. "He lives just off Hanover Square. He writes as Marjorie Banks Gilbert."

"Oh ho!" Dorothea laughed. "I have read this Marjorie Banks Gilbert! So she is a he! I am not surprised. He draws his heroines clumsily. His *The*

Noble Barbarian was very bad."

"Didn't that just come out last week?" Clementina asked Annabel in a stage whisper.

"Yes, I think so. But I thought she said she never read novels," Annabel replied.

Dorothea looked down her nose at them. "It is very difficult to hear what the two of you are saying when you mumble like that. But it all makes sense now. *The Fifty Shades of Udolpho* is so much better than his new book, and he knew it. So he contracted this one here—" she nodded at Titivillus— "to do away with the third volume, and make everyone angry and not wish to read it—"

"Except that it's had the very opposite effect according to Mr. Warburton. If Mr. Marjoribanks knows, he must be provoked beyond anything," Annabel added.

"But what do we do now?" Clementina asked.

Annabel hesitated and looked to Dorothea. "I think we must inform the other Ladies, since we now have evidence of wrong-doing of a supernatural nature."

Dorothea nodded. "I am in agreement."

"You know," Titivillus said. "If you just let me take that copy there, I could be on my way and done with this. It's the last one in London."

"Until someone outside London brings a copy in, or Aphrodite Press releases more copies, and then you—and we—will be back where we started." Annabel said. "No, we have to do something about destroying your contract and making sure Mr. Marjoribanks does not do this again. Let's bring it up in Monday's meeting—that's only two days from now."

"Oh, all right," Titivillus said, then turned its toothy grin on Clementina. "When do we start reading?"

The next evening at a concert at Sally's house, Annabel was happy to see Emily, radiant in deep primrose yellow, approach with her usual smile. Evidently, she was back in her friend's good graces after the scolding she'd been given on Wednesday.

"Annabel!" Emily took her arm and squeezed it. "I was expecting you to call on Friday for a good gossip. What happened? Did Quin take you to see E.C. Spruce?"

"A great deal happened. We'll be bringing it up at Monday's meeting. It's something the rest of us need to know about." She gave Emily an abbreviated version of the encounter with Titivillus and Gilbert Marjoribanks's wickedness, saying as little as possible about the visit to "Mr. Spruce."

"A demon!" Emily's eyes widened. "Annabel, you must have been so brave! I should not have liked to meet one. Was it very horrid?"

"It wasn't all that bad, really, aside from the smell." Annabel shuddered in remembrance. "I should warn Sally, if I can manage to speak to her alone this evening."

"Yes, you should. Come and sit with me after you do. I'm dying to hear more!" Emily called after her.

Annabel managed to drop a few hurried words in Sally's ear just before the concert started. "A demon?" Sally looked pained. "I loathe having to deal with them. I do wish we had a witch amongst our number—they're much better at that sort of thing. Too bad Lady Lansell isn't in town this Season, or I'd ask her to consult. Very well, we'll talk about it on Monday. Thank you for the warning." She banged the brass Chinese gong she held. "If you would all sit down, please, so that we may start the performance!" she called, her voice carrying as only Sally's could.

Annabel looked for Emily in the crowd but could not find her, so she slipped into a seat in the last row of small gilt chairs and prepared to enjoy the music. Just as the accompanist played the opening bars of the first song, someone took the seat beside her. She glanced up, and her smile faded.

It was the Marquis of Quinceton, looking more hungrily wolfish than ever.

He raised one eyebrow at her and she barely nodded to him. Thank goodness the music had started, saving her from actually having to speak to him. She did not allow her eyes to stray from the *basso* soloist after that brief nod, but she was sure she felt his eyes on her frequently over the course of the concert. She would have to think of what she would say when it was over; Hanscomb had told her that he had called on Friday while she and Clementina and Dorothea had been conferring with Titivillus and had seemed put out that she was not "at home."

Well, let him be put out! She had made it very clear that he would not be a part of their investigation. Nor did he have to play intermediary any longer; she had written a letter to Mrs. Denton with an edited version of what they had discovered (trying to explain Titivillus was beyond her pen) and the assurance that Mr. Marjoribanks would be, in some manner or other, dissuaded from engaging in such actions again.

After Signor Cassini had sung his last note and the applause had given way to a growing hum of conversation, Annabel braced herself for the demand for explanation she was sure would come. She did not have long to wait.

"Good evening, Fellbridge." He rose and bowed, then held his hand out to help her rise. "I hoped I would have the pleasure of seeing you here this evening. What did you think of Signor Cassini?"

She was so surprised not to be immediately attacked that she took his proffered hand and stood up. "He—ah—seemed to be in fine voice tonight."

"Yes, I thought so too. The Mozart was particularly well done, don't you think? His phrasing was especially nice." He held his arm out and again she took it, too surprised to do otherwise. Why was he being so. . . *affable*? She made some vaguely affirmative reply.

"I understand he'll be singing at Covent Garden in the next few weeks," he continued. "Lady Jersey was fortunate to get him this evening."

"Sally is very good at that. She is monstrous fond of the opera." In fact, she wasn't, but she had told Annabel that she took singing lessons and closely observed all the great singers and actors to pick up pointers in managing her wind abilities.

The marquis steered her toward the line exiting the salon. "I received a note from our friend in Hampstead today," he said quietly.

Annabel tensed; here it came. "I trust that she is well?"

"Quite well. She writes that she intends to come into the city early next week and asked me to inquire if she might do herself the honor of returning your call. She greatly enjoyed meeting you."

"I hope she does call. I enjoyed meeting her as well."

"I thought you might. Your situations are not unalike, are they not? She is an excellent person; I don't think you'll regret the acquaintance." He hesitated, and she waited for the inevitable: he had steered their conversation so adroitly toward the subject of Mrs. Denton that surely now he would be asking—*demanding*—to know if the ghost had been bearded—

"May I procure a glass of champagne for you?" he finally said. "We seem to be heading toward the refreshments."

Annabel nearly stopped in her tracks. "Why haven't you asked me about the book?" she blurted.

"The book? Which book?" He glanced at her, a faint smile lurking in the corners of his mouth. "No, I shouldn't tease. Why, do you wish me to ask about it? I had thought you made your feelings about my involvement in your activities concerning it abundantly clear."

She did not answer; it was all she could do to keep her temper, whether with him or with herself she was not sure. "You will undoubtedly be gratified to learn that your surmise was correct; a jealous author is behind the troubles."

"Ah. Yes, that makes sense."

"Though the fact that we were able to determine this without your protection might be less gratifying," she could not keep herself from adding.

"Fellbridge, believe me when I say that nothing was more gratifying than to see you here tonight, apparently unharmed and in excellent looks." He took two glasses of champagne from a passing footman and handed her one. "Very much in excellent looks," he added softly and raised his glass to her.

Annabel sipped hers gratefully, as its timely arrival saved her from having to answer him at once—though what she would say, she had no idea. He was not only odious, but also infuriating. . . and had made her blush like a miss in her first Season. She was grateful to see Emily wending her way through the press of guests toward them a moment later.

"Splendid concert," she announced, joining them. "Annabel, where were you? I saved a seat for you and made Lady Whitley very cross when I shooed her away from it." She didn't wait for an answer but turned to the marquis. "Quin, thank you so much for taking Annabel to see Mr. Spruce. However, I am very cross with her for not telling me all about her visit, as she was supposed to just now. What is he like? Is he dreamy, like a poet? Or stormy and dramatic, like his books?"

Ah, here was her chance. "Oh, you should not ask me. Mr. Spruce is Lord Quinceton's good friend. For my part, I believe he would be happy to tell you all about him. My lord?" She smiled at him brightly, and turned away.

"Well played, Fellbridge," she heard him murmur, just before the crowd swallowed her.

Chapter Five

At Monday's Lady Patronesses' meeting, after the usual business of making voucher decisions, Sally began the rest of the day's business by saying, "Annabel has something to tell us that we may find of. . . well, for lack of a better word, interest."

Georgiana Bathurst sniffed. "I trust that this won't take long."

"As long as necessary, Georgiana," Sally replied pleasantly but with a slight edge to her voice. "Annabel?"

Annabel rose from her seat. When would Georgiana forgive her for not being a forger? "I shall endeavor to be brief," she said, and launched into a description of the last several days, treading carefully around the visit to E.C. Spruce.

"A demon!" Maria Sefton said wonderingly when she was through. "This Mr. Marjoribanks summoned a demon to take the books? How dreadfully. . . excessive."

"Dreadful is hardly a strong enough word," Clementina put in, her voice hoarse. "I've had to read volumes one and two to Titivillus over the last two days. It keeps interrupting me to say things like, 'Aha! So *that's* why she did that! I should never have seen that coming if I hadn't already read it.' It's horribly irritating!"

"I can imagine, you poor dear." Emily patted her arm. "You're an angel to put up with that horrid creature!"

Clementina hesitated. "Oh, not really. Titi—er, Titivillus has sworn to bring me a copy of the third volume the instant its contract is voided."

"*Titi?*" Dorothea repeated. "Do my ears deceive me, or did I just hear you refer to that odoriferous blue hedgehog as 'Titi?'"

She blushed. "It can be quite sweet when it wishes to. It always sits next to the window to cut down on the odor and takes care to see that I have a footstool and cushions for my back before we begin to read."

Dorothea, eyes glinting mischievously, opened her mouth to speak, but Sally cut her off. "I am glad to hear that even demons can have manners, Clementina, and thank you for your help. Now, the question is, what shall we do about this situation? Clearly we cannot countenance authors summoning the denizens of hell to vanquish their rivals."

"Why can't we send Georgiana or Annabel to Mr. Marjoribanks' house to take away the demon's contract, as they did with the forged vouchers?" Frances asked.

"That won't do. What's to keep him from doing the same thing again tomorrow or the next time E.C.

Spruce or anyone else publishes a book more popular than his?" Sally answered. "No, I'm afraid we must be more direct than that. He must be confronted and told in no uncertain terms that such behavior is not acceptable in modern London. Summoning demons! The man must be positively *gothic*."

Emily smothered a giggle. Sally frowned at her. "The question is, whom shall we send?"

"Annabel ought to go, since she's done most of the work on this and should be on hand to see it resolved," Clementina said.

Annabel smiled at her. "Perhaps Emily should go as well, to ensure Mr. Marjoribanks deals with us honestly."

"Should Dorothea go, to stun him in case he becomes violent?" Maria suggested.

"Authors are not generally known for their violent tendencies, most of the time," Dorothea said. "But I will go if you wish me to. It might be amusing to see this summoner of demons."

"I wouldn't mind going. For my part, I wish to give Mr. Marjoribanks a piece of my mind for doing what he's done!" Frances put in.

"I appreciate your sentiments, Frances, but I believe *I* shall go," Sally said, after a moment's reflection. "We should present a temperate, measured demeanor when we confront him. I do not think that displays of overt emotionalism will be effective in this case. We must bring him to his senses with calm and logic. I am certain he must be a reasonable man."

Frances nodded, chastened, and Emily said, "When shall we go, then?"

"The sooner the better, I think," Sally said. "I

will come by for you tomorrow at two."

Sally and Emily arrived at Annabel's shortly after the allotted time. Emily moved to the rear-facing seat, leaving the preferred front-facing seat next to Sally for Annabel.

"You didn't have to do that," Annabel scolded as the footman let down the stair for her.

"Yes, I did. This is your investigation," Emily promptly replied. She glanced over the back of the landau as she sat. "Oh, it appears someone's coming to call on you."

Annabel looked quickly at the plain traveling coach just pulling up behind them. "It's no one's carriage that I know. Probably someone calling on the Maitlands next door." She sat down next to Sally, and they set out for Hanover Square.

"You look well," Sally said approvingly. They had agreed to appear in their most elegant afternoon costumes and hats to present as imposing an appearance as possible. Annabel hoped her topaz muslin and brown velvet spencer would help bolster her confidence; confronting Mr. Marjoribanks in his own home was going to be awkward in the extreme.

"I just hope he's *at* home," Emily said. "Wouldn't it be ridiculous if we called on an empty house? Oh, sorry, Annabel. Didn't mean to look."

Fortunately, he was at home. An astonished-looking, elderly butler let them into Mr. Marjoribanks' front hall, looked even more astonished as he surveyed their calling cards, and ushered them into a dark, over-furnished sitting room.

"I take it there's no Mrs. Marjoribanks," Emily murmured, looking at the dull maroon velvet of the curtains and the equally dark carpet. "No woman of any mettle would put up with a room that looked like this to receive callers in. It's positively funereal."

"Perhaps he finds it conducive to his writing," Annabel said. "Are his books very dark and brooding? I haven't read any."

"No. They're mostly about extraordinarily tall, firm-jawed, argumentative, and hot-at-hand heroes and rather colorless, adoring heroines who stand by admiringly while the hero lops the limbs off his adversaries and fall into fatal declines if he's killed."

"Oh dear. I hope Mr. Marjoribanks isn't like his heroes. Perhaps we should have brought Dorothea after all."

Sally frowned. "Don't forget, we are trying to convince him without a display of our abilities—"

She fell silent as the door to the sitting room opened and the butler announced, "Mr. Marjoribanks."

A small, stooped man of early middle age came into the room, clad in a dark coat of an old-fashioned cut and knee breeches; his graying, mousy hair was worn in a short queue. He paused just inside the threshold, rapidly blinking his small, dull blue eyes at them, and bowed. "Your ladyships," he said, his voice surprisingly deep for one of his slight stature. "To what may I ascribe this honor?"

Sally waited until the butler had ponderously closed the sitting room doors and gave Mr. Marjoribanks a brief curtsy and an appraising look. "Good afternoon, sir. I believe we have the honor of addressing not only Mr. Marjoribanks, but—ah, Miss Gilbert?"

Mr. Marjoribanks' sour expression deepened into outrage. "Who told you that?" he demanded.

"We have it on very good authority, sir," Annabel said.

He scowled at her. "Who told you? I'll warrant it was that scoundrel who calls himself my printer. I'll have the blackguard flogged through the streets!" he declaimed, puffing out his thin chest. "We had an understanding that my name would remain—"

Sally had put on her severest Lady Patroness manner. "Your printer did not tell us. We did not even consult with him. And be assured that no one else knows your identity, nor will anyone learn it from us. May I suggest we be seated? We have a serious matter to discuss with you."

Mr. Marjoribanks' frown deepened. "I'm a very busy man, my lady, and don't have time to make idle chatter with besotted readers—"

Emily snorted. "Does the name 'Titivillus' mean anything to you, Mr. Marjoribanks?" she asked.

He paled. "Wha—where did you hear about Titivillus?"

Sally sat down on the hideously dark sofa. "Please, Mr. Marjoribanks." She gestured to a chair opposite.

Mr. Marjoribanks stumbled toward it, then seemed to change his mind. He straightened his back and glared at Emily. "I haven't the faintest idea what you're talking about!"

"Sir, we've spoken with Mr.—er, with the demon Titivillus. We know what you engaged it to do, and we must say we think it reprehensible behavior and not the least the action of a gentleman. We are here to ask you to destroy the contract you made with it and never undertake such action again," Sally said.

"And I have no idea what you're talking about," Mr. Marjoribanks said, drawing himself up even more stiffly.

"It's true, sir," Annabel said gently. "We caught Titivillus in the act of taking a copy of the third volume of *The Fifty Shades of Udolpho*. It told us what you had compelled it to do; it's who told us your name and address."

Mr. Marjoribanks appeared in imminent danger of combustion. "Why, that villain—" He coughed. "That is, I've never heard such nonsense before in my life."

Sally sighed. "We should have brought Titivillus with us. Really, Mr. Marjoribanks, there isn't much use in denying any of this."

Mr. Marjoribanks gripped the back of the chair behind which he stood. "It is your word against mine, madam. And furthermore, what authority do you possess that you feel you can invade a man's home and throw such accusations in his face? If you were not a female of such elevated rank, I should know how to deal with you. As it is, I must ask you to leave my house with all due celerity." He went to the bell-pull by the fireplace. "Now if you will excuse me—"

But before he could pull it, a knock sounded on the sitting room door, and the lugubrious butler came in, bearing a small tray. "More callers, sir," he intoned, and presented the tray to Mr. Marjoribanks, who scowled and snatched up the cards it held.

"'The Marquis of Quinceton and Mrs. James

Denton,'" he read aloud. "More of your friends come to persecute me, hey?"

Annabel gasped. Mrs. Denton, here? But how? And *why*?

Sally glanced at her but spoke to Mr. Marjoribanks. "We are acquainted with the marquis, but we have no idea why he should be calling on you, and no idea whom his companion might be," she said calmly.

"Send them away." Mr. Marjoribanks made shooing gestures with his hands. "I am outraged—*outraged*—by these invasions of my privacy—"

Just then the sitting room door flew open, revealing Mrs. Denton in an elegant calling costume, with the marquis standing behind her. He caught Annabel's eye and nodded to her. But Mrs. Denton quickly drew her—and everyone else's—attention.

"*You!*" she exclaimed in tones equally accusatory and loathing, her flashing eyes fixed on Mr. Marjoribanks. "So you are my tormentor!"

Mr. Marjoribanks grew even paler but stood his ground. "My good woman, I have no idea who you are, much less what you are talking about—"

Mrs. Denton advanced into the room, somehow making her small frame look tall and terrible. "You are that heartless, soulless creature who is destroying my livelihood and taking the bread from the mouths of my poor, fatherless children! Oh, how can you hold your head up? How can you even meet our eyes?"

Since Mr. Marjoribanks was doing anything but that, his eyes swiveling in panicked fashion from window to window as if in search of escape, that question seemed unanswerable. When they came to rest on the figure of his butler, who seemed transfixed, his face grew furious. "You! Out!"

The butler started and scuttled from the room.

Sally, however, was undaunted. "Madam, I am receiving the impression that your errand might coincide with ours. If I might be allowed to ask who you are—?"

Mrs. Denton's face softened, and Annabel was sure she caught a twinkle in her eyes just before she raised one trembling hand to her forehead. "Oh, did you come to support me in my affliction? It is of the greatest comfort to know I am not alone, that my sisters are here to support me in my time of persecution—"

"You're her sister?" Mr. Marjoribanks said, turning furiously on Sally.

"I have never seen her before in my life," Sally replied coldly.

"I was speaking metaphorically," Mrs. Denton said, lowering her hand and looking haughtily at Mr. Marjoribanks. "Not that *you* would know a good metaphor if it clubbed you over the head!"

Emily made a choking noise, and a light of understanding appeared in Sally's eyes. "Ah. Do I have the pleasure of addressing E.C. Spruce?"

"You do," Mrs. Denton said with great dignity. "I am E.C. Spruce. I was forced to take on a man's name when I turned to writing to support my family."

Emily giggled. "So *you* took a man's name to publish under, and *he* took a woman's? It's all quite mad." Then her eyes widened. "Great heavens! *You're* E.C. Spruce? I'm actually talking to E.C. Spruce?" Her sentence ended in a squeal.

Lord Quinceton cleared his throat. "Mr., er, Spruce is the widow of one of my oldest school friends."

"Yes, except now I am all but ruined, because that man has used means most foul to suppress my books! Oh, what shall I do?" Mrs. Denton blinked several times, and tears were seen to well up in her blue eyes. "My poor, fatherless sons! We shall be cast out in the street to starve if my books continue to disappear." She raised her hand to her forehead again. "Oh, I am faint."

The marquis leapt forward, arms out-stretched to catch her. "My dear Eliza, you are overcome!" He glanced at Annabel, and she was sure he winked and gave her a tiny, encouraging nod. Good heavens, did he want *her* to join in as well? Mrs. Denton hardly seemed to need the help; she was making Mr. Marjoribanks' sitting room resemble the stage at Drury Lane. But it was too tempting not to leap in.

"It is quite disgraceful!" she said, coming to Mrs. Denton's side after a moment's hesitation. "This poor woman! What can be done? Her livelihood all but destroyed—"

Mr. Marjoribanks stood statue-like. "*You're* E.C. Spruce?" he croaked.

Lord Quinceton was helping Mrs. Denton into a chair. "Indeed, she is. And a braver, more gallant soul cannot be met. Of course, bearing up under this latest onslaught of fate may be her undoing. She has withstood so much, but even the strongest heart breaks when the burden is too great."

"Why, you—you *brute*!" Emily cast Mr. Marjoribanks a quite authentic-looking look of loathing. "Do you see what you've done? This poor,

poor woman!" She too crossed the room to join Annabel next to Mrs. Denton.

Mr. Marjoribanks opened his mouth and attempted to speak, but no sound came out, giving him the appearance of a beached fish. At last, he seemed to master himself. "Madam, I. . . I had no idea!"

Mrs. Denton sniffed frantically and groped in her reticule for her handkerchief. "It is scarcely to be expected that you would. No one was supposed to know who I am. Ohh!" She found her handkerchief, buried her face in it, and began to weep loudly.

"Madam, please—" Mr. Marjoribanks looked aghast. He groped for the bell-pull and jerked it four or five times. "Madam, you must compose yourself, I beg you! You will make yourself ill!"

"What if I do?" Mrs. Denton moaned. "I have nothing left to live for. My life is in ruins! Ashes! Dust!" Her sobs redoubled.

The sitting room door opened, and the butler cautiously poked his head into the room as if fearful of having it bitten off. "Sir?" he quavered.

"Jackson, in the top right-hand drawer of my desk you will find a sealed document bearing the word 'contract' written in my hand. Bring it to me immediately," Mr. Marjoribanks said loudly, above Mrs. Denton's sobs.

The butler cast her a terrified look. "At once, sir," he said and shut the door so quickly that Annabel was surprised that he didn't catch his nose in it. She risked a glance at Lord Quinceton's solemn face as he bent solicitously over Mrs. Denton; again, there was the hint of a twinkle there as he met her gaze.

"I trust you are satisfied, sir," Emily said severely to Mr. Marjoribanks.

He took a pace or two toward them then stopped, obviously afraid to venture closer. "I—I had no idea!" he cried, wringing his hands. "I didn't intend such an outcome! I merely thought—it's just that. . . that—that E.C. Spruce's books always do so much better than mine!"

Mrs. Denton gave forth a particularly heart-rending wail, and Mr. Marjoribanks blanched even whiter. He crossed the room in a dramatic rush and dropped to his knees at Mrs. Denton's feet. "No, my dear Mr.—er—Mrs.—er, madam. Cry no longer, for I will destroy the contract with the fiend Titivillus! He will steal no more of your work! Had I but known, I should never have done the foul deed! Never shall it be said that Gilbert Marjoribanks achieved greatness at the expense of widows and orphans!"

Mrs. Denton's shoulders positively shook, no doubt with the force of her tears. Annabel turned away, struggling to keep her countenance. If Mr. Marjoribanks were to know what effect his scheme had had on the sales of *The Fifty Shades*, he would probably sob as loudly as Mrs. Denton. They would have to take good care that he never found out.

There was a discreet knock on the door, and the butler came in, bearing a folded and wax-sealed document. "Sir," he said and handed it to Mr. Marjoribanks before beating a hasty retreat.

"Thank you, Jackson." Mr. Marjoribanks rose with great dignity, cracked open the wax seal, and unfolded the paper. He held it out toward the marquis. "My lord, see you this?"

Lord Quinceton straightened and surveyed the

paper. "Yes. It appears to be a contract drawn up between you and someone called Titivillus."

Mr. Marjoribanks threw back his shoulders and tore the page in two, then in half again, with a sweeping gesture. "There!" he cried, throwing the pieces to the floor and grinding them with his heel. "The contract is no more! We are free, free of its pernicious influence!"

Annabel pressed her lips tightly together. Good heavens, if the man wrote his books the way he spoke. . . !

Mrs. Denton gave one last great, gulping sob. "T-truly?" she said, lowering her handkerchief so that one astonishingly unswollen eye peeped out. "You've t-torn it up?"

"Truly, madam! And never again will I venture to do such a dastardly deed! The demon is vanquished!" Once again, he fell to his knees, seized Mrs. Denton's hand, and kissed it. "You have my word as a gentleman!"

"Oh!" She let the handkerchief fall and gave him a radiant smile. "Oh, I knew you could not be so cruel!"

"Thank you, sir," Sally said. "We are much obliged." She turned away, carefully not meeting Annabel's eyes.

An hour and a half later, after Mr. Marjoribanks had insisted on tea being served to help poor Mrs. Denton recover her shattered nerves and had begged her permission to call upon her in the near future to share war stories of their common profession, his five unexpected callers stood on the pavement before his house.

"Will you receive him if he calls on you?" Annabel asked Mrs. Denton.

"She'll have to. I think he's smitten. He might take it into his head to treat her like one of his reluctant heroines, and she'll find herself tossed across his saddle as he gallops across Hampstead Heath on his destrier," Lord Quinceton said, looking solemn.

Mrs. Denton snorted. "You're being absurd, Geoffrey."

"Says the woman who just out-Siddoned Mrs. Siddons."

She laughed. "I did, didn't I? I wasn't certain of what I would say to the man while we stood on his threshold, but as soon as that terrified-looking butler let us in, I knew. We used to do family theatricals when I was a girl; I shall have to tell my father that the experience served me in good stead. Ah, here we are."

Annabel started when she saw the carriage just drawing up behind Sally's. "Why, it was you at my house when we were leaving," she said to Mrs. Denton, who nodded.

"Yes, it was. We were on our way to call on you and saw you leaving. For some reason Quin thought there might be something afoot with my book and made my coachman follow you. We arrived here a few minutes after you did and made sure that this was Mr. Marjoribanks' house before we followed you in."

Emily was gazing at her worshipfully. "I still can't believe you're E.C. Spruce," she said and added, *sotto voce*, to Annabel, "And I still can't believe you didn't tell me!"

"I couldn't betray her confidence, Emily. You know that," Annabel muttered back.

"I know. You're far too good."

"Is she? I shall have to bear that in mind," Lord Quinceton said, suddenly looming next to them.

Annabel jumped. "Don't *do* that!"

"Did I startle you?"

"What do you think?" she snapped.

He made her a small bow. "Pardon me for interrupting your *tête-à-tête*, Fellbridge, but Eliza asks if you won't accept a ride home in her carriage, as she was coming to call on you anyway."

Annabel shook her head. "Thank you, sir, but as Lady Jersey was kind enough to bring me here, I think I—"

"Oh, go with them, Annabel. Sally won't mind," Emily said, and turned away.

Annabel hesitated and looked at Mrs. Denton, who was chatting with Sally, then said stiffly, "If Mrs. Denton wishes it, I would be glad to."

"What if I wish it too? No, never mind. I might not care for the answer." He paused, and asked, "*Are* you too good, Fellbridge?"

Annabel felt herself flush. "I have no idea what you are talking about."

"Mostly nonsense, but it was worth it to see that lovely blush creep up your cheeks. You are a deucedly attractive woman, you know. I've thought so ever since I first laid eyes on you."

Annabel tried to snort derisively, but she was too flustered. Was this his latest way to tease her—compliment her into utter confusion? "I doubt you even recall when that was."

"On the contrary, I recall precisely when it was: at a party at your parents' house to celebrate your engagement. I was on the list of guests requested by Freddy. It was the 28th of June 1801, at 9:22 in the evening. Or it might have been 9:23," he added, after a moment's consideration. "I'm afraid my vision was somewhat dazzled, which made reading my watch difficult. You were receiving with your parents and Freddy at the top of the stairs. You wore pink silk with a gold-spangled gauze overdress—if I had the dressing of you, you would always wear pink and gold—and a pearl and diamond set. Your hair was in long curls on your shoulders, and you looked absurdly young." A smile glimmered in his eyes as he looked at her, and he offered his arm. "And now that I have basely rendered you speechless and unable to resist, let us join Eliza, shall we?"

Author's Notes

I suppose I might be accused of going "meta" on my readers, because this story is about books, writers, publishers, and booksellers. Authors are supposed to write what they know, right?

But the 19th century book world is a little different from today's. Here's a brief guide to some aspects of literary life with which today's readers might not be familiar.

Three-volume Novels

Not to be confused with today's popular trilogies, three-volume novels were just that—a novel broken up into three separate books, with the divisions often occurring at a cliff-hanger point. They were long—on average, 150-200,000 words—so each volume was usually around three hundred pages. The format seems to be the result of economics. Books were expensive to produce (and to buy—each volume of a three-volume novel cost about the same as today's expensive hardcovers, relatively speaking.) Chopping a story up into three parts allowed volume one to go on the market, and proceeds from sale of that volume could go toward producing volumes two and three. Publishing one story in three parts also lent itself well to the fact that a great many people got their reading material from circulating libraries (more on those shortly): having a book divided into multiple parts meant that more than one person could be reading any given story at a time. Two-thirds of 19th century works of fiction first released in book form (not in serial form in a magazine) were published as three-volume novels, until their demise in the 1890s.

The Gothic novel craze

Ruined castles, gibbering skeletons, ancient curses, and deep purple prose... ah, the Gothic novel!

It all started in 1764, when Horace Walpole, son of prime minister Robert Walpole, published *The Castle of Otranto*, replete with ghosts, castles, and emotion... and therein lies the key to why Gothic fiction became so popular for the next sixty years: it was a reaction to the intellectualism of the Enlightenment, which had rung the death knell of common belief in things like witches and curses and other supernatural beliefs. People stopped believing that their horse had gone lame or their child taken ill because they had been "overlooked" by the old lady at the end of the lane with a wart on her nose and poor personal hygiene... but once the real fear of the supernatural waned, people missed the frisson of excitement that it had lent to life. Gothic novels supplied that frisson, and were hugely popular right through the 1820s, when the pendulum arced back first to historical and then to realistic fiction via Sir Walter Scott and Charles Dickens. Many authors of Gothic fiction were women, the most famous probably being Ann Radcliffe, who wrote, among other works, a huge bestseller called *The Mysteries of Udolpho*. Hmm.

Circulating libraries

If you were a reader of the middle or upper classes in the 18th and 19th centuries, chances were that you were an enthusiastic subscriber to a circulating library. For an annual fee (usually a few guineas—which meant that you were a person with some disposable income), you could borrow books much as we do at today's free public libraries; the higher the fee you paid, the more books you could borrow at any given time. Like today's libraries, there were late fees and fees for damaged books, and members who lived at a distance could still borrow books by post. At first, only the larger cities and resort towns like Bath had circulating libraries, but over the course of the century, even small towns might have one. Circulating libraries also carried periodical and some even functioned as publishers; the Minerva Press, mentioned below, started life as a circulating library. Several even sold things like hats and ribbons. They were also important as a social venue, especially for women. Though a few survived into the early decades of the 20th century, the rise of the free public library and the drop in the price of books mostly spelled their demise not long after the Second World War.

Allardyce's

Readers of my young adult Leland Sisters stories will recognize Allardyce's Bookshop, Mr. Allardyce, Melusine Allardyce, and her annoying younger brother from *Bewitching Season*. There's another reference to the Leland Sisters world in this story as well—did anyone spot it?

The Aphrodite Press

I based the Aphrodite Press, the publisher of *The Fifty Shades of Udolpho* whom Annabel and Frances and Emily visit, on the Minerva Press, which was the foremost publisher of Gothic novels and sentimental fiction in the 1790s through the 1820s. . . and really, don't you think Aphrodite would have been a much better goddess to name such a publishing house after?

Titivillus

On researching the phrase "printer's devil," I was delighted to run across Titivillus, a demon first mentioned in the thirteenth century as the infernal being responsible for causing monks hard at work in the scriptoria of their monasteries to make mistakes in their copying. I am sure he was able to adapt quite easily to the printing press and typesetting and seems to be alive and well in the computer age as well.

Mrs. Siddons

Sarah Siddons (1755-1831) was the premier tragic

actress of her day, first at Drury Lane and then at Covent Garden before her retirement in 1812. She was known in particular for her powerful portrayal of Lady Macbeth; audience members on occasion had to be carried from the theater to recover, so affecting were her performances.

Gilbert Marjoribanks

Mr. Marjoribanks is of course a fictional character, but I could not resist basing him slightly on a character from one of my favorite books of all time, also set in Regency England. If you can guess which book that is, then please drop me a note at marissa@marissadoyle.comand we can geek out over it together.

LYRICS AND LARCENY

Chapter One

London, early May 1810
A Friday afternoon

Emily Cowper was a darling and her dearest friend. Nevertheless, on occasion she made Annabel Fellbridge want to shriek.

Like right now, for instance. Here they were, comfortably ensconced in the library with a tea tray and a plate of Annabel's favorite rout biscuits and her cook's special macaroons, ready for a delightful gossip. Annabel had just told her about her last encounter with the Marquis of Quinceton on Tuesday after they'd confronted the author Mr. Gilbert Marjoribanks over his unscrupulous summoning of a demon to steal another, more popular author's books—and Emily looked as though she were about to nod off.

"What do you think he could have possibly meant?" Annabel bit into a rout biscuit and chewed thoughtfully. "It was the most extraordinary thing

I've ever heard, him recalling all the particulars of my betrothal party and exactly what I was wearing that evening. Disconcerting does not begin to describe it. Why should he remember *that* in such detail?"

Emily sat with her feet curled under her in a corner of the shabby brocade sofa. "Why shouldn't he?" she said.

"But it was nine *years* ago! Doesn't it strike you as somewhat odd?"

"Not particularly." Emily actually yawned. "If it troubles you so much, why don't you ask him why he remembers it so well?"

"I could never do that!"

"Then do stop worrying about it. Really, Annabel, when it comes to Quin, sometimes you're positively gothic. Are you certain that you don't have a secret *tendre* for him that you just won't admit? He *was* looking particularly handsome the other day."

"Emily!"

She laughed. "With that kind of response, I may just assume the answer is 'yes.' Speaking of handsome men, how was your drive with Lord Glenrick this morning?"

Annabel smiled. "It was very pleasant."

She had made Lord Glenrick's acquaintance just recently—she had a lot of catching up to do after her years away from London—and couldn't help being flattered by his very marked attentions to her. He was heir to the duchy of Carrick, after all, and (as Emily had said) was charming and good-looking, so how could she not be flattered? If only Lord Quinceton had not warned her off him without supplying any reasons why she should be wary of him. . . oh, why did the infuriating man have to intrude into every thought—

"Very pleasant? Is that all you have to say?" Emily made a sound of mock exasperation. "Details, woman! I want details! Did he look down your front?"

Annabel inhaled a crumb of biscuit and broke into a fit of coughing. "Emily!" she said when she could breathe again. "Is that all you think about?"

"Did he?"

"I was wearing a spencer and a gauze scarf."

"Oh, you tease. He'll have to wait until the next ball, then."

"Actually, he invited me to the opera on Tuesday." Annabel was surprised to feel her cheeks warm just a little. Good heavens, she was as bad as a girl in her first London season!

"Did he? That's excellent. Take care that you don't disappoint the poor man—wear something to give him an eyeful. It would be great fun to be able to call you 'Duchess' someday."

Annabel was saved from having to reply to such an absurdity by Hanscomb's discreet knock on the door, followed by Hanscomb himself. "Excuse me, madam," he began. "Your—"

He was abruptly set aside and the door thrown open as a young man with a headful of untidy gold curls bounded into the room. "Yes, of course she'll see me, Hanscomb. Be a good old thing and push off, won't you?"

Hanscomb's face remained perfectly impassive, but Annabel winced for him. "Yes, thank you, Hanscomb, I'll see this scapegrace—who really needs to learn some manners," she said.

The youth halted, his face contrite. "Oh, I say—was I rude? I beg your pardon, Hanscomb—I'm just in a tearing hurry to see my best cousin. You'll forgive me, won't you? For old times' sake?" He turned a smile—half cajoling, half pleading, and wholly charming—on the butler.

The perfect impassivity of Hanscomb's face relaxed somehow without really changing. "If I may be so bold as to say so, you always could wrap the world round your little finger, my lord. Shall I bring up more tea, madam?"

"No, this will do us just fine," the young man said cheerfully, eyeing the plate of biscuits, then noticed Emily. "Oh, hallo, it's you. I know you, don't I? Seen you around, at any rate."

Annabel nodded her dismissal to Hanscomb, waited until the door had closed behind him, and turned to the young man. "Hartley, I don't care if you've known Hanscomb forever—you simply can't behave that way with him. And what are you doing here? I thought you were up at Cambridge."

"I was. But I'm here now." Her cousin Hartley, Viscount Mompesson, plonked himself down next to Emily on the sofa, strategically in front of the plate of biscuits, and attacked. "I have to talk to you, Annabel," he said around a mouthful of macaroon. "You're the only one who'll listen."

Emily raised an eyebrow. "Should I assume that you won't want me to listen as well?"

"Hmm? Oh, no, you're all right. You can stay if you like." He took another two macaroons, sat back against the sofa cushion, and sighed. "It happened, Annabel. I never thought it would, but it did. I'm in love."

"Oh." Annabel sat back too and stared at him. Hartley was the son of her Cousin Medea—Lady Mompesson—and had inherited the title on his father's untimely death last year. As the only son after five older sisters, he'd been coddled and indulged all his life; miraculously, he hadn't turned out insufferably spoiled—at least not too much. He'd been saved by being a bookish boy, obsessed equally by the Greek poets and by the study of birds. He'd excelled at Cambridge, earning a first in Greek last year, and had been determined to remain in his college as a junior don, flatly refusing to submit to the course of balls and house parties his doting mother had planned to find him a bride worthy of him.

She should not have been surprised at his reluctance; Hartley had always scorned society in general and girls in particular. Annabel knew he only liked her because she hadn't been afraid to climb trees with him to study birds' nests on summer visits to his family's estate in Cornwall. Though he'd managed to acquire some amount of social address at university, he'd never been comfortable with the female sex. Annabel had fully expected him to remain a confirmed bachelor, happy with his Hesiod and Pindar and collection of stuffed songbirds.

"That's splendid news!" she said. "Do I know her? Your mother must be delighted." Though *delighted* and *Cousin Medea* weren't words often uttered in the same breath—

He shook his head. "She isn't," he said frankly. "That's the problem. You've got to help me bring Mother around."

Oh dear. Hartley hadn't fallen in love with a

tavern wench or someone completely inappropriate, had he? "Bring her around?"

"Yes. She's got some idiotish notion that Demetria isn't good enough for me. Just because she's a singer—"

"Demetria? You don't mean Demetria Pouli, do you?" Emily put in.

Hartley turned to her, his face alight. "You know her?"

"I know *of* her," Emily said cautiously.

"Who is she?" Annabel asked.

"You haven't heard? She's a soprano from Greece, and everyone's trying to book her for concerts, but she's terribly exclusive and will only sing if she thinks she'll be appreciated. Oh, and no one less than an earl need apply. From what I understand, she's good enough to get away with it." Emily sat up, warming to her topic. "I keep hearing descriptions of her like 'unearthly' and 'heavenly' and 'spellbinding'.

"They're nothing more than the truth. And why should she sing for just anyone?" Hartley put in hotly. "Most of London can't tell the difference between her and a street-vendor calling his wares anyway. Annabel, she's. . . she's an angel. Not just because of her voice or her looks, though she's the most beautiful girl I've ever seen. But she's the sweetest, kindest. . . and she understands me. We can talk about poetry because she knows it all and loves it as much as I do." His eyes softened. "Do you know, I saw her sing a robin onto her hand when we went walking in Green Park, and it perched there on her finger, completely unafraid. Even the birds love her."

"Does she return your sentiments?" Annabel

asked carefully. Hartley sounded serious—more serious than she'd expected. But if this girl was just on the catch for a rich husband—

"I—I *think* she does. I've told her how I feel, as well as I can without frightening her—" He jumped up from the sofa and began to pace. "You don't understand—she's like a bird herself, so timid and shy—she's just nineteen and far from home. I know what you were thinking, and she's not some brazen hussy on the hunt. She's the most modest little thing ever—a regular nun. I don't think I've even caught a glimpse of her ankles."

Well, that put a slightly different complexion on the matter. "What about her family? Does she have any?"

He threw himself back onto the sofa next to Emily and gave a mirthless laugh. "Far too much, as far as I'm concerned. There's an uncle—he's her guardian, and a brute, I expect, despite all his bowing and scraping. Some aunts or great-aunts or something—all draped in black so you can scarce see if they even have faces—who are her chaperones. The only way I was able to take her walking was because I slipped 'em a few guineas so they'd walk ten paces behind us instead of between us. And servants, too. They all follow along in her wake when she so much as sets a toe out of the house, like a damned chorus." He fixed his gaze on the tea tray and brooded.

Annabel caught Emily's eye and inclined her head ever-so-slightly toward Hartley. Emily's eyebrows rose, but she nodded and fixed her fine dark eyes on him. Ordinarily, Annabel would not ask her mind-reading friend to spy on a relative's thoughts, but this was shaping up to be a serious matter. If

Hartley was truly in love and not just infatuated with this girl because she was pretty and knew a little poetry—well, Annabel needed to know before she agreed to help him. Cousin Medea was convinced that nothing less than a duke's daughter would do for her Hartley—heavens, if the king's daughters hadn't all been over thirty except for the invalid Princess Amelia, Annabel would not have put it past her to cast her eyes in *that* direction for a wife for him. A singer, and a foreign one at that, would *not* be on her eligible list, for she simply would not believe her precious lamb capable of refusing to marry at all if he couldn't have the girl he wanted.

"Hartley, don't you think you ought to ascertain what her feelings are before you worry about bringing your mother round to accept her?" she asked. "It might well be that she's simply not interested in marrying a stranger in a foreign land—"

He sat up, his expression resolute. "No—I—I'm quite certain she loves me. But she's afraid. She may be young, but she understands what we face. That's why I need you, coz. Would you—would you call on her? Make it a proper social call? If one of my family does, it will make her braver—and make everyone understand how serious I am. If I can't marry Demetria, I won't marry anyone. I don't give a damn what my mother says, I won't be saddled with some simpering female just for the sake of spawning a brat to continue the family line. Cousin Horace can be viscount after me, for all I care." He scowled. "And I don't give a damn about Papa's will, either."

"His will?" Annabel prompted.

"Yes. When he fell ill, he let mother talk him into putting in a codicil that if I married without her consent, I wouldn't inherit any of the non-entailed property before I married—and if I married without her approval, I wouldn't get it till I was thirty. Well, I'm not going to wait that long and let Demetria slip through my fingers."

Trust Cousin Medea to mishandle Hartley so badly; blindly opposing him was the absolute worst thing she could have done. Annabel glanced at Emily, who nodded slightly. She'd already guessed that Hartley was sincere, but Emily's confirmation helped. "All right, Hartley, I'll call on your Miss Pouli—"

He leapt up, his scowl dissolving. "You will?" He stepped over the tea table, grabbed her hands, and yanked her up out of her chair to fold her in a suffocating embrace. "You'll love her. I know you will. You won't be able to help it. And then you can tell mother how wonderful she is since she won't listen to me."

"I truly don't think I have that much influence with your mother."

"May I go with you when you pay your call on Miss Pouli?" Emily shrugged at Annabel's look of surprise.

"Both of you? That would be brilliant! Mother won't be able to say that no one knows her anymore." Hartley was grinning from ear to ear. "Here's her address. They've taken a house off Cavendish Square." He scribbled something on a calling card and handed it to Annabel. "I knew you'd help me," he added, gave her a smacking kiss on one cheek and bolted out the door.

"Well!" Annabel stared after him. "That wasn't quite what I was expecting. Hartley's in love with someone other than himself!"

"As far as I could tell, without being too nosy."

Annabel nodded. Emily was scrupulous about not peeking into others' thoughts unless there was a very good reason for her to do so. "Thank you for checking. I didn't like to ask, but. . ."

Emily waved a hand. "It wasn't difficult. I didn't have to look very hard; men in love are usually quite easy to read."

"Men in love, or men in lust?"

She grinned. "Men are usually in lust. Love is something again. He's in love."

"Well, that's good to know. I wish we could convince his mother of the fact. It was kind of you to volunteer to come with me to call on this Miss Pouli."

"Having both of us call will be even better if you're trying to make a point about her being socially acceptable." Emily nodded sagely, but her eyes gleamed. "Besides, I'd dearly like to talk to her about doing a performance at my house. How can she say no to a countess who pays an actual call on her?"

"And here I thought you were doing it from the sheer goodness of your heart." Annabel looked at the card Hartley had given her. "Holles Street. Funny, I would have thought they would be staying at a hotel rather than taking a house. When would you like to go?"

"Perhaps they like their privacy. Temperamental artists and so on." Emily shrugged. "As for when, the sooner we go, the sooner I can get my invitations sent. How about tomorrow?"

Annabel considered. Tomorrow was a quiet day. "Yes, that will do." She hesitated. "I. . . I almost wish I could go shadow-cloaked and just observe instead of having to think about being sociable."

Emily raised an eyebrow. "Why? This seems like a fairly straightforward call to me."

"That's because it isn't your cousins you'll have to deal with. Have you ever *met* Medea Mompesson?"

"Ah. Yes, I have, now that I think about it. At Almack's with one of Hartley's sisters, the year I came out." Emily made a wry face. "But still, you can't go cloaked. That would defeat the whole purpose."

"I know," Annabel sighed. But she still wished she could. Something bothered her about the whole affair: it just wasn't like Hartley, despite all his protestations, to fall merely for a pretty face. Maybe she *was* the paragon he'd painted her. . . but what if she wasn't and had set out to entrap him?

"Well, never mind. I'll do most of the talking and let you do the observing. But I think you're worrying unnecessarily. What's more natural than a young man falling for a beautiful, unattainable girl?"

Annabel sighed again. "You're probably correct. I hope we'll find out tomorrow."

The next afternoon the two of them, properly attired in afternoon walking costumes—Emily in a high-necked dark lilac sarsenet mantle, Annabel in a blue demi-pelisse—drew up in Annabel's landau before the Poulis' hired house in Holles Street. It was not precisely a fashionable street but certainly a respectable one, lined with small but well-kept houses.

"I hope she's in," Emily murmured as Annabel plied the knocker.

"Maybe Hartley warned her we were coming," Annabel murmured back. A twitch of the curtain at the window to their right caught her eye, and a small, dark face with a beaky nose scowled at them through the lacy fabric. Annabel pretended not to notice.

A moment later, the door was opened by a neatly-dressed but very un-English-looking maid. Annabel recognized the face that had examined them with such disfavor. "What do you want?" she demanded.

"Is Miss Pouli at home?" Annabel gave the maid her card, as did Emily.

"Hm." The maid examined the cards closely. "I will ask. You wait." She shut the door firmly, leaving them on the doorstep.

Emily stared at the closed door. "Well, they're foreigners, I suppose," she said after a startled pause.

Annabel opened her mouth to reply, but before she could, the door was flung open. A small, slender girl with a luminous olive complexion and a demure riot of dusky curls caught up in a yellow ribbon dropped them a flustered curtsy. "My ladies, I humbly beg your pardon—Stasia didn't know what to do with you," she said in a clear, flute-like voice. "I am Miss Pouli. Please, won't you come in?" She stepped aside and gave them an anxious look.

"Thank you, Miss Pouli. I am Lady Fellbridge, and this is Lady Cowper. Hartley has told me so much about you that I wanted to make your acquaintance." She stepped past Miss Pouli into the house, Emily close behind her.

"Oh!" A faint rose color suffused the girl's

delicate features. "Hartley said—I mean, Lord Mompesson—oh, you are too good! Will you—will you do us the honor of sitting down?" She gestured to a pair of closed doors to their right—the same room, Annabel presumed, from which they had been observed. The maid who'd answered the door was hovering by them, glaring suspiciously; only when Miss Pouli hissed "Stasia!" did she start forward and open them.

The salon was a somber chamber, weighed down with heavy mahogany furniture and dark paneling. Two old women—at least, Annabel got an impression of great age from them—sat side-by-side on a sofa not far from the window. They wore featureless black gowns and heavy, almost nun-like headdresses with black lace veils obscuring their faces. Anchoring the room at the other end was a large, stout man of middle age, leaning against the chimney piece. He was fashionably dressed, aside from a dreadful yellow and black striped waistcoat that made him resemble an alarmingly large bee. As they entered the room, he made them a low bow.

"Your ladyships! Such an honor! We welcome you to our temporary home!" he declaimed in a deep, carrying voice—at least, it sounded very much like an actor's speech.

"M-my ladies, if I may have leave to present—" Miss Pouli was still flustered. "My honored aunts, Mrs. Kanakaris and Mrs. Oikonomou, and my uncle, Mr. Skourletis. Here are Lady Fellbridge and Lady Cowper. Lady Fellbridge is Har—I mean, Lord Mompesson's cousin."

For a second, no one moved. Then the two ladies on the couch inclined their heads with great dignity. Mr. Skourletis bowed again.

Annabel curtsied. There was another awkward silence, and then Miss Pouli took a deep breath. "Will you—will you be pleased to sit?"

"Thank you." Annabel smiled at her as she sat down on the sofa near the fireplace. Hartley was right; Miss Pouli was a modest little thing, not the least bit brazen or encroaching. She had a certain sweetness that was immediately likeable and went a fair way toward laying to rest Annabel's concerns for Hartley. She patted the cushion next to her invitingly and smiled up at Miss Pouli. The girl ducked her head shyly and sat down beside her.

Emily took a chair opposite them. "It's our honor to meet such a well-respected artist," she said to Miss Pouli. "I've not had the pleasure of hearing you sing, but I hope to do so very soon. Do you plan to be in London very long?"

"At least through the season, your ladyship," Mr. Skourletis answered. "We did not know that London was such a city of music lovers, did we, Demetria? It is humbling to be in a place that so cherishes its artists."

Annabel avoided catching Emily's eye. To say that the *ton* held concerts or visited art shows because it truly respected art was a trifle naïve—and she did not get an impression of naïveté from the man. His manner of speaking was polished to the point of oiliness, but something about his expression told a different tale. He was clearly sizing them up, deciding how they should be played. Well, someone had to be the businessman in the family—but she couldn't quite bring herself to like him.

"I think your view of Londoners is a little rosy,"

she said coolly. "But there are some true music lovers among us. What other cities have you visited? You seem so young—surely you are just beginning your career?"

"It has been difficult, with the present unpleasantness on the continent," Mr. Skourletis said before Miss Pouli could open her mouth. "But we came most recently from Denmark. Demetria was much admired in Copenhagen."

"Indeed." Annabel knew little about Denmark, apart from the fact that its former queen had been sister to King George and that it had managed to keep from being overrun by Napoleon chiefly by allying itself with him. A practical move, she supposed, if not a popular one in Britain. . . and when was the child ever going to be allowed to answer a question on her own?

She looked meaningfully at Emily, who gave her a small nod and said brightly, "Mr. Skourletis, am I correct in assuming that I should apply to you about engaging Miss Pouli to sing at a small soirée at my house?" She hesitated, then smiled. "Well, perhaps not so *very* small. . ."

His eyes gleamed. "My dear Lady Cowper, I know that I speak for my niece when I say that she would be honored to sing for you. When had you thought to hold your soirée?"

Annabel smiled to herself as Emily pretended to dither about dates and times, the better to keep him occupied so that she could have a chance to talk with Hartley's Demetria without her uncle. . . unless the aunts would step in—

But no, they sat almost eerily unmoving, though she had the sense that they were listening closely to everything that was said. She would almost have thought they were statues or at least asleep if they hadn't nodded their greetings before. Well, if they wanted to listen without participating, they were welcome.

"I assume you know that Hartley asked me—well, us—to come. My friend Lady Cowper asked to accompany me so she could meet you as well," she said quietly.

"I am—it is most kind and—and condescending in you—" the girl began, blushing prettily. "Hartley—Lord Mompesson—has been *so* kind—"

Annabel repressed a smile. "If he has, then you've wrought miracles, Miss Pouli. He's been a selfish little beast all his life, and if he's suddenly turned kind, that's all your doing."

"Oh, no! I cannot believe that!" Miss Pouli had the air of a kitten leaping to the defense of a mastiff. "He's the sweetest, gentlest—you should hear the things he says to me! I am convinced no girl has ever had such lovely things said to her!"

Annabel expected she would be bored silly if she did get to hear Hartley's love-making but refrained from saying so. Instead she said, "Should I understand that you reciprocate Hartley's feelings? I called him a selfish little beast, but I am fond of him—we were great friends, growing up—and I think the right wife could be the making of him."

Miss Pouli looked in danger of collapsing into blushes and stutters once more. But then she straightened her back and met Annabel's eyes. "I *do* love him, Lady Fellbridge. I love him with all my heart," she said. "I know that his family would not approve—"

"I would not assume that his *entire* family would be opposed to your marrying him." Annabel raised one eyebrow ever so slightly, and the girl suddenly grinned a charming, impish grin. "But his mother has her heart set on a very grand marriage for him. He's her only son, and she's always cherished splendid dreams for him—most of which are completely ridiculous if you know him. Still, she's a rather forceful personality."

Miss Pouli positively wilted. "Then all is lost."

"Not necessarily. Medea Mompesson may be ambitious for her ewe lamb but she also loves him dearly. If she could see how happy you make Hartley, I hope she would in time come around." Maybe. Cousin Medea could also be astonishingly stubborn.

"But how? Oh, dear Lady Fellbridge, you must help us!" She clasped her hands under her bosom and gazed piteously at Annabel.

"Now, now, Demetria!" Mr. Skourletis suddenly boomed. "Do not forget that you have a concert tonight! You must not overexcite or tire yourself." He went to the bell pull by the fireplace.

"No, uncle." Miss Pouli seemed to deflate.

Annabel glanced up at Emily, who made an apologetic grimace. "I beg your pardon—if we had known you were resting before a performance, we would have come a different day," she said, standing up.

"No, I'm glad you came to see me today!" Was that a look of defiance Miss Pouli cast toward her uncle?

"Where do you sing tonight?" Emily asked.

"At Lady Jodrell's." All the defiance and spirit seemed suddenly to drain from her.

"I know that you will have them all spellbound," Annabel said kindly.

She was unprepared for Demetria's reaction. The girl turned white, then red and looked as though she were about to burst into tears. "No. Oh, no! I—I hope not!"

"Good-bye, your ladyships," Mr. Skourletis said. He wore a peculiar expression, trying to smile at them and frown at Miss Pouli at the same time.

"I shall show them out," Miss Pouli said, as the sour-faced maid Stasia opened the door to the salon.

"I kept him talking as long as I could," Emily muttered under her breath after they'd made their farewell courtesies and fallen into place behind Miss Pouli.

"I know. It was fine," Annabel muttered back.

In the hall, away from her uncle, a little of Miss Pouli's animation returned. "Oh, thank you, Lady Fellbridge," she said. "I know Hartley and I can trust you."

"Yes, you certainly can."

"Don't let us keep you," Emily said kindly. "I shall look forward to having you sing at my house next week."

She sighed, and the hint of animation drained away. "Yes, I—thank you, Lady Cowper."

Annabel exchanged another quick glance with Emily. Why did the girl seem to stiffen up whenever someone referred to her singing? "And I shall look forward to hearing you," she said.

A look of horror crossed Miss Pouli's delicate features. "No! Oh, Lady Fellbridge, I—please, I beg you, don't ever come to hear me sing!" And with that, she almost pushed them out the door.

"Good heavens!" Emily said, when they were back in Annabel's carriage. "What was that about?"

"I don't know. I'm just as mystified as you are." Really, it had been extraordinary—the child had been so eager and confiding one minute, and the next—?

"Well, I hope you won't pay her any heed. She'll be singing at my party next Sunday evening, and if you aren't there, I shall go forth and drag you over if necessary." Then Emily grew thoughtful. "What did you think of her family? Mr. Skourletis talked too much and those aunts spoke not a single word. It was peculiar, wasn't it? What did you learn from Miss Pouli? Is she truly in love with Hartley? I suppose I could have looked, but I didn't want to unless you asked me to."

"I'm fairly certain she loves him. I said I would help them." Annabel raised her parasol against the sun. Emily was correct—it had been peculiar, but she could not put her finger on precisely how. Once more, she wished she could wrap herself in a shadow and sneak back into that dark, heavy room.

Chapter Two

Annabel usually kept her Sunday mornings solitary for various homely tasks: writing to the boys, reviewing the weekly report from her farm bailiff at Chalfont on the progress of the spring planting, and contemplating the upcoming social events of the week and figuring out which dresses she could safely re-appear in based on the likely guest list.

So it was with some surprise that shortly after she had curled up on the library sofa with Will's carefully penned letter and Martin's blotted and untidy one, she looked up to see Hanscomb hovering in the doorway.

"I beg your pardon, my lady. The dowager Viscountess Mompesson is downstairs," he said, sounding a trifle out of breath.

"Great-aunt Philippa? Good heavens!" Annabel hurriedly rose. The dowager Viscountess Mompesson was her mother's aunt—and Hartley's grandmother. This unexpected visit *had* to have something to do with him. "Is she, er, capable of coming up here?"

Hanscomb paled slightly. "It might be best if your ladyship came down to receive her. Ascending the stairs might be possible, but getting her safely down again would be a different matter."

Annabel got a mental image of Hanscomb slinging Great-aunt Philippa over his shoulder like a sack of corn and trotting down the stairs with her, and restrained a smile. "I understand. Where is she?"

"Resting on the stairs when I left her."

"Well, let's get her into the Pink Chinese Salon. It's closest."

"Very good, your ladyship. With your leave, I shall bring sherry in a moment. The Viscountess seems in need of a restorative."

Annabel stopped. "Is she ill?"

"Not ill, my lady. Upset, I would say."

"Thank you, Hanscomb. Please do." Oh dear, what had happened now? Had Hartley eloped with his Demetria?

She followed Hanscomb down the stairs. As he had said, Great-aunt Philippa was perched on a stair, leaning on her stick and breathing heavily.

"Auntie, what a pleasant surprise," she said, when she and Hanscomb had edged past her and hoisted the frail old woman to her feet. Goodness, she wasn't going to expire on the spot, was she?

"Annabel!" Great-aunt Philippa panted when she'd regained her balance. "Annabel, I must talk to you! No one else will believe me!"

"Yes, certainly," she said soothingly. "Why don't we sit down someplace more comfortable and you can tell me all about it?"

"Anything's got to be more comfortable than these stairs. My backside ain't what it used to be, y'know," Auntie said. "All the padding's gone."

Hanscomb's face remained carefully unsmiling. As soon as Annabel could afford it, she would have to raise his salary.

But Great-aunt Philippa tottered with remarkable agility into the Pink Chinese Salon, so christened by Will and Martin for the excessive amount of *famille rose* porcelain, bought by Freddy's father, on display there, and tossed back the sherry Hanscomb brought her with an appreciative smack of her lips.

"Not bad. Must be something Freddy put down before his wine merchant got tired of not being paid," she said. "Thank you, m'dear, I needed that."

"You're very welcome. Auntie, I'm always glad to see you, but what is wrong? You said—"

"Pour me another jot of that, and I'll tell you." Auntie held out her glass, which Annabel refilled. She downed it in two gulps, then slumped in her chair with a sigh.

Great-aunt Philippa had been a great belle in her day, back when George II was on the throne. At over eighty she still managed to be a social butterfly, gadding from rout to dinner to ball, often without benefit of an invitation as most of her friends had long since gone on to their reward. She was tolerated by their descendants for old times' sake and was hardly ever ejected from any event she decided to attend. Annabel liked her; she had something of a reputation for dottiness, but Annabel guessed it was more her tendency to feel free to utter whatever thought came into her head, as only the very old could get away with. At least her outspokenness was sensible and honest, if occasionally embarrassingly so.

She topped off her glass once again and took the chair to her right, as Great-aunt Philippa's left ear was quite deaf. . . not that the right one was much better. "Well, Auntie?"

"Well!" Great-aunt Philippa echoed. "I meant what I said. I've told Medea and Sarah and Selina and Susan—couldn't Medea have called one of those girls something other than a name beginning with 'S'?—and none of them will listen to me. They say I imagined it all, or that I dreamed it. But I know what I saw," she concluded darkly. "And someone has to do something about it or poor Hartley's heart will be broken."

Annabel touched her arm. "Aunt Philippa, please—go back to the beginning. I don't know what you're talking about." But a distinct sinking feeling had begun in her chest. This had to be something bad about Demetria Pouli if Hartley's heart was at stake.

Auntie peered at her closely. "You know about Hartley, don't you?"

"He came to me a few days ago to tell me he was in love with a Greek singer named Demetria Pouli."

"And?"

"And I went to call on Miss Pouli the next day. She seems a very nice girl though I can't vouch for her family. I think she's genuinely in love with him."

"At last, *someone's* done something sensible!" Auntie said to the ceiling. "I was going to do the same, but Hartley neglected to give me her particulars. Where's she living?"

"They've taken a house in Hollis Street."

"Hmmph. Could be worse. Well, I didn't have

her direction, but I heard Lady Jodrell—knew her grandfather, an old flirt of mine, the rogue!—was having the chit in to sing last night, so I went to at least get a look at her."

Annabel suppressed a smile. "What did you think?"

"Oh, she's a taking enough little thing—all eyes and hair, I thought, but some men like that sort of thing. It's what she did that's flummoxed me. Have you heard her yet?"

"Not yet. My friend Lady Cowper is having her to sing at a soirée next week."

Auntie clutched her arm. "Don't go. Or at least, don't wear any jewelry you value."

"What?"

"You're thinking I'm slipping my mooring, aren't you? But I know what I saw. Listen first, before you say anything." She took a deep breath—and broke into a fit of coughing. Annabel pounded her back and poured her more sherry, then sat back to listen.

"As I said, I wanted to have a look at the gal, so I went to Lady Jodrell's," Great-aunt Phillipa wheezed. "I found myself a seat with a good view—didn't want the harpsichord lid, or fortepiano or whatever you call 'em these days—blocking my line of sight. I waved to a few friends—la, Lizzie Shaw looks old!— and settled myself down to listen."

Annabel hesitated. "Er, can you actually hear music anymore?"

Great-aunt Phillipa shrugged. "Sometimes I can if it's loud enough. I didn't really care if I heard the child or not—I just wanted to look at her. You can tell a lot just by looking. I couldn't hear a note she sang, but I could see her prodigious well. I expect she's quite good—she holds herself with confidence when she sings. But that's not all."

"Go on."

"I closed my eyes, just for a minute—'pon rep, I don't know what it is with you modern gals, setting out so many candles at night. Fewer give a much more flattering light." Great-aunt Philippa shook her head. "I declare, I was quite dazzled."

"How unpleasant," Annabel murmured sympathetically.

"So I closed my eyes, to rest 'em for a moment—and when I opened them again, that was when it happened."

"What did, Auntie?"

"Someone was looking at my pearls."

"What?"

"The Mompesson pearls—no, I haven't given them to Medea. She'd look so dreadful in them with that sallow skin of hers that they'd probably shatter from sheer mortification. I was wearing 'em last night, and when I opened my eyes, someone was bent over my chest, examining them. I was looking down at the top of their head."

"Auntie, that's, ah. . ." Annabel hesitated. "That's. . . very interesting. What did you do?"

"Do? Nothing! I'd had a chance to glance around me, and that was even stranger."

"What was?"

"Everyone around me was asleep. I expect the whole room was. O' course, a number will drop off at a concert—my husband used to snore disgracefully at the opera—but the whole room?"

Annabel bit her lip. Part of her wanted to laugh

at the image summoned by her great-aunt, but the small hairs on the back of her neck were bristling. A whole roomful of people lulled to sleep? How? And what connection—if any—did Miss Pouli have to it? "What happened next?"

"Oh, I shut my eyes again right away. I didn't want to let on that I'd seen anything and find m'self going home with a slit throat. They let go my pearls, and after a few seconds, I felt my hand being taken, and someone tugging at my sapphire ring. It's the first time I've been grateful for my rheumatism—the ring won't budge past my knuckles unless I use soap. And then the scoundrel gave up and let me be. I kept my eyes shut for a minute or two more, then opened them just a crack again. Whoever'd been pawing at me had moved onto the lady in the next chair. Eh, she was a sour-faced thing!"

"The lady next to you?"

"No, the one who'd been pawing me. She had a face that would curdle new milk."

"Hmm. What happened after that?"

"I managed to get a good peek around when she was busy. In addition to Sour-face, there was a large, fleshy man with the most shocking bad taste in waistcoats also moving among the audience. He's something to do with the Pouli chit—I saw them talking before she started to sing. I actually saw him take a penknife and pry a gem out of someone's bracelet. And then he went through Lord Gerton's pocketbook and pulled out a handful of guineas."

"My word!" That could only have been Mr. Skourletis, Miss Pouli's uncle. And the sour-faced person could very well have been Stasia, the unpleasant maid who had opened the door to her and

Emily the other day. What about the silent aunts? Were they part of this as well? "Was there anyone else helping them?"

"No, just those two. They didn't need any help. They moved through the crowd sharpish enough."

"What was Demetria—Miss Pouli—doing while all this was happening?"

"Oh, she was still singing away—not that I could hear her. But she'd changed. She wasn't pouring herself into it anymore, but looked—sad. Scared even, I would say, singing to a room full of sleeping people."

Annabel sat back and looked at her great-aunt. The entire gathering at Lady Jodrell's somehow had been sent into an unnatural sleep whilst their valuables were stolen. Had the dowager viscountess finally crossed the line from amusing outspokenness to—well, true dottiness? "Auntie—are you certain?"

Great-aunt Philippa drew herself up in indignation. "Annabel! You're becoming as bad as Medea!"

"No, I'm not. But you have to admit that it sounds... outré. What happened then? Did everyone stay asleep?"

"No, of course not! That scoundrelly pair made their rounds through the room, and then the man— he seemed to be the ringleader—told Hartley's inamorata that he was done and she could release them. Those were the very words he used, 'release them'—I read his lips, so I'm certain that's what he said. I sneaked a peek at her and she was still singing, but eventually everyone around me started to wake up. It was a gradual thing, them slowly regaining their senses. They blinked and hid yawns and glanced around at their neighbors as if to be certain they hadn't been caught napping. And then the girl must have stopped singing because everyone clapped prodigious loud and then got up to go get champagne, as if nothing had happened. I clapped and got up too, because I didn't want that man or that sour-faced creature to notice me—they were at the edge of the room watching the crowd sharpish enough as it woke up."

Annabel began to doubt her doubt. That was not a detail a person suffering from delusions would be likely to imagine. "Did no one notice they were missing anything?"

"I don't know. I called for my chair as soon as I could." Great-aunt Philippa was probably one of the last people in London to have her own sedan chair and bearers. "I didn't want to be there any longer." She looked unhappily at Annabel. "What do we do? If that Pouli girl's nothing but a thief, we can't let Hartley marry her, no matter how nutty over her he is. And how did she do that? Did her singing really put everyone to sleep?"

Annabel took her hand. "I don't know, Auntie. But—I believe you."

"You do?"

"Yes. I wish I didn't but I do. Let me think about it for a day or two. Who else was at the concert?" Asking around to get other accounts of the evening might be the place to start.

"Oh, the usual." Auntie waved her hand vaguely. "I don't know anyone's name these days—oh, wait, I said Lizzie Shaw was there, didn't I?"

Lady Elizabeth Shaw was, if anything, older and dottier than Auntie. "Then I'll make some inquiries. And Auntie—don't tell anyone. If you think of someone else who was there, tell me. But for now, let's keep this between us."

Great-aunt Philippa nodded. "But what about Hartley? He wants my help with convincing his mother to give her consent to his marrying the chit."

Annabel bit her lip. "Don't say anything to him, either. Pretend you're ill or otherwise indisposed. I expect you can devise some way to put him off."

She sighed. "I don't know. He's a demmed persuasive boy when he wants to be, but I'll think of something." She leaned over and took Annabel's hand. "Thank you for believing me, child. Just because I'm old doesn't mean I've lost all my faculties."

After she and Hanscomb got the old lady safely into her sedan chair, Annabel went back up to the library to think. This was. . . bad. Assuming that Auntie hadn't dreamed the whole thing—and the more she thought about it, the more convinced she was that the old dear hadn't—then there was something very strange about Demetria Pouli and her family. It looked as if they were a pack of hardened thieves, preying on the *ton*. . . yet she'd been certain that Demetria was genuinely in love with Hartley.

This would bear further investigation—perhaps, in the end, by the Lady Patronesses. Ought she to bring it up at tomorrow's meeting?

Lord Glenrick and Frances came for her in Glenrick's highly varnished landau on Tuesday to bring her to the opera with them. Glenrick himself came to the door for her; she was standing in the front hall drawing on her gloves when Hanscomb opened the door to him.

"Lady Fellbridge!" He was across the hall in an instant, seizing her hand and bowing low over it.

She laughed. "My goodness, sir! One might think we hadn't seen each other in months!"

"It feels that way," he said, releasing her hand. His eyes widened as they swept up her figure, lingering on her décolletage. "May I say, madam, that I have never seen you in such fair looks?"

"Thank you, sir. You are very kind." Her golden-brown crepe dress wasn't new but from two years ago, refurbished by her maid Winters, and was cut low in front with gold lace and bugle beading on the bodice. She hadn't thought much about it when she dressed for the evening, aside from being pleased at having a new (well, new-ish) dress to wear. . . but Lord Glenrick certainly seemed *taken*.

"Not in the least." He intercepted Winters, who was approaching with her evening cloak, and took it from her, then himself settled it over Annabel's shoulders. "And you are very ravishing," he murmured. "I am almost regretting we must go to the theater. I would rather keep you to myself to gaze upon than permit all of London to feast on the view."

She laughed, but a little thrill of pleasure ran through her. Freddy had never paid her compliments, even when he was courting her. They went straight to the head like champagne, she had noticed. "I don't think all of London will fit in the theater."

"Enough of it will to rouse my jealousy." He took her hand and raised it to his lips. She could feel the warmth of his hand even through her gloves, and met his eyes. They were just as warm. He seemed determined to conduct a flirtation with her, it would seem. Did she wish to join him?

Frances greeted her cheerfully in the carriage. They had seen each other just the previous morning at the Lady Patronesses meeting—where Annabel had decided *not* to bring up her concerns over Demetria Pouli. After Emily's musical evening this coming Sunday would be time enough once she'd had a chance to do her own investigating. If it should turn out that Demetria's family was indeed robbing the *ton*, telling poor Hartley would not be easy. . . but she was not going to think about that tonight.

"I haven't been to the King's Theatre in ages," she said as they clattered down the street. "My father always calls it the Dovecote because the boxes remind him of pigeonholes."

Frances giggled. "I never thought of that, but he's absolutely right. How funny! Maybe they should rename it." She paused. "I wonder if they'll have to call it the Regent's Theatre some day?"

"Frances," Lord Glenrick said, his voice lightly reproving.

"Oh dear, I had not heard—is the king unwell again?" Annabel asked.

The king's health was an issue of concern and had been for a long time, ever since he suffered his first fit of madness over twenty years ago. Though he had always been restored to health again afterward, the fear was there, if not expressed aloud, that one day he would again fall ill and this time not recover. The Prince of Wales had nearly been named Regent during his father's first illness amid a great deal of controversy. What would happen today, when England was standing alone in Europe against France, if the king were to become irretrievably mad?

Lord Glenrick shrugged. "He's seventy-two years old, can hardly see for cataracts, and is practically crippled with rheumatism. I cannot help but think that going mad again would be the kindest thing to happen to Farmer George. And not just him."

Annabel looked away. She was aware that some thought the king had outlived his usefulness to the country—indeed, had never been very useful in the first place, but—but he was the *king*. Something about the way Lord Glenrick carelessly tossed off those words—a certain cold callousness—gave her a chill. A few prominent politicians were excessively vocal about their desire for the king to step down. Lord Glenrick would seem to be one of them.

"My dear Lady Fellbridge." He leaned forward. "I have distressed you. I sincerely beg your pardon."

She tried to smile. "No, I'm being silly. It's simply that the king has always been very kind to me whenever I have met him."

"The king admires a beautiful woman as much as the next man." His eyes were caressing.

Annabel was glad when their arrival at the theater put a timely end to the conversation. Not that she objected to Lord Glenrick's implying that she was beautiful—that was quite pleasant. Perhaps she'd forgotten how to accept compliments gracefully?

Lord Glenrick had taken a box on the third tier, which would give them an admirable view of the stage. But for a moment Annabel forgot all about the upcoming performance when she entered the box behind Frances.

"Good evening, ladies," the Marquess of Quinceton said, rising from a chair.

"Quin! You're early!" Frances held out her hand to him.

He bowed over it politely. "My apologies. Should I have been late instead?"

She giggled. "No, this is much better." She turned her back to him and waited pointedly until he helped her off with her cloak and draped it over her chair.

"Fellbridge." He bowed to Annabel then, a smile lurking in his eyes.

"Lord Quinceton." She supposed she should not be too surprised that he was here; Frances was nutty about the man. But she also knew that Lord Quinceton didn't return Frances's regard and was quite the opposite of nutty about Lord Glenrick. So why had he accepted their invitation this evening?

She felt Lord Glenrick behind her, waiting to help her off with her cloak, and reached up to unfasten it. To her surprise, Lord Quinceton's eyes widened as much as Lord Glenrick's had as the cloak fell away. Good heavens—she would not have guessed that he was susceptible to a pretty dress as well.

They took their seats; Annabel was further surprised when Lord Quinceton settled next to her. "Not bad, Fellbridge," he murmured to her. "Though I still think pink flatters you best."

Would there come a day when he would be unable to make her blush? "I don't know why you should take the least notice of what colors flatter me, sir."

"Why shouldn't I? You do not have to look at yourself; others do. I like what I see around me to be as aesthetically pleasing as possible."

"I cannot think that you see me frequently enough for me to offer any offense to your aesthetic sense."

"No, I don't. But I cannot say for certain as I don't have sufficient evidence to draw a conclusion." He regarded her solemnly. "How many times per week must we meet before I can judge? Five? Ten? More?"

Once—as little as a few weeks ago?—Annabel would have cut him off with a well-chosen snub. But tonight there was something about the tilt of his eyebrows and the set of his mouth that made her choose to fence with him instead. It was simply too tempting. "But that might be dangerous, my lord, in case there's a chance that my appearance does in the end offend you. Surely such an experiment would be ill-advised," she said demurely.

"Come now, Fellbridge—surely you of all people do not fear to offend me?"

"On the contrary, sir. I should never wish to offend anyone"—she lowered her gaze, then raised it to his—"unintentionally."

He grinned. But before he could reply, Frances tapped him with her fan. "Quin, who is that across the way—there, in the second box over? Your eye-sight is much keener than mine."

Annabel opened her own fan and waved it before her. Sparring with the Marquis was certainly good for the circulation; her heart was beating faster, and her breath too had quickened. It could be a perilous pastime, though—perilous because she might grow to like it too well. She should mind her manners and pay attention to Lord Glenrick, who had listened to them in silence.

"This Madame Bertinotti"—tonight's perform-ance was a benefit concert for the theatre's newest prima donna—"is she as good as Madame Catalani? I've never heard her sing," she said, turning to him.

He drew his chair a little closer to hers. "In her own way. Less bravura than the Catalani, more lyrical. Though I hear there's a singer in town right now who puts both of them in the shade. I can't think of her name right now, but it's something foreign—"

Oh goodness! He couldn't mean— "Not Miss Pouli?"

"Yes, that's it. Have you heard her? I haven't yet, but she's evidently all the thing—"

"She's very good," Lord Quinceton interrupted.

Annabel looked at him, surprised. "You've heard her?"

"This past Saturday, at Lady Jodrell's. I did not know you were so fond of music, Fellbridge." He raised an eyebrow at her.

Annabel ignored his implied question. "What did you think of her performance?"

"She's not as powerful as Madame Catalani, but I thought she had a peculiarly sweet voice."

"Did anything. . . happen at the concert?"

"Happen?"

"Anything out of the ordinary?"

He considered for a moment, and an odd ex-pression flitted across his face. "Perhaps something did. Why do you ask? Don't tell me another of your investigations is at hand?"

Annabel chose a coolly dignified response,

which was opposite her actual state of mind. "I am merely interested. Emily Cowper has engaged her to sing at her house next week."

"Has she? How interesting. I shall have to ask for an invitation. Unfortunately, though, now is not the time and place to further discuss the matter." He nodded toward the stage, where the curtains were drawing back.

Annabel seethed through the first half of the concert and did not hear a note of Mozart. At the interval the gentlemen disappeared to procure refreshments, so she tried Frances. "Have you heard anything about Demetria Pouli?"

Frances thought for a minute. "No, though the name seems familiar. I suppose everyone's talking about her, so that's why. Why do you ask?"

Annabel started to deny any real interest, then changed her mind. "She may require some looking into by the Lady Patronesses, but I don't want to bring it up until I know more. If you hear any gossip about her, please let me know."

"Ooh, my goodness! Yes, of course." Frances looked as if she wanted to ask for details, but the gentlemen's return with champagne curtailed further discussion. Instead, Annabel girded herself to question the Marquis again.

But he wouldn't be questioned. "I beg your pardon, Fellbridge. If you would care to hear what I thought of Miss Pouli's concert, the discussion will have to take place elsewhere. It hardly seems polite to discuss her performance here."

Annabel did not ask him when politeness had become such a concern, tempted though she was. "Very well. Where and when?"

He smiled. "In my curricle. I'll pick you up at three tomorrow if you are not already engaged. We can consider it part of my consideration of your aesthetics, of which I believe I ought to undertake an examination."

Oh, the *beast*. She bit back the impulse to say that her "aesthetics" were none of his business and that she was otherwise occupied tomorrow. But this was too important; she would have to resist his needling. "I am not. Three o'clock, then."

Chapter Three

To Annabel's surprise, the first words out of the Marquis' mouth once she was settled next to him in his curricle the next afternoon were, "What do you want to know about Lady Jodrell's concert?"

"What?" Curse the man! Why did he have to be so good at putting her off balance? She had been prepared to spend the next ninety minutes coaxing and cajoling an account of the evening out of him. Instead here he was, docile as a lamb, practically begging to answer her questions.

"You expressed an interest in my experience as a guest at Lady Jodrell's house where Demetria Pouli gave a recital on Saturday. Assuming you're willing to answer a question or two in return, I'm willing to answer yours."

She looked at him through narrowed eyes. "What kind of questions?"

"So suspicious, Fellbridge! Nothing too diffi- cult, on my honor. And yes—to answer your unspoken inquiry, I do have some modicum of honor."

"Why, I didn't say a thing!"

"I know you didn't. I thought I would beat you to it, just in case. So—Lady Jodrell's. It was the usual musical evening—until the music itself began."

Annabel steadied herself—he wasn't being so lamb-like after all—and asked, "What about the music was unusual?"

Lord Quinceton frowned as he turned them into Hyde Park. Annabel reluctantly admired his choice of timing for this outing; there were few fashionable people taking the air at this hour, which would permit them to talk uninterrupted by the necessity of greeting friends and acquaintances. "It's hard to put it into words," he eventually said. "She has a lovely voice, very sweet—ethereal, you might call it. Haunting. I was thinking about its unusual qualities when I fell asleep."

Annabel's heart sank. "You fell asleep? You're quite certain?"

"Yes. It's not something I ever do, so I was somewhat surprised to wake up and realize that I had. That is why I was intrigued by your question last night."

"Did you notice if you were the only one, or had others slept as well?"

He thought for a moment. "I'm certain I wasn't the only one. I noticed several people seated near me rubbing their eyes and yawning at the recital's end in the manner of someone waking from sleep. I felt quite refreshed, if that makes a difference. It must have been a good nap."

Just like what Great-aunt Philippa had

described seeing. "What about afterward? Anything unusual?"

He shook his head. "Just the usual twittering from people who say they are much fonder of music than they actually are. I left for my club shortly after."

She took a deep breath. "Were you—that is, did you notice that you were missing anything when you got home?"

His eyebrows rose. "Missing anything?"

"Your watch—or money—anything valuable?"

"No, I don't believe so."

"What about Miss Pouli? What was her demeanor throughout the evening?"

"Very modest—shy, almost. She changes when she sings—becomes much more assured." He paused, frowning again. "At the end of the concert, when I woke up as she finished, she seemed different again. She showed not just the usual weariness you'd expect to see in a singer after a performance—there was that, but she also seemed. . . it's difficult to say. Something between angry and sad. If her people hadn't packed her away saying she was too tired to talk to guests, I would not have been surprised to see her burst into tears. It's not what you expect to see with these aspiring *prima donnas*—they're usually performing as much after their concerts as during them."

Good heavens. Annabel sat back and thought about his account. He had slept when he never dozed off at musical performances (how astonishing—both her father and Freddy had always promptly begun to snore at the first note of a piano or harp.) He had noticed that others near him had slept as well. And Miss Pouli's behavior—that too was very odd.

"Are you done with your interrogation?"

"What? Oh, yes—thank you."

"Then it's my turn." He slowed his horses to a walk. "Why did you want to know all this?"

Annabel gulped. Would part of the truth suffice? "It's my cousin, Hartley Mompesson. He's in love with Miss Pouli and wants to marry her. His mother is dead set against it, and he asked me to help convince her otherwise. Before I agree to help, I want to make sure Miss Pouli isn't someone he should think twice about wishing to ally himself with."

"Your cousin being Medea Mompesson?"

"Yes."

"Poor girl." He grimaced. "What about Miss Pouli? Have you made her acquaintance?"

"I paid her a call the day after Hartley came to see me. My cousin Medea of course has refused to do so."

"Charming. And your verdict?"

"She seems a pleasant enough girl in person. I think she's genuinely in love with him and that they would deal famously. But after what my great-aunt said she saw—" she stopped.

"What did your great-aunt see? Which great-aunt, anyway?"

Oh, why had she let that slip? "It's nothing important."

"Going back on your word, Fellbridge?" He shook his head in mock sorrow. "And after I answered *your* questions?"

Annabel sighed. "My great-aunt Philippa Mompesson. She's Hartley's grandmother. She was at Lady Jodrell's too."

"Ah. And what did she see there?"

"I cannot say without breaking a confidence."

"In that case, I suppose I can't tease you any further." He glanced at her sideways, brows drawn. "Since you seemed unsurprised at my account of the evening, I'll wager hers wasn't much different, though. Very interesting."

Annabel lifted her chin. "Have you any further questions, Lord Quinceton?"

"Yes. I would like to know. . ." He paused, and she braced herself. "How goes the planting at Chalfont?"

Had she heard him correctly? "I beg your pardon?"

He raised an eyebrow at her. "The spring planting? At Chalfont Abbey? That is the name of your home, I believe?"

She stared at him, waiting for the catch. Surely he was setting up some elaborate joke at her expense, or—or something. "You want to talk about the spring planting at Chalfont?"

"I do believe that's what I said. Would you feel better if I told you about mine first? My bailiff informs me the barley around Sayre Hill is doing well, thanks to regular rainfall in our district, and the wheat seems to be recovering from the late frosts in April, though with the current cool weather, its growth may slow. How does yours?"

Good heavens, he wasn't joking. Very well, if he wanted to talk agriculture, she'd talk agriculture. She launched into the most recent report she'd had from Soames, her farm bailiff, and gave him a detailed description of not only her wheat and barley, but also the root crops (turnips good, potatoes suffering from the cold), pasturage, and how this year's lambs and the new merinos were settling in. To her surprise he listened with every appearance of interest, asking questions and nodding at her answers until for a while she almost forgot she was talking to the infamous Marquis of Quinceton and not Soames or one of her tenants.

"I have another question," she said, breaking a short silence between them.

"You want to know why I asked you that."

"Er, yes. It's not the—the—"

"The usual topic of conversation between a man and a woman driving in Hyde Park? No, it isn't. It isn't even the usual topic of conversation between, say, two men at their club, which means I have no one else with whom to discuss something I find of absorbing interest and was curious to see how you would do with the subject. Is that reason enough?"

She shook her head. "It's a little hard to credit that the Marquis of Quinceton is a farmer at heart, like Mr. Coke of Norfolk."

"Why should the Marquis of Quinceton not be concerned with his farms, since they provide so much of his income?"

"There's concern, and then there's true interest. Your reputation would indicate your interests lie elsewhere."

"Do they? Why, what do you know of my interests? Or, for that matter, my reputation? Come, Fellbridge, tell all."

Annabel fought back a wicked smile. "Oh, I can't, sir, even though I'm sure one or two of the stories I've heard must be grossly exaggerated."

His eyes widened, then he gave a shout of laughter. "A direct hit! I deserved that, though, didn't I?"

"Only a saint could have ignored that opening."

"Which means you're not a saint. And yet I seem to recall Emily Cowper recently accusing you of being too good. Which is it, Fellbridge—saint or sinner?" Then, before she could respond, he changed the subject. "I am going up to Hampstead one day next week. Would you care to accompany me?"

Hampstead could only mean a visit to his late friend's widow, the authoress Eliza Denton. "Oh, I would not wish to intrude—"

"Eliza specifically requested that I invite you."

Annabel hesitated. Did that mean he was only asking her because Mrs. Denton wished it, or did he also want her to come—not that she should care, of course, but still. . . "Yes, I'll come, if it isn't an intrusion. I would enjoy seeing her as well."

"Thank you."

The rest of their drive was spent in companionable silence, rather to her surprise. Surely it could not be that she was beginning to get used to the man. . .

Did she even want to?

Why was the Marquis of Quinceton seeming to try to insinuate himself into her life? He did not behave as a potential suitor might (she carefully did not think of Lord Glenrick)—his persistence in addressing her as "Fellbridge" and interest in talking about their farms made that clear. Yet his hungry wolf gaze had not gone away. . . and his comment about his first view of her at her betrothal party still shook her whenever she thought of it. His teasing sometimes drove her mad. . . and then, a moment later, he could speak sensibly on sensible topics. And he had cooperated with her questions about Miss Pouli's behavior at Lady Jodrell's without hesitation.

Why did he have to be such a puzzle?

On Sunday evening Annabel arrived at Emily's house a half hour early for the soirée to warn her about what might happen. She probably should have done so earlier, but it had been a busy week; Will had come down with a feverish cold, and she had hurried up to him at Windsor with a box full of her mother's sovereign remedies to prevent it from settling into his lungs. She hadn't returned till yesterday afternoon, having regretfully canceled a drive with Lord Glenrick to Hampton Court.

"*Now* you tell me," Emily said with a groan when Annabel told her what had occurred when Miss Pouli sang at Lady Jodrell's house. "Should I lock up the silver?"

"I don't think so. They'd soon stop being invited to houses if they were that obvious about their thievery. It sounds as if they're very careful; they didn't touch the Mompesson pearls, which everyone has seen, but popping a stone from a setting could easily be attributed to loss rather than theft. I would like to be in hiding when they arrive and see if I can learn anything. And we'll both pay close attention during the concert, of course. Depending on what happens, we may need to bring this up at tomorrow's Lady Patronesses meeting."

How she would bring this up with Hartley would be a different matter. How could she tell him that his angel's family were practiced jewel thieves? All she could hope was that the Lady Patronesses would investigate and Miss Pouli and her strange entourage would flee London—which would be a resolution of sorts, but perhaps not the best one for the two people most intimately involved, Hartley and his Demetria.

Emily showed her the small room she'd set aside for Miss Pouli's use, and Annabel wrapped herself securely in a shadow and withdrew to a corner, listening as the guests arrived and stood chattering about the adjoining salon. She didn't have long to wait: a scant ten minutes after she'd settled in her corner, Miss Pouli, looking charming in a simple gown of pale lilac muslin, Mr. Skourletis, and the sour-faced maid Stasia entered the room.

"Hmmph," Mr. Skourletis said after a quick examination of the room. "This will do, I suppose. Cowper's loaded, they tell me."

Miss Pouli looked unhappy. "Can't—can't we just leave everyone alone tonight? Lady Cowper was so kind to call—and Lady Fellbridge will be here, I believe. I could not endure it if they—"

"What, do you think we follow you around while you sing for these high-and-mighty folk out of the goodness of our hearts? Stop whining, stupid girl. If they paid what you were really worth, we wouldn't have to steal from them. They owe it to you." Mr. Skourletis sat down in the upholstered chair Emily had had brought in for Miss Pouli's use and eyed the tray a housemaid had left on a side table. "Bah," he said. "The English and their tea. If I never drink a drop of it again I will die a happy man."

"I quite like it," Miss Pouli said, straightening her shoulders defiantly.

"It is bad for the stomach," Stasia said. She

pushed Miss Pouli into a straight-backed chair and began to fuss over her hair.

"I *like* it," Miss Pouli said again and winced as Stasia tugged at her curls with a comb. Mr. Skourletis continued to lounge in the chair and glower at the tea tray, then got heavily to his feet and opened the door leading to Emily's larger salon a crack. He peered out for a few seconds, then closed the door and turned to Miss Pouli.

"Enough of your vapors," he scolded. "You'll do as you're told. It looks like a good crowd tonight; we should be able to take in plenty."

Miss Pouli positively wilted under his glare. "Not—not Lady Fellbridge or Lady Cowper. You leave them alone, or I shall—I shall do something dreadful!"

He sneered. "Such as?"

This time, she stood her ground. "You know what I could do," she said quietly.

"And you know what *I* could do—to you and your aunts." He seized her upper arm, shaking her roughly. Annabel nearly leapt at him from her corner; the poor child would be badly bruised.

Miss Pouli whimpered but exclaimed, "Brute! You leave my poor aunts alone! What have they ever done, except suffer under your tyranny!"

Stasia made an impatient clucking noise. "Stop it, both of you. We're here, so we're gonna get what we came for. We'll leave your precious ladies alone— now sit still while I finish." She finished combing the girl's hair, dabbed at her nose and forehead with a swan's down puff dipped in rice flour, and bade her bite her lips until they were rosy. "There. Now go and tell Lady Cowper you're ready. I think the sooner we finish here, the better. It'll all go as we planned—you'll see. And the more we take tonight, the sooner we can leave this nasty, dirty city." She pulled Miss Pouli out of her chair and pushed her toward the door. Mr. Skourletis followed them, adjusting his cravat and straightening his green and red brocade waistcoat as he plastered a wide, false smile on his face and passed through the door behind them.

Annabel waited a moment, then slipped out behind them, still wrapped in shadow, and made her way to the empty sitting room across the front hall where she could safely discard it. She brushed it away and leaned against the fireplace where a small fire burned to combat the evening's chill, thinking.

That had been instructive, but not as much as she had hoped: it was clear that Miss Pouli's family was engaged in thievery from her audiences, but how were they doing it? What caused everyone to fall asleep so deeply that Mr. Skourletis and Stasia could rob them with impunity? It had to have something to do with—

The door opened, disrupting her thoughts. She turned, and to her surprise beheld the Marquis of Quinceton in the doorway. "I wondered where you were hiding, Fellbridge," he said.

"I wasn't hiding!" What was he doing here? Emily hadn't mentioned she was inviting him.

"The concert will be starting shortly. Are you afraid of facing the music, as it were, after our conversation in the park last week?"

"Of course not. I just came in here to. . . to check my earrings. They felt loose." She turned back toward the fireplace, where a looking-glass hung over the chimney piece, and pretended to survey them.

He came into the room and stopped behind her. Before she could move away, he'd reached over her shoulders and tugged ever-so-gently on each earring. His fingers just brushed the edges of her ears. "They seem secure to me," he said, his breath stirring the fine hairs on the back of her neck beneath the cluster of curls Winters had patiently labored over.

Annabel's own breath caught in her throat. She looked up at his reflection in the looking-glass and saw his hungry-wolf expression was there, along with something else she wasn't certain she could identify. Then he stepped back and she turned; his face now wore only a polite smile. "Will you join me? I believe neither of us wishes to miss the concert." He bowed slightly and held his arm out to her.

She took it without a word and let him lead her back to Emily's salon and seat her next to him in a small gilt chair near the back of the room, where they had a good view of both Miss Pouli and the listeners. Annabel tried to keep her attention on the room—she noticed that Miss Pouli sang without accompaniment, as there was no piano or other musician near the table where she would stand—and off the memory of Lord Quinceton's touch.

This would not do. The man was impossible—or she was, to be so easily rattled by the merest brush of his hand!

She knew what Emily would say, indeed had already said many times: that she needed a man in her life. But Annabel was not convinced it was so: she was a mature woman and had survived very well for years without masculine companionship—and in fact secretly wondered at how so many women, Emily among them, could be so in thrall to their *amours*.

Conjugal life with Freddy certainly hadn't given her an elevated opinion of it. She suspected that there was something wrong with her, some vital quality missing, that made her indifferent to such matters.

Yet just now the lightest graze of a finger against her ear, a whisper of breath on her skin, were making her wonder if there wasn't something after all to Emily's contention that a night spent in her lover's arms was the nearest she would come to heaven in this lifetime.

But. . . but why had the Marquis of Quinceton been the one to bring her to this realization? She had no feelings for the man beyond the barest level of tolerance, though she was perhaps enjoying fencing with him more than she expected—

At the front of the room Miss Pouli had taken her place beside a table which held a tall vase of white lilies. Annabel straightened in anticipation as the girl curtsied to Emily and then to the room. Next to her, Lord Quinceton shifted in his chair and glanced at her. She met his gaze and looked quickly away.

And then Miss Pouli began to sing.

Annabel forgot everything as that glorious voice filled the room. She recognized the piece—it was by Mr. Beethoven—but it resembled no Beethoven she had heard before. . . and any other rendering of it would now fall flat in comparison. It was just as Lord Quinceton had said: such haunting sweetness, combined with a power and a range that was astonishing. No wonder Hartley had been captivated by her!

"Oh," she murmured to Lord Quinceton. "You were right. Her voice is exquisite."

He didn't seem to hear her; Annabel expected he was as absorbed by Miss Pouli's singing as she was. She applauded energetically when the piece was over, wondering what would come next.

This time it was what sounded like a folk song. Was it in Miss Pouli's native Greek? Whatever it was, her voice was as mesmerizing as it had been in the Beethoven. . . as was her next song, and the next, and the next after that, the songs blending into each other seamlessly and naturally, like threads in a tapestry. No one applauded after that first piece; it would have destroyed the gossamer web of song that filled the room. Only when she sang her last low, quavering note did the listeners stir and break into thunderous applause and cries of "*brava!*"

Annabel was certain she had been awake for the entire concert: no one could have dreamt of such beauty. Besides, she knew her eyes had been open for the entire time: she had not seen any sign of Mr. Skourletis or Stasia among the audience. Had Miss Pouli prevailed after all in her desire not to rob Emily's guests?

"And?" she said, turning to Lord Quinceton as most of those guests rose and surged toward Miss Pouli and Emily, who had come to stand beside her. "What did you think of that? Not the least like the concert at Lady Jodrell's, was it?"

He shook his head. "On the contrary. There were some differences, but I think you had better press on in your investigation, Fellbridge."

"Why, what do you mean? Nothing happened!"

"Something certainly did happen."

"But I was awake the entire time! I heard her! More importantly, I didn't see anyone's jewelry being stolen."

"No, you weren't asleep. You sat with your eyes

fixed on her the entire time with a charming little smile playing about your lips. It was all I could do not to—" He coughed. "Everyone sat that way. Not asleep, but not awake, either. Mesmerized. And her guardian or whoever he is and her maid went quite freely among you all, helping themselves to various valuables. That's why you asked if I'd lost anything at Lady Jodrell's, isn't it?"

Annabel ignored his question. "I don't believe it! Why weren't you mesmerized too?"

"Because I had these." He held out a hand. Two large plugs of wax lay in his palm.

Annabel stared at them. "I don't understand."

"I plugged my ears before she started to sing, and then just did what everyone else did while those two pawed through jewels and pockets. They left you alone, incidentally. Miss Pouli has enough decorum not to steal from a possible future relative, it seems."

Annabel swallowed hard and watched Miss Pouli. She looked tired and strained, her eyes darting toward Mr. Skourletis who stood at the edge of the crowd smiling his nice-nasty smile. There was no sign of Stasia. Had they really somehow mesmerized the entire room?

"Why did you do it?" she asked him. Miss Pouli was looking very pale now, and Mr. Skourletis had come to her side and was talking to Emily.

"Because of you and your questions. They got me wondering, so I asked Emily for an invitation. I can only be grateful for the benefits a classical education can confer."

"What?"

"Odysseus. It's the first thing that I thought of when you told me—"

"Annabel! Wasn't that wonderful?" Frances Dalrymple was suddenly beside her, taking her arm.

Frances! Of course she should have known that Emily would have invited all the Lady Patronesses. How many of them had actually come? She'd been so busy spying on Miss Pouli that she hadn't had time to look. Had any of them noticed anything? "It was wonderful!" she agreed with false heartiness.

"I am delighted to see you back in town, Lady Fellbridge. How does your son get on?" Lord Glenrick was there too, smiling warmly at her. "I trust he is better; you still owe me your company on a drive to Hampton Court, and I shall be unrelenting until I collect my debt."

"That's a debt I will be delighted to pay," she said, but Frances was tugging on her arm.

"Come with me! I simply have to meet this Miss Pouli," she said.

Annabel was surprised; usually if Lord Quinceton was present, Frances had eyes only for him. But she let Frances steer her away from the two men; it would give her a chance to ask Frances if she'd noticed anything out of the ordinary.

By the time they made it to the front of the room, Miss Pouli had left and the crowd had dispersed in search of supper and champagne. "Evidently her singing exhausts her, so she did not wish to stay for supper," explained Emily, who had waited for them. She was radiant. "Wasn't that splendid? I've never heard such a voice!"

"Neither have I, but you had better listen to this." Annabel told them what the Marquis had done and gave Frances a quick explanation of their suspicions about Miss Pouli. "I'm bringing it up at tomorrow's meeting," she concluded. "If you can think of any little thing that you noticed tonight that might help us, please say something."

Emily looked as though she'd bitten into an unripe lemon. "Oh, no! And I was positive everything had gone well!"

"So was I, but it seems we were wrong. Were any other of us here tonight?"

"Lady Patronesses? Yes; besides you two, Georgiana came. I think she's in the supper room. Shall I go find her?"

Annabel did not have the stomach for Georgiana's icy politeness right now. "No, we'll ask her tomorrow at the meeting. You, er, didn't peek at Miss Pouli, did you?"

Emily shook her head. "It didn't even occur to me to do so. I thought everything was fine and your great-aunt had imagined it all."

"I don't think so. And I don't think Lord Quinceton would have imagined such a thing or even made it up to tease me." She glanced across the room to where he still stood by their seats alone with Lord Glenrick, his head bent at a listening angle as Glenrick spoke—

Her gaze sharpened. There was something odd about the tableau—the way the Marquis held his shoulders so stiffly and his hands clenched behind his back, unlike his usual relaxed stance. His countenance was pale and his mouth a thin line. What could they be talking about that was putting him into such a state of. . . of—what *was* it? If Annabel hadn't known better, she would have thought he looked caught somewhere between anger and apprehension. But surely she was imagining things.

Chapter Four

The following day, Annabel arrived at Almack's a few minutes early; she and Emily had agreed to do so to prepare to bring their recommendation for an investigation of Miss Pouli. But the regular Lady Patronesses' meeting had not even commenced before Georgiana Bathurst, looking as though she'd run all the way from her house to King Street, stormed into their chamber and up to Emily.

"Did you find it?" she demanded, ignoring Annabel's presence. "It has to be at your house!"

"What does? Georgiana, what are you talking about?"

Georgiana grasped her arm. "My necklace! It must be there!"

Emily shot Annabel a quick look and detached Georgiana's hand from her arm. "Come, let us sit down so you can start at the beginning. You've lost something, I apprehend." She steered Georgiana to a chair and sat down next to her. Annabel followed, a horrid sinking feeling in her middle.

Georgiana sat but clutched at Emily's hand once more. "My necklace! I wore my great-grandmother's topaz necklace to your soirée last night. We went to the ball at Viola Blether's house afterward, but it wasn't till I returned home that I realized it was no longer around my neck."

Emily evidently shared her sinking feeling; she didn't bother asking if Georgiana had inquired with Lady Blether if her necklace had been found there. "I don't know exactly where your necklace is, but I'm afraid I have an idea about how it went missing," she said gently.

Georgiana's face crumpled. "I didn't think the clasp was that loose! I know it's old, but I would never have worn it if I'd known—"

Annabel stepped forward. "That's not what Emily means, Georgiana."

Georgiana cast her a cold look. "I do not recall asking *your* opinion, Lady Fellbridge."

Annabel sighed and looked up at Sally; the rest of the Lady Patronesses were clustered around them, wearing expressions ranging from concern (Maria) to boredom (Dorothea.) "Sally, might we start with a meeting instead of vouchers today? We would like to discuss a matter we think needs investigating— something that might shed light on Geor—on Lady Bathurst's loss."

"We?"

"Emily and Frances and I."

"All of you? That sounds serious." Sally nodded. "Very well. Ladies, your seats."

A quiet cough startled them. "And gentlemen, too, if ye please," a voice added.

Sally's head whipped around. "William! This is

a pleasant surprise."

"That's the best kind, no?" William Almack, the Lady Patronesses's late founder, didn't attend every meeting, but his presence, if invisible, was always welcome.

When they had all settled around the table, Sally asked, "Who will speak?"

"Annabel will. She's the one who knows the most about the matter," Emily said.

Georgiana made a small sound of derision. Sally frowned at her and said, "Annabel, you may begin."

Annabel took a deep breath and told them about Hartley's and Great-aunt Philippa's visits concerning the lovely, if larcenous, Miss Pouli.

"Philippa Mompesson." Mr. Almack chuckled. "Now there's a name I haven't heard in a long while. She was quite a girl in her day. . . begging your pardon, Lady Fellbridge."

Annabel smiled. "Oh, she's still quite a girl, sir. And despite her age, I'm certain she is a reliable witness to what happened at Lady Jodrell's house. . . especially in light of what the Marquis of Quinceton experienced last night." She told them about the evening at Emily's, first her own account and then Lord Quinceton's. "So we cannot know for certain, but I greatly fear that Georgi—er, Lady Bathurst's necklace may have been taken by Miss Pouli's accomplices."

"Oh," Mr. Almack said, on a long gusty sigh. Annabel couldn't help wondering where he'd found the breath for it. "Not again."

"What?" Emily said. "Do you know what's going on?"

"Oh, no!" Maria added. "Are you thinking what

I'm thinking, William?"

"I fear so, Lady Sefton."

"You—you don't think so, do you?" Georgiana had straightened in her chair. "But it's been years since we've seen one!"

"All the more reason for it to be likely it's them, ma'am," Mr. Almack said.

"What," Sally interjected sternly, "are you talking about?"

Maria hesitated, glanced at Georgiana and the chair occupied by the incorporeal Mr. Almack as if for approval, then turned to Sally. "It sounds very much to us like London's being visited by a Siren."

"A Siren? You mean, the mythical creatures who sing sailors to their deaths?" Clementina looked amused.

"They're not mythical," Maria said soberly. "We haven't had one in London since the Peace of Amiens back in 1802, so it's not surprising you young ones haven't met one yet. But this is exactly what happens when one is around."

"Nay, definitely not a myth, more's the pity," Mr. Almack added. "Every few years one will turn up, wandering the capitals of Europe, using their voices to steal. Then they go home until the money grows short and do it over again. I imagine the war's kept them away from London all these years." He chuckled. "That's one thing we can thank Boney for— he's kept the Sirens away!"

Good heavens! Annabel shook her head. So Hartley's darling Demetria was a Siren! "What about her family? That awful Mr. Skourletis and her aunts? Are they even actually related to her?"

"They may very well be relatives," Maria said.

"It's hard for a beautiful young girl—or what looks like one, anyway—to move about in society with impunity. She has them with her to lend her respect-ability."

"I suppose." Somehow, though, she couldn't see Miss Pouli as a calculating schemer. . . unless the girl was a superb actress. And why would she have behaved as she did in the little room in Emily's house when she would have thought herself unobserved?

Georgiana buried her face in her hands. "A Siren," she mumbled. "I'll never get my great-grand-mother's necklace back!"

Sally gave her a sympathetic look. "What do you suggest, William? We can't let them stay in London, robbing our friends."

"Ye have to scare them off somehow," Mr. Almack said. "Make it clear to them that they've been discovered and that they need to leave town."

"But you have to proceed with great caution. Sirens can be quite nasty, if you're not careful," Maria added.

"I see," Sally said grimly. "Which one of you will undertake this investigation?"

"Alas, I must step aside," Dorothea, who'd been unusually quiet thus far, said. "We—ahem!—are distantly but alas undeniably related, you know."

"Gorgons and Sirens? Really?" Maria looked fascinated. "I didn't know that."

"It is not something we Gorgons care to admit in public." Dorothea gave a little sniff of distaste. "Sirens are often so *common*."

Sally frowned. "That's too bad. You might have been helpful if matters did get difficult with them—but I understand. Well? Anyone else?"

"Me," Annabel said. "I should like to do it, if I may."

"Are you certain?" Sally leaned forward and looked at her hard. "While I appreciate your offer, you just handled the Spruce-Gilbert incident. We don't expect anyone to lead consecutive investigations."

Annabel returned her gaze steadily. "I know. But this is a family matter as well—my cousin is in love with Miss Pouli."

"Poor boy." Maria shook her head. "It won't be easy telling him. I'll help you, Annabel. I speak Sirenese. It's very close to many of the bird languages, you know. And I've seen them before."

"Thank you, Maria!" Annabel hesitated. "Do you not wish to lead the investigation, since you have the experience?"

"Oh, I'm happy to defer to you. Besides, this Miss Pouli seems to like you. That will go a long way when dealing with Sirens, believe me."

Two days later, Annabel and Maria waited in Annabel's library for Miss Pouli. They had met Monday afternoon to plan their strategy; Maria had suggested inviting her for a drive as a way to separate Miss Pouli from Mr. Skourletis and the others and confront her. But Annabel had chosen to invite her to drink tea instead; there would be much less likelyhood of being overheard here in the house than there would be in her landau, with a coachman and groom in close proximity. She had sent Miss Pouli a note of invitation on Tuesday morning and added a post-script that she hoped Miss Pouli would be able to come unattended, so that they could discuss a matter of *relative* importance. Miss Pouli had accepted by return note, saying she would do her best to come alone; she had evidently caught the veiled reference to Hartley.

The weather was rainy and chill, which made Annabel glad they hadn't gone for a drive. She directed John the footman to build a roaring fire; she had an idea that Miss Pouli would find it comforting, being from a warm country. Mr. Almack had said it was necessary to frighten Sirens away, but Annabel suspected that taking a different road with Miss Pouli would be more effective. The poor child had already seemed frightened half to death the other night at Emily's.

Miss Pouli, in a maidenly white muslin dress and sage-green spencer that complemented her olive complexion, arrived precisely on time. Annabel went down to greet her, ignoring Hanscomb's visible-only-to-her (*how did he do that?*) disapproval at so signal a distinction being conferred upon so humble a guest. But she didn't want the girl, for whatever reason, to take fright and flee.

"Miss Pouli! I'm so glad you could come," she said, taking her arm and drawing her gently up the stairs. "One of my friends is here; I hope you won't object to making her acquaintance."

"Oh, Lady Fellbridge—you are too kind—" But she looked apprehensive.

"Not in the least," Annabel said cheerfully. "Are you singing a great deal this week? You mustn't over-tire your voice."

"No, Lady Fellbridge—that is, I will be singing tomorrow for Viscountess Stonear." The prospect seemed to fill her with anything but pleasure. "She is not—is she a friend of yours?"

"We're not well-acquainted, no."

That seemed to reassure her; she managed a smile as they entered the library. Annabel shut the door behind them.

"Maria, here is Miss Pouli who sang so enchantingly at Emily's on Sunday," she said. "Miss Pouli, this is my friend Lady Sefton." She led Miss Pouli to the sofa nearest the fire, where Maria waited.

Miss Pouli's smile had vanished at the mention of singing on Sunday, but she curtsied prettily to Maria.

Maria smiled and opened her mouth. An extraordinary thread of sound, melodious syllables mixed in with whistles and clicks, issued forth.

Miss Pouli's eyes widened and her countenance grew even paler. Annabel tensed, waiting for her to flee, but instead she collapsed onto the sofa and stared up at Maria, visibly trembling, then burst into tears.

Maria sat down beside her, putting her arm about Miss Pouli's shoulders. To Annabel's relief, her next words were in English. "There, child, no need to cry. No one's going to hurt you."

Miss Pouli sobbed harder. Maria tucked a napkin from the tea tray into her hand and raised her eyebrows at Annabel. They both waited, and when the tears showed some sign of abating, Annabel poured a cup of tea and taking a seat on Miss Pouli's other side, put the cup into her hands. The girl started, then lifted it and gulped it down between hitching breaths.

"You—you know," she said, when she could talk.

"Yes," Annabel said simply.

"How do you know my language?" she said, turning to Maria. "You speak it so well—surely you're not—"

"No, I'm not," Maria said quickly. "I just, er, happen to know a lot of languages. But for now we shall keep to English so that Lady Fellbridge might understand what we say. Will you tell us how you came to be in London? We've not seen a Siren here in many years."

Miss Pouli stared at them piteously. Annabel poured her more tea, which she drank gratefully; then she took a deep breath. "It was Mr. Skourletis. He's not really my uncle—he is nephew to the late husband of one of my aunts. He made us come—it was his idea to make me sing people to sleep so that he could rob them. He thought we should come to northern Europe—that no one here would know about us and we could take as much as we liked and then go home again. We began in Copenhagen, then came here. I didn't want to—I hate taking people's pretty things and having to lie, but he—he made me do it! Every single time I've sung, it's because he's made me!" She dissolved into tears once again.

Maria leaned toward Annabel behind the sobbing girl's back. "This might not be as difficult as we feared," she murmured. "I've never heard of a Siren who didn't enjoy every minute of this game." More loudly she said, "My dear Miss Pouli, if we were to help you, would you truly stop singing in order to steal from people and return to your home?"

"Oh, yes!" She emerged from her napkin. "I

never want to have to sing in front of lots of people again! Only. . . only—"

"Hartley," Annabel said.

Miss Pouli broke down once again. "Oh, my darling, darling Hartley!" she wailed. Maria handed her another napkin, and they waited until she had mastered her sobs again. "Lady Fellbridge, I love him more than anything," she said, still sniffling and hic-cupping. "If I leave London, I will have to leave him."

"I don't see why you should have to leave, if you're married to him."

For a moment, an expression of pure joy shone on Miss Pouli's tear-stained face. Then it vanished like the sun behind a cloud. "There's nothing I would rather do," she said simply. "All I want is to marry him and help him with his studies and watch birds with him and take care of him, but I can't—I *can't*! Mr. Skourletis has threatened to do all manner of terrible things to my poor aunts if I accept Hartley and stop singing. . . and he will do something even more dreadful to Hartley!"

Why, the scoundrel! "If he thinks he can offer violence to an Englishman in his own country—" Annabel began, but Miss Pouli shook her head.

"It is worse—*far* worse—than that!" she ex-claimed. "Mr. Skourletis swears that if I try to marry Hartley, he will tell him about—about. . . no, it is too terrible!"

"What will he do, child?" Maria asked.

Miss Pouli drew a deep, shuddering breath. "He will—he will tell Hartley about my *feet*!"

Annabel was conscious that she was staring at Miss Pouli in what was probably a very foolish man-ner. "Your. . . what?"

Maria's expression was sober, but there was a hint of twinkle in her eye. "Annabel, you may not be aware that Sirens have. . . ah. . . birds' feet."

Miss Pouli buried her face in a fresh napkin. "I will never live down the shame—never! He will surely never want to look at me again if he knows!"

Annabel would not allow herself to meet Maria's eyes. Miss Pouli *did* wear her gowns very long. . . and hadn't Hartley said something about never having had even a glimpse of her ankles? "Miss Pouli—Demetria—if you do marry Hartley, he will probably see your feet at, er, some point in your married life. It just happens in—in the course of things."

"*Ohh!*" Miss Pouli wailed into her napkin. "I never thought of *that*!"

"Yes, but you're forgetting that Hartley *loves* birds," she put in quickly. "I am persuaded he would think your feet are perfectly *charming*."

"Of course he would," Maria said stoutly.

Miss Pouli lifted her face from the sodden napkin, her eyes wet but starry. "Do you think so?"

"I am quite certain," Maria said. "But my dear girl, I rather expect you have things a little backwards."

"Do I? How?"

Maria hesitated. "I know it appears that Mr. Skourletis is in charge, but I have seen your kind visit London before and do precisely this—steal from wealthy music lovers, accumulate a—ahem!—a nice nest egg, and return to their home to live on the proceeds until the money runs out and they do it all again."

Her eyes grew round with wonder. "You *have*?

But he was certain he was being terribly clever! And my aunts never said a word!"

"He was not being in the least clever, if it makes you feel better. If I were to venture a guess, I would say that it's your aunts calling the tune here—ah, if you'll excuse the expression. They are Sirens too, I expect."

"Yes, they are," Miss Pouli breathed, wide-eyed. "But—but why?"

"He is a very convenient front for them. It is difficult for a woman to do business in the wider world; having a man to manage matters on their behalf makes it much easier. They can supervise from the background as your chaperones, while he thinks he is running everything."

Annabel looked at Maria in astonishment. "Really?" Those two still, silent statues she and Emily had seen at Holles Street—*they* were behind all this, not that horrid man?

Maria nodded placidly. "That's what we've always seen in the past. Now, the question is, will they permit you to marry Hartley? I don't worry about your Mr. Skourletis, though he sounds a most unpleasant person. If *they* approve, I expect he won't be able to gainsay them."

Miss Pouli still appeared stunned at Maria's revelation. "Truly? He shouts at them so dreadfully—"

Maria took her hand. "I would not be surprised if that were for your benefit," she said gently. "I expect they know how you feel about having to do this. But I also expect that they've convinced you that you are protecting them from him by agreeing to sing."

"Oh," Miss Pouli, wide-eyed, sat back against the sofa cushions. "I had not thought—that is, yes, I can maybe see that. . ." She looked at Maria, then Annabel. "What do I *do*?"

"Are you quite certain that you wish to marry Hartley?" Annabel asked. "It will mean remaining in England rather than returning to your home."

Miss Pouli swallowed but nodded her head. "I love him with all my heart, Lady Fellbridge. If—if you don't think he will be disgusted by my feet. . ." She took a deep breath. "I will have to be brave, won't I?"

"Yes, dear," Maria said.

"Then I will—for Hartley's sake!"

Annabel looked at Maria. "Then—then if you will undertake not to sing at anyone's house again"—Maria nodded her agreement—"the next step is for us to speak to your aunts. Do you think you can claim illness and not go to Lady Stonear's tomorrow?"

Miss Pouli looked frightened but nodded. "I must."

"Good girl." She hesitated. "I think it would be best if Mr. Skourletis were not present when we pay our call." If Maria was right, the last thing they needed was his interference while they spoke to Miss Pouli's aunts.

"I may need a day to arrange that," Miss Pouli said slowly. "Not tomorrow—would Friday be convenient? I will send you a note."

No, not tomorrow; she was engaged to visit Mrs. Denton with Lord Quinceton. "Maria? Will Friday do?"

"Friday is quite convenient."

"Then Friday it is. We'll await your note." Then she and Maria coaxed Miss Pouli to drink another cup of tea, and Annabel rang for her maid Winters to bring a cool wet cloth sprinkled with lavender water to bathe her eyes. After they sent her home again in Annabel's carriage, Annabel sighed and looked at Maria. To be honest, she had always found her a little on the. . . well, silly side. But it was clear there was a great deal more to Maria Sefton than she'd suspected.

"Do you think we'll be able to carry this off?" she asked.

Maria looked thoughtful. "I don't know. I hope so. Sirens are like magpies—very acquisitive. But they also have a strong family feeling. I think the way to go is to appeal to both sides of their characters: convince them that they'll be making the girl happy as well as settling her most creditably if they give her permission to marry your cousin. The question is, will it work?"

"I hope so."

"I do too." Maria hesitated, then said, "Though I do wish we could bring Dorothea with us, just in case things turn unpleasant. Sirens can be very. . . excitable."

"I'd noticed."

Maria smiled. "Poor child. Well, I doubt it will get to that point."

Annabel hoped she was correct. Manipulating shadows and being able to talk to animals (and their relations) were not the best defensive skills against angry Sirens with taloned feet. . . but surely it would not come to that.

COUNTESS OF SHADOWS   265

That night turned out to be an unexpectedly sleepless one for Annabel; she tossed and turned, thinking about the morrow. She would be driving to Hampstead with Lord Quinceton, which meant two hours each way in his curricle with no one to speak to but him. After the events of Sunday evening at Emily's, she had no idea what to say to or even *think* about the man. Eventually she decided that she would pretend that nothing had happened, and instead would treat him with friendly but empty cordiality, all surface with nothing beneath it. Perhaps if she ignored the confusion she truly felt, it would just. . . go away?

When he arrived for her at noon, she gave him a polite smile along with her hand so that he could help her up into the curricle. Now, to find something unremarkable to comment upon less obvious than the weather— "Good day, my lord. Is that a new watch-chain?"

He didn't answer at once, but swung himself up beside her, settled a rug over her legs to ward off the day's damp chill, and took the reins, tossing a coin to the boy who'd held the horses' heads. "Yes, it is. . . but really, Fellbridge! Do you mean to discountenance me utterly by such a remark?'

"What? Why should it discountenance you?" There he went, wrong-footing her within moments of their meeting. She should have known better than to try to make light conversation with him; he probably wasn't capable of it.

"Do you mean to admire my new watch-chain, or disparage it?" He guided the horses into a smart trot up the street.

"If I meant to disparage it, I would hardly have brought it up as a topic of conversation."

"No? Why not? Ah, yes—I forgot that you are good. I shall assume you approve of it, then. But truly, what has shaken me to the core is that you even noticed it. Dare I presume to hope that you have come to regard me as more than a mere acquaintance? Someone about whom one notices details as trivial as a new watch-chain?"

She sought desperately for a reply. "I—I am known for my remarkable powers of observation, Lord Quinceton."

He smiled. "Ah. Well parried. I concede the point and make my salute. . . but nevertheless I shall continue to hope I was right." He drove silently for a few moments, then looked at her sideways. "Am I?"

She returned his look and quailed. His light, teasing smile had changed into something even more terrifying: *sincerity*, which could only be answered in kind. He had backed her into a corner because he was right: she *had* begun to regard him as something more than an acquaintance. What the nature of that regard was, she didn't care to examine too closely right now—but she should keep in mind that the man was a noted fencer with both steel and words, drat him.

"You have conceded the point. . . and thereby won the bout," she finally said. "It is not the usual way of things, I believe."

He was startled into a laugh. "What is this, Fellbridge? You're giving me the win? Are you feeling quite the thing? It was an unorthodox strategy, I agree—and one I should probably keep in mind for future engagements with you."

She took refuge in lightness. "Future engagements? Oh no. I'm scarcely a worthy opponent for such a nonpareil as you."

"You underestimate yourself, madam. You could slay me far too easily with one small, very dull weapon."

"What weapon is that?"

He raised his eyebrows. "I should not tell you, lest you be tempted to use it on me. . . but it's an odd weapon, one you would not even be aware of using, probably, if it comes to that. By then I would probably welcome my death."

"Well? What is it, then?"

He smiled at nothing. "Your indifference."

She drew in a quick breath. But he was already speaking again. "And what came of your investigation of Miss Pouli after Sunday's revelations? I regret that we were unable to continue our conversation on the topic."

They hadn't continued it because he had disappeared after she observed him speaking with Lord Glenrick—not that she'd been paying special attention, of course. "I do wish you would stop using that term. I am not *investigating* anything. I merely do not want to see my cousin make an alliance that will lead to his unhappiness."

How could the man imbue a silence with such skepticism? "Oh, come now, Fellbridge," he finally said. "We both know very well that the child is a Siren and busily engaged in robbing London blind. I assumed you had come to that conclusion as well?"

If she thought he had wrong-footed her before, this was far worse. "A—a Siren, Lord Quinceton? That's a—an interesting theory."

"You're a very poor liar, you know—which pleases me no end, but that's not the matter at hand.

What else could she be, under the circumstances? What are you going to do about her and her accomplices? Surely you don't want a jewel thief in the family?"

"She's not a thief!" Annabel was stung into retorting. "She's being forced into this by her aunts and that awful man she's compelled to pretend is her uncle. She would like nothing better than to stop this horrid business and settle down in the country with Hartley—"

"So you've spoken with her, then," he broke in, calmly. "Was that wise?"

Oh, confound him! "There was absolutely no danger. Miss Pouli is a very well-behaved girl—er, creature." She hesitated. "How—how did you know what she was?" And why was he accepting the presence of a supposedly mythical creature in modern London so calmly?

"I told you—the benefits of a sound classical education. I always had a fondness for the tales of Odysseus and his wanderings. Hence the wax plugs in the ears—though I found that I had to hum to myself as well—her voice is very penetrating."

Odysseus and the Sirens—so that was what he had meant. She sighed. "I assume, my lord, that I can count upon your discretion."

"You can, though you probably don't need to—who would believe me if I told them what she was?"

Hmmph. "Thank you, I think."

He smiled briefly. "You're welcome. Now, what is your intention? If it's to help Miss Pouli escape her unpleasant relations, I applaud your chivalry—and will expect to be informed of the time and place of your attempted liberation."

"Good heavens, we're not going to abduct her. We merely intend to call upon her au—" Annabel narrowed her eyes. "Why do you want to know?" she demanded.

"Because this time I do not intend to stand by while you face a potential—er, antagonist—alone," he said. "Dealing with Gilbert Marjoribanks's demon—a demon!—was bad enough."

"Titivillus was nothing to be afraid of," she protested. "He was actually very sweet to Clem—" She stopped and pressed her lips together.

"That may well be, but you have no idea if Miss Pouli's aunts—I assume that was what you were going to say?—are dangerous or not—"

"No."

"They're not dangerous? How do you know?"

"I meant 'no' as in, 'no, you will not be accompanying us when we speak to Miss Pouli's aunts.'"

"You say 'we.' Will your cousin be coming with you?"

"Hartley?" Goodness, she hadn't even thought of that. Hartley's was not the first name that sprang to mind when thinking of people who might be helpful in a delicate and potentially hazardous situation. Besides, Miss Pouli ought to be the one to inform him about her unusual antecedents. "No, not Hartley."

"Who, then?"

There would be no putting him off, would there? "Lady Sefton," she said reluctantly, not looking at him. It was no use; she could feel his incredulity even before he spoke.

"*Maria Sefton*? Are you quite mad, Fellbridge? Of what earthly use will she be—and why does she even know about this matter?"

"Maria will be very useful."

"May I inquire how?"

"No." She hesitated, then said, "In the instance of Titivillus and Mr. Marjoribanks, you had some right to be informed of what was happening because of your particular relationship with Mrs. Denton and her family. In this case, no such relationship exists— and you therefore cannot have any real expectation of being involved in the matter."

She stole a glance at him. Even in profile, his scowl could be plainly seen.

The remainder of their drive to Hampstead passed in silence. Annabel told herself she should be glad of it, but she wasn't; it was a thick, uncomfortable silence that made her want to squirm. Nor were matters improved by the weather: with a half-hour yet to go before reaching Mrs. Denton's house, it began to rain. Lord Quinceton had already raised the canopy over them, but it was still a damp, miserable, cold ride.

Mrs. Denton, thank goodness, had a roaring fire and a large, sustaining tea awaiting them in the comfortable ground floor sitting room. She fussed over Annabel, settling her in a chair close to the hearth and making her drink a cup of hot tea immediately before she would herself sit. Lord Quinceton remained silent—but not for long, as it turned out.

"Eliza, there's no reason for you to be so concerned for Fellbridge's well-being. She isn't," he said in a conversational tone, watching them from the sofa.

Annabel put down her teacup. "Lord Quinceton, may I respectfully invite you to close your mouth and keep it that way?"

The corners of the mouth in question twitched—in amusement or annoyance, she couldn't say. Nor did she care. What possessed him to resume their conversation about Miss Pouli *now*?

Mrs. Denton frowned. "Geoffrey, what trouble have you got yourself into now?"

"Me? I haven't got myself into any trouble. She, on the other hand. . ."

"You haven't?" Annabel put in. "How interesting you should say that. You certainly looked troubled to me at Emily's when you were talking with Lord Glenrick after Miss Pouli sang."

His expression darkened, and he almost glared at her. "Damn it, Fellbridge, that has nothing to do with you, and I'll thank you not to involve yourself!"

Annabel raised one eyebrow. "Indeed, sir. I might say the same thing."

Now *that* had been interesting. She had mentioned the episode almost at random, trying to divert him; evidently there was more to it than had met the eye. What *had* the two men been discussing, and why was Lord Quinceton so upset by it? She caught Mrs. Denton's questioning look and answered it with a small shrug.

"Well, then." Mrs. Denton made to rise from her seat. "If the two of you wish to quarrel, I shall ask to be excused. I am at a tricky section in the new book I'm working on, and should probably go back to my desk."

"I beg your pardon," Annabel said quickly, reaching out to her. "*I* certainly didn't intend for that to happen."

"Eliza, maybe you can talk some sense into this stubborn female," Lord Quinceton said.

"No." Annabel returned his black look. "I don't wish Mrs. Denton to be bored with the matter."

"I doubt I could be bored by anything that has the pair of you so exercised," Mrs. Denton observed, and smiled at Annabel. "Truly, if there is anything I can possibly help you with, Lady Fellbridge—you did so much for me—"

"The situations are not without similarities," Lord Quinceton interrupted. "Fellbridge has managed to tangle herself with a supernatural creature once again." He gave Mrs. Denton a quick summary of Miss Pouli's depredations among the *ton*. "And now she proposes to visit the chit's family to convince them to let her marry her cousin without any idea of the possible danger involved, and to do so unaccompanied by anyone who might offer any protection against harm or insult."

"Such as you?"

"Yes."

Annabel expected Mrs. Denton to rally on her behalf, but she didn't. Instead, she turned to her with a troubled air. "Lady Fellbridge, I must confess that what Geoffrey says troubles me as well." Then she shook her head and smiled. "Sirens. You do find yourself in interesting situations, don't you?"

"Mrs. Denton, you know I am not a helpless female."

The other woman's eyes went to the tea table that Annabel had covered with a shadow on her last visit. "No, you are not. But—my dear madam, are you certain you will be safe?"

Annabel remembered Maria's wishing they could have Dorothea with them, but resolutely set the memory aside. "Quite certain," she said firmly.

They stayed until the rain began to slacken. When the Marquis excused himself to supervise his horses being hitched to the curricle, Mrs. Denton walked with Annabel to the door. She opened her mouth and closed it, then seemed to make a decision. "Lady Fellbridge, you said something that rather upset Geoffrey earlier."

"What *haven't* I said today that didn't?" Annabel said. "But yes, I know what you infer." She explained what had occurred—Lord Glenrick's confidential air, and Lord Quinceton's agitated one—as the two had spoken together. "And no, I have no idea what they might have been discussing."

"Is this Lord Glenrick a friend of his?"

"No, that's the odd thing. Lord Quinceton seems to actively dislike him and even warned me against him—and yet he accepted Lord Glenrick's invitation to the opera with him and his sister."

"His sister?"

"Lady Frances Dalrymple. She is a friend of mine." Annabel did not mention Frances' *tendre* for Lord Quinceton.

"Hmm. I suppose it's nothing. . . but it was very unlike him to behave in that manner." She hesitated. "If you could perhaps keep an ear open—not that there's anything I can do to help him if something is troubling him. But we're very, very fond of Geoffrey."

Annabel smiled. "The fact that you are is one of the things that keeps me from quite washing my hands of him."

Mrs. Denton's face clouded. "Oh, please don't do that. He would be devastated to lose you—your friendship, I mean."

"Oh, I am certain he would. Whom else would

he find to torment?"

She smiled unwillingly. "Don't let him fluster you. He doesn't mean three quarters of what he says."

"Yes, but which three quarters? Believe me, I don't let him trouble me." Which was quite untrue, but Mrs. Denton didn't need to know that.

Lord Quinceton appeared with the curricle then, the mud wiped from its gleaming sides and wheels, followed by Mrs. Denton's groom. Just as he was about to help Annabel into the seat, Mrs. Denton took her hand and pressed it. "Thank you for coming. I hope I shall see you soon."

"So do I," Annabel said, and meant it. "And please—it's Annabel."

"Annabel." Her anxious expression softened momentarily into a smile, but quickly clouded again. "Annabel, please—when you call upon this Miss Pouli's aunts, be careful."

Chapter Five

Annabel was relieved when Miss Pouli answered the door to her and Maria that Friday afternoon at the house on Holles Street.

"No Stasia?" she murmured as the girl shut the door behind them.

"I sent her on a list of errands as long as my arm," Miss Pouli confessed, her face lighting with a mischievous smile. "She'll be gone till six, I expect." The smile faded. "I wish I could be as certain about my—about Mr. Skourletis. He usually visits a coffee house a few blocks away between one and three, but we never know when he'll decide to come home early or stay late."

"Then we'd best get talking to your aunts," Maria said briskly. "Are they expecting us?"

Miss Pouli nodded. "I reminded them that you were Hartley's cousin, Lady Fellbridge."

"Well, that helps, unless—shouldn't Hartley be here as well to present his suit?"

"Among our people, it's the women who arrange

marriages"—she blushed prettily—"so they will not think it odd that you are here and Hartley is not."

Annabel thought it odd but didn't say so. Leave it to Hartley to have found a way, even if inadvertently, to get someone else to take care of the tiresome parts of proposing to his future wife.

"I should warn you," Miss Pouli said, pausing before the doors to the gloomy salon they had sat in before. "My aunt Thelxiope does not speak a word of English. Aunt Molpe's is not too bad, at all events."

"I gather she has visited England before," Maria said.

Miss Pouli had the grace to look uncomfortable. "Er, yes, I believe she has." She turned the door handles and opened them wide.

At Annabel's first meeting with Miss Pouli's aunts when she and Emily had called, they had been silent, almost motionless figures veiled in black. Today, they still wore black—but the veils had been thrown back. Annabel checked on the threshold and stared.

She had presumed, from the way Hartley and Miss Pouli had spoken of them, that they were old ladies. But the two faces that were turned expectantly toward her and Maria were not old—not young, perhaps, but certainly not the wrinkled, crone-like visages she had somehow expected. They appeared to be in that place somewhere between youth and age, no longer in their first flush but not yet old—but for them it was a glorious place where age tempered the insipidity of youth, and youth the harshness of age. Only a faint touch of silver showed in their thick, ink-black hair, and the merest hint of lines touched their foreheads and the corners of their dark eyes. . . .

and they were breathtakingly beautiful. Of course, she should have known they would be—they were Sirens, after all. It was a good thing that the Prince Regent, who was known to be attracted to more mature women, had not clapped eyes on them.

"Aunt Molpe, here are the ladies who wish to speak with you," Miss Pouli said nervously, then switched into the fluid whistling tongue of the Sirens, presumably for the other aunt, Thelxiope's, benefit.

Maria made them both a pretty curtsy and said something in Sirenese. Annabel curtsied as well and watched the aunts' faces as Maria spoke. They remained impassive, their glances moving between Maria and her.

"Sit," one of them said—presumably the English-speaking Aunt Molpe. "I wish to hear from you about this young man who wants to marry our Demetria." She nodded to the chairs opposite their sofa, facing the bright light from the window over which the heavy velvet draperies had only been half drawn.

They sat, Miss Pouli taking a stool next to Aunt Thelxiope, presumably to translate. Annabel took a deep breath and began. "Yes, my cousin Hartley would like to marry Miss Pouli. He is much in love with her, is master of a handsome estate in Cornwall, and as a viscount would give her an excellent position in society."

"Is he rich?" Aunt Molpe asked.

Annabel tried not to start. After all, that was why she was here—to negotiate a marriage, and money was a prime consideration. "He is—and he isn't. While he has possession of his family's title and house, most of the family's more liquid assets are under the control of his mother until he marries or turns thirty—and she can retain control of them until then if she does not approve of his choice of wife." She paused, to give Miss Pouli a chance to translate. "So for now, his income is adequate; no matter what happens, though, when he turns thirty he will be a very wealthy man."

"That is still several years away." Aunt Molpe frowned. "So why doesn't his mother want him to marry Demetria—yes, we know that she doesn't."

"Hartley is an only son and very precious to his mother—perhaps a little too much so. She has grand dreams for him, most of which have nothing to do with his own wishes. Those include his marrying someone of her choosing—someone from one of our highest families."

Aunt Thelxiope snorted and said something in Sirenese. Maria chuckled. "She says that your cousin Medea must be touched in her head—everyone knows that sons are worthless and only daughters matter." She said something back to her in Sirenese, and Aunt Thelxiope shook her head in a way that plainly said she thought English customs ludicrous.

"But I assure you, Hartley doesn't care for his mother's plans. He is quite clear on that point." Annabel hesitated, glancing at Maria, then said, "Surely it will be a burden lifted from your minds to know that your niece will be well taken care of—and not a charge to you." She and Maria had discussed this tactic—pointing out to the aunts that they would no longer have to support their niece. "Further, I might add that the climate of Cornwall is quite different to London's, much warmer and sunnier. There are palm trees on his property there."

Aunt Thelxiope said something, and everyone laughed. "My aunt says, 'anywhere has nicer weather than London!'" Miss Pouli translated, then added wistfully, "Truly? Palm trees?"

"Truly." Annabel smiled at her, then turned back to the aunts, schooling her face into a sterner expression. "However, if you give your niece permission to marry my cousin, the concerts and recitals will have to cease at once."

There was a heavy silence after Miss Pouli finished her whispered translation. "Why?" Aunt Molpe finally asked.

"For one thing, it would not be appropriate for a future viscountess to sing in public for money." She paused. "For another, it would not be acceptable for her to continue to steal from her future social circle."

If the previous silence had been heavy, the one that followed was oppressive. Then Aunt Molpe said, a little plaintively, "We only do it to support ourselves."

"I understand that. But if Miss Pouli is to marry Hartley, it has to stop. Besides, I think you are overlooking the obvious."

"Which is?"

"Which is that your niece will become the wife of a wealthy—or eventually wealthy—man, who will take no issue with supporting his beloved wife's relations." She paused, then added with quiet emphasis, "*Palm trees.*"

Aunt Molpe's delicately arched brows drew down, and she motioned to her niece and sister. The three dark heads drew together in conference.

Annabel scarcely dared to breathe. Hartley didn't know she had just offered his house to a pair

of Sirens *d'un certain âge,* but if that was the only
way to win him his Demetria, he could not complain
too loudly. Of course, there were still Cousin Medea's
protests to overcome—

"That was a good start," Maria said quietly,
turning toward Annabel to give the three a modicum
of privacy. "But we shouldn't assume victory yet.
Sirens are funny. Proud, I suppose you might say.
Plus I think they enjoy the sport of singing roomfuls
of people to sleep."

The conversation amongst the Sirens grew
louder and more strident, sounding like a small flock
of squabbling sparrows. Annabel watched them co-
vertly; Miss Pouli, surprisingly, seemed to be giving
her aunts as good as she got. That was a promising
sign; Hartley would not be able to run completely
rough-shod over her if she didn't choose to let him.

How much longer the aunts and Miss Pouli
might have debated if not for the interruption that
occurred then, Annabel could not guess. But interrupted they were: the doors to the salon banged
open, and an angry voice shouted, "Blast it, someone
locked the door! I had to come in through the
damned kitchen! Where has that lazy slut Stasia gone
off to—oh."

The look on Mr. Skourletis's face was so
comically dismayed when he stopped complaining
long enough to take notice of the visitors and the
aunts' unveiled state that Annabel was hard-pressed
not to laugh. She restrained herself, however, and
actually felt a tinge of admiration for how quickly he
composed himself.

"But look—we have guests! What an
unexpected. . . pleasure." He delayed the word just

long enough to imply its reverse, then finished the effect with a deep bow.

"Yes, Uncle—Lady Fellbridge and Lady Sefton were kind enough to pay us a call," Miss Pouli said calmly enough. But Annabel saw that her hands were twisting in her lap, betraying her agitation.

Mr. Skourletis noticed them, too, and his smile grew wider and falser. "But my dear niece, you are overcome by the honor! We cannot let you be too excited—don't forget that you have another recital tomorrow—"

"Demetria will not be singing tomorrow," Aunt Molpe spoke up suddenly.

"What?" Mr. Skourletis's brow darkened.

"What?" Miss Pouli and Annabel echoed. . . and then turned to grin at each other.

"You heard me, Stavros. Demetria won't be singing anymore because she's going to be a viscountess and viscountesses can't sing," Aunt Molpe said.

"Well, they can, but that will do," Maria murmured.

"A vis—" Mr. Skourletis had begun to turn purple. "That Mompesson lout," he snarled. "No, she isn't. She's going to keep singing as long as I say she should. What are you doing, you foolish old woman, encouraging these fancies?"

Annabel winced at "old woman." Evidently Aunt Molpe took exception to it as well. "If she wishes to marry her viscount, she can, you fat stupid man."

"I am going to marry Hartley Mompesson, Mr. Skourletis," Miss Pouli said. Annabel noticed she hadn't called him uncle. "Lady Fellbridge and my aunts have agreed upon it."

"We have?" Annabel muttered to Maria.

"Evidently," Maria answered. She appeared to be enjoying herself hugely.

"They have, eh? Then maybe your Lady Fellbridge should agree instead to get herself out of this house and never come back." He crossed the room in a few long strides, grabbed Miss Pouli by the arm, and yanked her to her feet. "Tell the nosy ladies to go home now, Demetria. They're not wanted here."

"No!" She wrenched her arm from his grasp and stood with her shoulders thrown back defiantly. "I will not!"

"No?" Mr. Skourletis put his hand into his coat and drew out a small pistol. He pointed it at Annabel. "Now what do you say?"

Annabel's breath caught. No one had ever even *threatened* her before, much less pointed a firearm at her. The pistol looked enormous, even though she knew it was not; the small dark hole of the barrel looked like the entrance to Hades. . . No! This would not fadge. *Do something, Annabel!* she told herself fiercely.

"You—you bully!" Demetria burst into tears. "I *hate* you!"

"That was not a clever thing to do, Mr. Skourletis." Maria no longer sounded amused. "In fact, it seems to me to have been the action of a cowardly and not very intelligent man who can't think of any other solution to his problems apart from violence. Threatening a lady is not regarded lightly in this country. In fact, I think you will find it highly unpleasant to remain here much longer—"

"Aaaaieeeee!" One of the aunts—Annabel did

not move her head to see which—let out a long, keening wail.

The combination of Demetria's sobbing, Maria's stern lecturing, and the aunt's eerie cry created a wall of sound that made Mr. Skouletis cringe and wince. The pistol wavered—and Annabel seized a handful of shadow from a fold of her walking dress and hurled it at the gun just as a flurry of movement behind Mr. Skourletis made her look up in surprise.

Something—someone—appeared behind him and brought an object down upon his head with an unpleasant thud. The now-invisible pistol discharged harmlessly into the wall, and Mr. Skourletis collapsed heavily onto the floor next to the sofa, revealing the Marquis of Quinceton behind him, still clutching a heavy figurine in one upraised hand.

"Quin!" Maria gasped. "Upon my word, Quin, I don't know when I've been so relieved!"

He set down the statue and, ignoring both Maria and the alarmed shrieks of the aunts and Miss Pouli, stepped over Mr. Skourletis's inert form and up to Annabel. "Are you all right?" he demanded, taking her by the shoulders.

For a moment Annabel was again unable to speak. It had all happened so quickly—staring down the barrel of Mr. Skourletis's pistol—the cacophony—the gunshot—and an instant later, Lord Quinceton's stormy face filling her field of vision. "What did you hit him with?" she asked when she thought her voice would work properly.

His expression relaxed a small degree, and he let his hands fall. "A bronze statue of Hippolyta, I think. It was on the window ledge."

"How appropriate."

He smiled. "Yes, I thought so."

He stood there before her, not moving, while the three Sirens continued to fuss and Maria joined in in Sirenese, trying to calm them. Annabel wondered why he was looking at her that way, rather as if *he* were frightened—after all, *she'd* been the one who'd had a pistol pointed at her. Then she narrowed her eyes. "What," she asked, "are you doing here?"

He raised an eyebrow. "Saving your life?"

"Thank you, but I think we had matters well in hand."

"If that was 'well in hand', I don't want to know what chaos would look like."

"They can bear a remarkable degree of resemblance to each other at times."

"Fellbridge, the blackguard was aiming a pistol at you."

She would not let him see how her knees were trembling. "He might just have been trying to frighten us. Actually shooting me would have created many more problems for him. And besides, he might have been a bad shot."

"Not at fewer than ten paces, I shouldn't think. And to answer your question, I'm here because I asked Miss Pouli to allow me to be present when you called on her aunts, in case something precisely like this were to happen. She understood my concerns and agreed."

Oh! Annabel glowered past him at Miss Pouli, who was still embroiled with her aunts. "You expected Mr. Skourletis to attack us?"

"Let's just say I thought it might be a possibility, were he to interrupt your discussion. If nothing had happened, I would have remained quietly behind the curtains until your departure, and no one would have been the wiser."

"You mean *I* wouldn't have been any wiser," she replied tartly. But beneath she was concerned: Maria had spoken in Sirenese in front of him—would he simply assume it was some exotic Greek dialect? And she had thrown a shadow at Mr. Skourletis; what would he make of that? Had they said or done anything else here that might give away the fact that they weren't just an ordinary pair of ladies of the *ton*? Oh, she could just *shake* Miss Pouli right now!

"You have to admit that Eliza and I were right," he said, breaking into her thoughts.

"About what?"

"About not wanting to let you come here unprotected. Too bad I didn't make you place a wager on it." He shook his head regretfully.

She would not give him the satisfaction of knowing that Maria—yes, and she—had shared his concern. "I never gamble."

"No. Rather a shame, really."

Just then, a loud rapping from the front of the house interrupted them all. The aunts abruptly stopped twittering. Miss Pouli stared, hands clasped at her breast.

"Is someone going to answer that?" Lord Quinceton asked, sounding bored. But Annabel had learned to distrust that particular note of boredom in his voice and shot him a suspicious look. He returned it blandly.

"Y-yes, of course," Miss Pouli said, and hurried out of the room.

"I do hope it isn't more callers," Maria said.

"How will we explain that?" She nodded to Mr. Skourletis, still unconscious on the floor.

"Indeed, we probably should do something about him," Lord Quinceton replied.

Not to mention his pistol. Annabel darted furtive looks at the floor, wondering where it had fallen.

A muffled shriek from the front hall made her look up sharply. A moment later Miss Pouli returned, no longer frightened but radiant. With her was Hartley Mompesson, his arm about her waist. . . followed by Hartley's mother Medea, the dowager Lady Mompesson, a look of profound and determined displeasure on her bony features.

"Cousin Medea!" Annabel exclaimed. "Good heavens, what are you doing here?"

"I might ask the same of you, Annabel." Lady Mompesson's expression darkened further when she took in the aunts and Lord Quinceton, then changed to astonishment when she spotted Maria. "Lady Sefton! What are you—I mean, what an unexpected pleasure!"

Maria nodded politely. "Isn't it, though?"

"Oh, don't be daft, mother. Annabel's been helping me convince Demetria to marry me. She was supposed to convince you too, but it doesn't seem she's got round to that yet. Wish you'd hurried it up a bit, coz," Hartley said cheerfully.

"It will take more convincing than your cousin is capable of—my word, who is that?" Cousin Medea was staring at Mr. Skourletis's prone figure.

"Good lord, Demetria, isn't that your uncle?" Hartley asked, craning his neck. "Odd place to nap, but then I never thought much of him, even if he is family." He kissed the top of Miss Pouli's head, then sniffed the air. "Damned if I don't smell black powder. Who's been shooting in your parlour, darling?"

Miss Pouli shuddered. "I do not wish to speak of it. And no, he is not my uncle. He is a horrible, horrible man, and I'm glad you hit him so hard!" she said to the Marquis.

"You laid him out?" Hartley whistled. "Couldn't you have waited till we arrived? That must have been something to see."

"You knew Lord Quinceton would be here?" Annabel knew she'd been right to be suspicious.

"Knew it? He invited us—well, maybe invited isn't quite the word." For once, Hartley actually looked sheepish. "He said I should stop letting you do all my work and get my own proposing taken care of. So here I am." He squared his shoulders and drew Miss Pouli with him over to the aunts—then checked in surprise. "Where are those ghastly veils you used to wear? By Pindar, you aren't a couple of elderly antidotes after all!"

"Pindar? You know Pindar?" Aunt Molpe said.

"What? Yes, of course—my subject's Greek poetry of the—" he stopped and stared; Aunt Molpe had turned to whisper something to Aunt Thelxiope, and now the pair of them were giggling.

"Thelxiope knew him in Aegina—knew him *very* well," Aunt Molpe said, and elbowed her sister. They both giggled again. "He wrote her some poetry—I think we have it somewhere, don't we?" She spoke in Sirenese to Thelxiope, who nodded and replied. "Yes, he did, she says. She's quite fond of it and brought it with her—she'd be glad to show you—"

"You *knew* Pindar?" Hartley appeared thunderstruck. "But that's impossible! He died in 440—"

"Hartley, there's something I need to tell you. *Now*." Miss Pouli, her visage awash with color, pulled him across the room to the fireplace.

"*You* told Hartley to come here?" Annabel demanded of Lord Quinceton.

He gave a modest shrug. "It seemed the sensible thing to do."

"First Miss Pouli and now Hartley? Who's next? My mother?"

"No, though as I recall she's a delightful woman whom it would be a pleasure to see again. But it. . . annoyed me that your cousin was expecting you to take on the management of his marital plans. I merely represented to him that it was an unreasonable expectation and that he didn't deserve his prize if he wasn't willing to work for it."

Annabel still frowned at him. . . but drat the man, he was right. She had agreed to help Hartley because that's what everyone in the family had done all his life; she hadn't given the least thought to whether she *should* help him in this instance. But being right about the matter didn't oblige Lord Quinceton to step in and do something about it.

"I gather I am supposed to be gratef—" she began, but was interrupted by an imperious voice.

"Annabel!" Cousin Medea, who had been making polite conversation with a bored-looking Maria, swept toward them. "Annabel, I do not know what Hartley has told you about this regrettable situation or why you are here, but I do know that he"—she cast a deeply disapproving look at Lord Quinceton—"is not someone with whom it does you credit, as a young widow, to associate. Remember your family!"

"You enlighten me, madam. I was not aware that widows' weeds and nuns' veils were synonymous," Lord Quinceton said politely.

Annabel ignored him. "Since when, cousin, does being acquainted with a perfectly respectable person who is received at Almack's and every other home in London blacken my reputation?"

Cousin Medea's nostrils flared. "Don't take that tone with me, young lady. You've been seen driving with him several times now, I hear. The Marquis may be received, but that doesn't mean he *should* be!"

Annabel lifted her chin. "He was a friend of Freddy's."

"And you take *that* as a recommendation? I honestly don't know what your parents were thinking when they married you to Fellbridge. He may have been your husband, but he was not anyone I should have chosen to allow near *my* daughters."

"Having seen the Misses Mompesson, I rather doubt it would have been a concern," Lord Quinceton murmured.

Annabel was just able to turn a snort of laughter into a cough. Cousin Medea drew herself up. "How dare you, sir! Annabel, I demand you ask this—this *person* to leave!"

"As this isn't my house, Medea, I scarcely think I can." She took a deep breath and fixed Cousin Medea with a stern look. Enough was enough. "Nor do I want to. I know you're family, but that does not give you the least right to criticize my choice of companions. If I wish to converse, or drive, or otherwise enjoy Lord Quinceton's company, I shall do so, without reference to what you might say."

Two spots of red appeared on Cousin Medea's

cheeks. "Well! I shall have some words to share with your mother, young woman! In my youth, we were taught to hold our elders' opinions in respect!"

Annabel smiled sweetly. "Yes, things have changed somewhat since the seventeenth century."

She turned away, ignoring the older woman's sputters. By George, she had forgotten what a termagant Medea could be! Perhaps she should have kept better control of her tongue—not that Mama would blame her in the least, if Medea went bearing tales. But she was an adult and should be able to regulate herself better if she were to serve as a model for Will and Martin.

To calm her beating heart, she surveyed the room. Hartley and Miss Pouli were huddled together in the far corner—at least Hartley didn't seem in danger of exploding at anything he was being told—and Maria had rejoined the aunts and was chatting with them. Mr. Skourletis remained unconscious on the floor, though it looked as if someone had nudged his limbs into a less sprawling position.

"My dear Fellbridge, that parting shot at your aunt was a leveler," Lord Quinceton said in her ear. "And you quite put me to the blush, I must say. Did I truly hear you say something about enjoying my company?"

Oh! She had almost forgotten he was there, so angry had she been at Medea. Then recollection of what she had said flooded back. Good heavens—she had actually defended him—and her keeping company with him—right in front of the man! He would undoubtedly roast her about it for the rest of the Season. "I—I should not have said that," she said, not looking at him.

"Maybe not, but I'm glad you did. I've rarely met anyone so in need of a set-down. It looks as if she's moving on to a less formidable target."

She turned. Cousin Medea was bearing down upon Hartley and Miss Pouli. "Oh, confound the woman! She will antagonize Hartley entirely if she tries to scare off Miss Pouli, but I don't think she'll listen to reason."

"Annabel!" Maria called. She was gesticulating from where she stood by the aunts. When Annabel, trailed closely by Lord Quinceton, had joined them, she said, "Annabel, Mrs. Oikonomou and Mrs. Kanakaris"—she indicated Aunt Molpe and Aunt Thelxiope respectively—"are quite willing to allow their niece to marry Hartley."

"We have all sorts of stories to tell him about the poets we knew," Aunt Molpe explained. "No one ever wants to hear our stories. It will be a nice change to know someone who will."

"But what do we do about his mother?" Annabel looked over at the trio near the fireplace. Cousin Medea was quite looming over poor Miss Pouli, who appeared terrified. "Even if Hartley defies her and marries Demetria, they'll still have to deal with her for the rest of their lives."

"We discussed that, and these ladies have volunteered to help—ah—shall we say, *manage* her."

Lord Quinceton suddenly laughed. "Oh, I'll bet they have!"

"Hush, Quin." But Maria was smiling. "It's perhaps a trifle drastic, but I think that it would be for the best. I even expect she'll be happier, in the long run."

Annabel gasped. "Good heavens—you don't

mean—"

"She won't know a thing—it will be just a short song," Aunt Molpe assured her. "My sister here would like to do it—she's very good, I promise."

"I don't care a fig for any of that, mother. I'm marrying her, and that's it!" came Hartley's raised voice from across the room. He stormed over to them, dragging Miss Pouli with him. Behind them trailed his mother, plaintively calling, "My darling boy, you are distraught and don't know what you're saying—"

"Oh yes, I do," he said, and stopped before the aunts. "Ladies, you know how I feel about Demetria," he said, fixing each of them in turn with a level, direct, and most un-Hartley-like gaze. "I am asking you for her hand in marriage."

"Oh, Hartley!" both Miss Pouli and Cousin Medea cried, in very different tones. Medea recovered first.

"Hartley, dearest," she said, grabbing his arm with both hands and digging her nails in. "I am persuaded that your senses are quite disordered— that you've taken one of your childish passions—"

"It may be passion, but it's anything but a childish one. Will you allow her to marry me?" He was still gazing at the aunts.

Aunt Molpe beamed. "We would be most happy—"

"No! I forbid it!" Cousin Medea shouted, by now alarmingly red in the face.

"Annabel?" Maria asked urgently.

"Hartley and his wife will thank you, Fellbridge," Lord Quinceton said. "And so will most of London, I suspect."

Annabel hesitated—but a quick glance at Hartley's determined face and Miss Pouli's tear-stained one decided her. "Yes, if you please," she said to Aunt Molpe.

"Good!" Aunt Molpe's eyes gleamed. "Lady Mompesson, perhaps we need to discuss this a little further. Won't you please—?" She took Cousin Medea's arm and propelled her across the room to the fireplace, followed by Aunt Thelxiope.

Maria immediately stuck her fingers in her ears. Annabel quickly followed her example, as did Lord Quinceton.

"What—" began Miss Pouli, and then she broke into a smile and reached up to tenderly cover Hartley's ears with her hands. "I'll explain later," she mouthed at him.

An hour later Annabel, Maria, and Lord Quinceton prepared to take their leave of the aunts. Hartley and Miss Pouli accompanied them to the door.

"Well, I do believe that matter has been settled in a satisfactory fashion," Maria said to Annabel.

Annabel glanced behind her into the salon, where Cousin Medea sat on a sofa chatting amiably with the aunts. Aunt Molpe had been right: it had been a short song, but evidently an effective one. Annabel had never seen her cousin look so relaxed and cheerful. "Yes, I think it has. You'll not forget tomorrow, will you, Hartley?"

"Forget to get rid of that carbuncle? Of course not!" Hartley said indignantly.

A few minutes before, the aunts' maid, Stasia, had returned from her errands and gone into strong hysterics at the sight of Mr. Skourletis seated in a chair, clutching his head and groaning. On revealing that the pair of them had intended to marry as soon as they left England, it had been decided that Hartley and Lord Quinceton would accompany the two to the docks tomorrow and pay their fares on the next boat they could find heading for the continent—*anywhere* on the continent. One loose end neatly tied up. . . but there was another.

"I am still not clear, sir, on why you decided to involve yourself in my affairs," Annabel said severely to Lord Quinceton.

"Nonsense, Annabel. I'm very glad that Quin was here. He took care of that tiresome man for us so that the aunts didn't have to intervene. The situation would have been much trickier if they had needed to do so. This way, they could pretend to be the victims of Mr. Skourletis even though we all know better. Everyone saved face."

"Except me," Annabel couldn't help muttering.

"Fellbridge, I see nothing about your face that needs saving. . . but if there is ever any other part of you that does, I shall always be happy to step in and do so." He bowed to them, gave Annabel one more challenging smile, and took his leave.

"Oh, Lady Fellbridge, I do beg your pardon," Miss Pouli said. "I know I should have asked you first about letting Lord Quinceton be here, but he was so sincere when he called that I just couldn't say no. I knew exactly how he felt—if it were me and Hartley, I would want to be able to protect him—"

"It's not in the least degree the same thing!"

Annabel snapped. But when Miss Pouli recoiled, she relented. "Never mind—no harm done, I think, and it *has* all worked out." She leaned forward and kissed her. "Welcome to the family, my dear."

At the next meeting of the Lady Patronesses the following Monday, Annabel could not help feeling a little nervous. Not that she was unhappy with how Hartley's matter had turned out—he and Miss Pouli had called yesterday to inform her that a date for their wedding had already been set, and were clearly deliriously happy together. But that wasn't quite the end of the story.

She carried out her usual duties as a Lady Patroness—reviewing voucher requests and discussing the other more mundane business of the week. When that was done and Sally said, "And now for our other business," she took a deep breath.

"Annabel? Do you have anything to report on our troublesome Sirens?"

"I do. They won't be troubling London any longer." She explained the aunts' agreement to move to Cornwall with Hartley and Demetria and the banishment of Mr. Skourletis.

"You're certain they won't get up to their old tricks?" Dorothea said suspiciously. "Sirens. . ." Her lip curled.

"Miss Pouli has promised faithfully to keep them in Cornwall. They disliked London weather intensely, so that will help."

"And your cousin is happy as well! That was

very efficient of you. Well done!" Sally beamed at her.

"There's one more thing," Annabel said. She opened her reticule and removed a small pouch from it. "Georgiana, I believe this belongs to you." She passed it to Sally, who raised an eyebrow and leaned forward to hand it to Georgiana.

Georgiana gave Annabel a suspicious look but opened the pouch. . . and let out a shocked cry. "My great-grandmother's necklace!"

Maria nodded. "Annabel told Miss Pouli's aunts that although she understood that returning any currency Mr. Skourletis stole from guests at concerts would be very difficult, she did think that it was necessary for them to return as much jewelry as could be identified. They reluctantly agreed." Maria reached beneath her chair and pulled out a much larger bag. She lifted it onto the table with a grimace at its weight. "Finding the owners of some of the loose gems Mr. Skourletis and his accomplice pried from settings may be difficult too, but we will do our best."

"How will you return them?" Frances asked, wide-eyed.

"Oh, I expect we'll find a way. It may take a while, but Annabel has already volunteered to slip into houses to return the pieces we know the owners of. If you could all help us figure out what belongs to whom, it would be a great help."

"Annabel, you are a paragon." Emily, sitting next to her, patted her arm. "I can return any pieces stolen at the recital at my house and say that the maids found them, if that will help."

"Believe me, it will." She was going to be very busy for the next few days, sneaking around Mayfair wrapped in a shadow, returning stolen jewels.

"Ahem." Across the table, Georgiana cleared her throat. "If—if you would like some help returning jewelry, I think my sciatica has eased up—Annabel." She met Annabel's eyes, her expression apologetic and a little shamefaced.

There was a collective indrawing of breath around the table, including Annabel's. Then she smiled back at Georgiana and said, "Thank you, Georgiana. I would very much appreciate that."

"Well, I'm glad *that's* finally taken care of, because I'm going to need all of you over the next few days," Sally said. "We have something very odd to look into."

"All of us?" Clementina asked. "What could you possibly need all of us for?"

"Something you were probably going to do anyway: go to the Royal Academy Exhibition and look at the pictures. Several times."

Annabel looked at Emily, who raised an eyebrow in return. Going to the annual show at the Royal Academy was one of those things that the *ton* did, whether or not they cared for art; she had indeed planned on going some day this week now that Hartley's business was settled. Should she invite someone to go with her? It would be amusing to go with the Marquis of Quinceton and hear his acerbic comments on modern art—

She hoped Emily hadn't heard her thinking that.

I hope you enjoyed these installments of *The Ladies of Almack's*! There's more—much more!—to come. If you'd like to keep up with the news from King Street, you can sign up for my newsletter for new release announcements, extras, and more about the ladies:
https://marissadoylenewsletter.link/

Also, if you enjoyed reading these stories, please consider telling your friends who might also enjoy them or posting a review on the site where you purchased them or on your favorite social media site such as Goodreads or LibraryThing.

Author's Notes

Benefit Concerts

The concert Annabel attends with Lord Glenrick, Frances, and Quin was the May 9 benefit performance for Teresa Bertinotti, one of the new premier singers at the King's Theatre. Leading stars at the various theaters often negotiated benefit performances into their contracts—concerts for which they'd receive most of the evening's proceeds, as a sort of bonus. Bertinotti chose to sing from *Cosi fan Tutti*, a work of Mozart's that had only recently premiered in London. Funny to think about a time when a Mozart opera was "modern" music, isn't it?

Marriage Laws

Young Hartley Mompesson asks Annabel and his grandmother to help convince his mother to allow him to marry Demetria Pouli. At this time there were a few ways to marry: a couple could obtain a special license, which would enable them to marry anywhere and at any time, as long as an Anglican minister performed the service. If either party was under twenty-one, parental consent was required. Posting the banns was much cheaper—this meant that a couple's intent to marry was announced in church at the parish in which they would be marrying over three Sundays, after which they could marry; again, parental consent was theoretically required, but if a couple managed to post banns in a different parish without anyone snitching to Mom and Dad, they could get away with being underage. For the wealthier classes, where estates and inheritances were involved, consent to marry could be tied up in all sorts of unpleasant knots, such as what Hartley faces. This points back to the fact that for many parts of society, marriage was indeed even more of an economic transaction than it was a sentimental one.

Mr. Coke of Norfolk

In a time when most of the wealth of the aristocracy came from the agricultural activities on their land holdings, remarkably few landowners took all that much interest in figuring out how to maximize those activities. . . until Thomas Coke came along. He was a member of Parliament and prominent among the liberal Whigs (and supported American independ-ence) but he's probably best known as an agricultural reformer. On his estate in Norfolk, Coke improved the poor soil by selective planting of different grasses and, with the better grazing land, went on to be a pioneer in sheep breeding. He died in 1842 at the age of 88, having finally accepted a peerage for both his political and agricultural work.

Sirens

In Greek mythology, the Sirens were beautiful but sociopathic entities who used their beautiful voices to lure sailors into sailing their ships into destruction on the rocks of their island. Physically they were said to be a combination of bird and woman, and ancient authors came up with differing combinations of the two. I rather liked the idea of them, from later antiquity, as beautiful women with birds' feet, so that's how I depicted my Sirens. They were also given different names by different poets, among them the two I chose for Miss Pouli's aunts, Molpe (pronounced "**mole**-peh") and Thelxiope (pronounced "**thelk**-si-**o**-peh"). Oh, and by the way—"pouli" is bird, in Greek. I love playing with character names and either often try to make them mean something appropriate, or else research the heck out of them and make them as plausible as possible for their characters' time and place.

Hippolyta

Back to mythology again. Lord Quinceton wallops Mr. Skourletis with a small bronze statuette of Hippolyta, who was the daughter of the god Ares and queen of the Amazons. Definitely a fitting instrument of the scoundrel's downfall, don't you think?

Palm Trees in England? Really?

Yep, really. . . at least in Cornwall. Located at the southwest tip of Britain, Cornwall has the mildest and sunniest climate of any region of the country. Why? Because it sticks out into the Atlantic where the warm Gulf stream current flows past, and as a result tropical and semi-tropical plants, including palm trees, can be grown in more protected areas along the south coasts.

Dramatis Personae

Or, a brief list of who was *really* who

For those among you who are not hard-core Regency fanatics, the following are highly idiosyncratic biographical sketches of the historical figures mentioned in this first story.

But first, a quickie tutorial on title usage in England

Peers (anyone of the rank of baron, viscount, earl, marquis, or duke) have a family name or surname like their less exalted fellow humans, but then also have their title, and can be referred to by both. Let's look at an example. . .

John Smith is the Earl of Noodle. He is commonly known as Lord Noodle; his friends might just call him Noodle, or he might be referred to as John Noodle to differentiate him from his late father,

George Noodle, if the family is being gossiped about; but Noodle is not his surname—that's Smith. He will never be referred to as Lord John Smith or Lord John Noodle; men referred to as "Lord First-name Surname" are usually the younger sons of marquises and dukes, who are given the courtesy title of "Lord."

His wife, Mary Smith, the Countess of Noodle, is commonly known as Lady Noodle; she might be referred to as Mary Noodle to differentiate her from her mother-in-law Jane, the Dowager Countess, who is still alive and gadding about in society, and the name might stick even after the Dowager countess is no more just because everyone has gotten used to it. Mary will *not* be called Lady Mary Noodle, or Lady Mary Smith; women referred to as "Lady First-name Surname" are the daughters of the higher nobility—earls and above—and are permitted the use of the courtesy title of "Lady." A widow of a peer keeps her rank and title unless she remarries, when she then takes her new husband's rank (and title, if any.) In social practice, many women who married men of lower rank still kept the courtesy title they were born with.

Fred Smith, Viscount Macaroni, is Lord Noodle's eldest son. Most members of the higher nobility have multiple titles, so an eldest son (and ONLY an eldest son—there are a whole set of rules around heirs apparent—direct offspring—and heirs presumptive—brothers and nephews and cousins—that we won't get into right now) is permitted to "borrow" his father's second most prestigious title as a courtesy (though if there is a third title and if Fred has a son, the lad might get to use that one if grandpa allows it.) Fred's younger brothers are just plain

Honourables (only younger sons of marquises and dukes use the courtesy title of "Lord", don't forget) but his sister is Lady Susan because the daughters of earls (and marquises and dukes) have the courtesy title of "Lady."

There are other rules—dukes have their own special set. So. . .

Aurelius Smith is the Duke of Megapounds. Unlike his cousin John Smith, Earl of Noodle, he is *never* known as *Lord* Megapounds. He might be addressed just by his title, Megapounds, by his friends and acquaintances. . . or he might be addressed as "Duke" by others of his (relative) social class or as "your grace" by his inferiors. When he's being gossiped about, he might be referred to as Aurelius Megapounds or as "the seventh Duke" to differentiate him from his father Julius Megapounds, the sixth Duke. Aurelius's wife Ruby Smith, the Duchess of Megapounds, is likewise addressed as "Duchess" by friends and acquaintances, or as "your grace" by her inferiors, or as Ruby Megapounds to differentiate her from her mother-in-law the dowager duchess, Pearl Megapounds.

Now for the who's who. . .

Sally Jersey

Sarah Sophia Child Villiers, Countess of Jersey (1785-1867), known as Sally Jersey to differentiate her from her mother-in-law, also Lady Jersey (and well-known as a mistress of the Prince of Wales). She was also known by the ironic nickname "Silence" as she was reputed never to stop talking, and was a Lady Patroness of Almack's and very influential in society for many years, though never as actively interested in politics as were many of the other Lady Patronesses. Fascinatingly, she inherit-ed the senior partnership in a bank—Child & Co.—from her maternal grandfather (as well as his fortune—she was one wealthy woman!) and on attaining the age of twenty-one took her role very seriously and was active in the bank's management for her entire life. She is reputed to have had many love affairs, including one with Henry "Cupid" Templeton, Emily Cowper's squeeze.

Georgiana Bathurst

Georgiana Bathurst, Countess Bathurst (one of the exceptions to all my rules above; in this case, the title and family surname were the same), 1765-1841. Georgiana was born a member of the Lennox family, descended from King Charles II and his mistress Louise de Kérouaille, and niece to the famous Lennox sisters, one of who nearly married George III. Aside from the basic information around her ancestry, her marriage to the 3rd Earl Bathurst who held several government positions, a list of her children, and the fact that she served as a Lady Patroness, almost no information about her seems to be commonly available. . . which left me free to create a personality for her.

Emily Cowper (pronounced "cooper")

Emily Mary Cowper, Countess Cowper (another exception where the surname and title coincide), 1787-1869. Born Emily Lamb, daughter of the well-known Lady Melbourne (another mistress of the Prince of Wales), sister of William Lamb, later

Viscount Melbourne, Queen Victoria's first prime minister, and sister-in-law of crazy-cakes Caro Lamb, lover of Lord Byron. She was married at a young age to Peter Clavering-Cowper, 5th Earl Cowper who was ten years her senior. She bore him a son, then embarked on a series of love affairs in London while he remained more or less contentedly in the country at their estate in Hertfordshire. Her grand passion was Henry John "Cupid" Temple, 3rd Viscount Palmerston, who was the probable father of a few of her children and whom she married in 1839 after her first husband's death. She was a political hostess *par excellence,* being the sister of one Prime Minister and the wife of another. She was one of the most popular of the Lady Patronesses, known for her kindness and social *élan.*

Clementina Sarah Drummond-Burrell

Clementina Sarah Drummond-Burrell, later Lady Willoughby de Eresby, 1786-1865. Clementina was a Scottish heiress and daughter of an earl; her husband, Peter Burrell, added her last name to his own so that they became known as Mr. and Mrs. Drummond-Burrell. Later her husband inherited a pair of baronies from both his father and (unusually) his mother; the older, more prestigious title was his mother's Willoughby de Eresby one, so that's the one they used. While Peter pursued a political career which Clementina's fortune subsidized (as well as his habits as a dandy), Clementina pursued a social one, becoming a hostess of some renown. She was reputed to be proud and haughty in nature and a stickler for correct behavior, which inspired the power I gave her, though some historians contend that it was her mother-in-law, not her, who was so snooty. Unusually for the time (and among her fellow Lady Patronesses) Clementina's marital reputation remained unstained, and she and her husband appear to have enjoyed a faithful, devoted relationship.

Maria Sefton

Maria Molyneux, Viscountess Sefton and later Countess of Sefton, 1769-1851. While much is known about her husband William's career as both a politician and a noted friend of the Prince of Wales (as well as a founder of the exclusive Four-in-Hand Club), very little is known about Maria beyond her connection with Almack's as a Lady Patroness. Might that excessive prudence and avoidance of publicity be a function of the fact that her parents, Lord and Lady Craven, had both lived rather scandalous lives and had divorced, a rarity at the time? She was reputed to be extremely good-natured, however, and an excellent if self-effacing hostess for her busy husband.

Dorothea Lieven

Dorothea von Lieven, Countess (and later Princess) Lieven, 1785-1857. Born in Riga, Latvia, Dorothea was a Russo-German noblewoman (she was educated at a convent in Russia and served as a maid-of-honor to the Tsar's mother) who was married (at age fourteen!) to General Count Christopher von Lieven. He was sent by Tsar Alexander I to serve as the Imperial Ambassador to England in 1812 (ssh, yes, I know that's two years after the setting of my stories. I invoke my creative license.) Dorothea took to London like a duck to water. She adored politics, knew everyone, and was the first foreigner asked to serve as a Lady Patroness at Almack's. She was known to be haughty and snobbish, had multiple affairs (including one with Count Metternich of Austria and again with "Cupid" Palmerston), received her own secret diplomatic assignments from the Tsar, and generally had a grand time of it for twenty years, until her husband was recalled to Russia. Not long after that she left him to live in Paris, where she established a salon and went on her merry way with a finger in every diplomatic pie until her death.

William Almack/Mr. Willis

Although he is referred to by contemporaries as a Scot, it is not known either when or where William Almack was born (though Thirsk in Yorkshire is a likely bet—so *not* a Scot, though maybe of Scottish heritage.) Earliest reports of him are as valet to the Duke of Hamilton, but he soon went into business as a proprietor of a tavern and then as the owner-manager of a gaming club in Pall Mall to which he gave his own name—and which eventually became known as Brooks's, one of the best known of London's men's clubs and still in operation today. In 1764 he built his famous Assembly Rooms in King Street and gathered his Lady Patronesses to administer them. . . though perhaps not in quite the way told in this story! On his death, he left Almack's to his niece and her husband, Mr. Willis, who continued to run it and seems to have passed it onto other descendants, as the club was renamed "Willis's Rooms" in 1871.

The Duke of York

The second son of King George III, Prince Frederick, Duke of York and Albany (1763-1827) was associated for most of his life with the army, for better and worse. He saw active service on the continent and was made Commander in Chief of the army, a post he resigned in 1809 after being dragged into a scandal involving his mistress's illegal selling of army commissions; after it was shown that she'd been paid off by the Duke's chief accuser, he was reinstalled as C-in-C in 1811. While not a particularly able or competent field commander (that nursery rhyme about the noble Duke of York marching his ten thousand men up and down hills for no very good reason is often identified as our Fred), he was responsible for a great deal of modernizing and improving of the army, which (as the Duke of Wellington often said) made possible Britain's successful Peninsular campaign against Napoleon. He was married to Princess Frederica of Prussia, an endearingly eccentric woman who avoided London and lived at their estate, Oatlands, with dozens of dogs and other more exotic animals, but they had no children.

Lord Palmerston

Mentioned above in Emily Cowper's entry, Henry John Temple, 3rd Viscount Palmerston (1784-1865) was a British statesman, serving as Prime Minister twice (from 1855-1858 and from 1859-1865), as War Secretary, and as Foreign Secretary. He was charming, intelligent, handsome, and something of a ladies' man (as can be seen from the number of Lady

Patronesses he conducted *amours* with), but remained single until the love of his life, Emily Cowper, was widowed. Their subsequent happy marriage, lasting until his death, was (according to contemporary observers) one of "perpetual courtship.

About the Author

Marissa Doyle graduated from Bryn Mawr College and went on to graduate school intending to be an archaeologist, but somehow got distracted. Eventually she figured out what she was *really* supposed to be doing and started writing. She's channeled her inner history geekiness into a successful young adult historical fantasy series and continues happily to write fantasy of various types for teens and adults. She lives in her native Massachusetts with her family, including a bossy but adorable pet rabbit, and loves quilting, gardening, and collecting antiques. Please visit her at her website, www.marissadoyle.com, and at her history blog, www.nineteenteen.com.

To keep up with new releases, news, and other fun stuff, sign up for Marissa's newsletter:

https://marissadoylenewsletter.link/

About Book View Café

Book View Café is an author-owned cooperative of professional writers publishing in a variety of genres, from fantasy to romance, mystery, and science fiction as well as select non-fiction.

Book View Café authors include New York Times and USA Today bestsellers; Nebula, Hugo, and Philip K Dick Award winners; World Fantasy Award, Campbell Award, and Rita Award nominees; and nominees and winners of multiple other publishing awards.

To keep informed of new releases, specials, and other news, sign up for Book View Café's monthly newsletter at www.bookviewcafe.com.